Even Light Cannot Escape

CRAIG CAUDILL

CHARACTERS

<u>Private Citizen, Harrodsburg, Kentucky</u>
Calvin Willett

<u>Escort, Lawrenceburg, Kentucky</u>
Celine "CeCe" Oliver

<u>Sutherland Tailoring, Harrodsburg, Kentucky</u>
Marcel Sutherland, CEO
Valerie Sutherland, Marcel's Wife
Brock Skinner, Investor
Frank Romine, Data Specialist

<u>Vigneron Winery, Hazard, Kentucky</u>
Maude Skinner, Proprietor and Brock's Wife
Truman, German Shepherd Guard Dog

<u>Ohio Valley Distillers' Guild</u>
Clive Natoli, Lobbyist
Pearl, Office Manager

<u>Private Citizens, Hazard, Kentucky</u>
Perry Oliver
Rhonda Oliver

<u>Investment Banker, Lexington, Kentucky</u>
Willard Lentz

<u>Barclay Farm, Charlestown, Indiana</u>

Nigel Barclay

Jaeger Barclay

<u>Professional Chess Player, Virginia</u>

Leslie Blazek

<u>Mechanic, Midway, Kentucky</u>

Thad Cameron

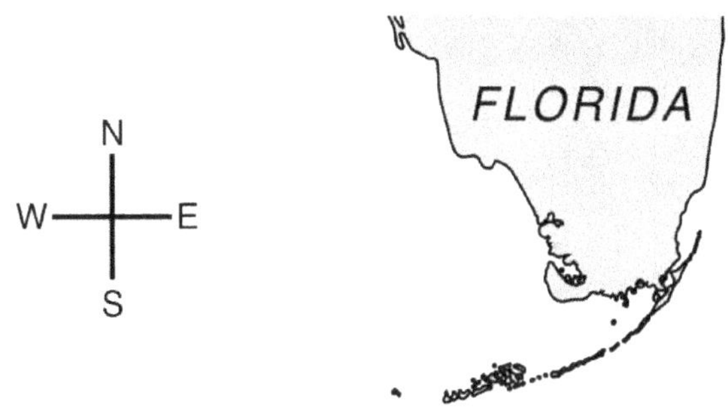

N
W E
S
FLORIDA

CUBA

GRAND CAYMAN
CAYMAN
TRENCH
HELL

This book is a work of fiction. Any references to historical events, real people, or real places are used fictitiously. Other names, characters, places, and events are the product of the author's imagination, and any resemblance to actual events or places or persons, living or dead, is entirely coincidental.

Copyright 2023 by Craig Caudill

All rights reserved, including the right to reproduce this book or portions thereof in any form whatsoever.

Book Cover design by ebooklaunch.com

Map Illustration by jenniferforrestdesign.com

For the wonderful times Jo and I had with friends
on the lake.

Chapter 1

In the middle of August, the clear, cerulean sky, reminiscent of an Edward Hopper painting, triggered a clarion call for the usual gang to show up at the dock for a party that Sunday. The dead-calm, noonday air offered little relief from the scorching sun beating down on the lake, and the churning crowd embraced the hot weather with customary fervor. Pork sandwiches, green beans, coleslaw, and watermelon had been laid out in aluminum tins on the bar courtesy of Sir Oink BBQ. Frank Sinatra crooned through speakers mounted under a corrugated metal roof over the boat slips, storage lockers, and makeshift loo.

A weathered pontoon boat claimed one slip, and a magnificent 1967 vintage Century Resorter 19 languished on the lift rails of the other. The inboard pleasure craft reached perfection the year it was produced but cost too much to make since it was still hand built from wooden planks. Mahogany had become extremely expensive and hard to come by. Fiberglass blown into a mold was faster and cheaper, hence the sad ending of the wood-boat era. A jocular nitwit standing close by commented, "If God had intended for boats to be made of fiberglass, he would have made fiberglass trees."

The sunny day party tradition was to collectively tackle a Sunday *New York Times* crossword puzzle while swimming, boating, sunbathing, and guzzling margaritas, or piña coladas. If a person didn't drink, they didn't fit in, yet oddly enough, the owner of the dock, Cal, and his date, CeCe, never touched the stuff. Calvin Willett was relaxing under the billowy red umbrella that shaded the round table anchored to the wooden deck of the dock. His date had her legs outstretched on the padded bench of the pontoon. Cal barked, "Give us a clue, CeCe."

There were other attractive girls on the dock that day, none in the same class as CeCe, who was wearing a floppy hat and one-piece aquamarine bathing suit that had a frumpy-looking skirt and ruffles over the shoulders. The outfit did little to hide her remarkable beauty. She was an athletic version of Brigitte Bardot, boasting an alluring smile that buckled knees. "Cardamom-containing coffeehouse creation. Seven letters."

"That's too easy." Cal tossed his head back and looked away. "Anyone have that one?" he asked the group milling around, talking amongst themselves. Everyone turned, shook their heads, and then went about their business.

Lake partiers were lovable, social creatures who had a knack for in-the-moment humor. That's what made it fun to be around them. They were plagued by arrested development and lacked curiosity—not a good formula for solving *NYT* crossword puzzles. Cal knew that and did his best not to belittle anyone. "Chai tea fits," he said.

"It does," CeCe confirmed.

Cal slowly got to his feet and boisterously called out the question: "Boat ride, anybody?" He knew there'd be more takers than room. CeCe always went along, so there were three spots left to be filled on a first-come basis. Cal spun the wheel of the lift until the rails bottomed out. He eased himself into the driver's seat of the boat and keyed on the engine while the other eager beavers climbed aboard. The gurgling of the water-level exhaust pipes sounded like Roman soldiers marching to war. "Untie us," Cal commanded in the stentorian voice of a Roman general. He backed out of the slip when the ropes were freed.

Inboard boats were beautiful machines, but they had one glaring weakness: the fixed prop and rudder behind it made the watercraft hard to maneuver at low speed compared to an outboard lower unit swiveling a prop in the desired direction with every turn of the steering wheel. Skiers preferred inboards for many reasons, most notably the quality of the wake generated by the low-profile rudder and prop. Century Resorters were the finest ski boats on the market in 1967. Most, like Cal's, were upholstered in red and white when they rolled off the assembly line sixty years ago.

Cal steered away from the fierce waves and other boat traffic, working his way into a shallow cove near the dam. The sting of the sun had become pronounced. "Okay, CeCe, what else you got?"

"Light cannot escape from it. Nine letters."

A young girl in the backseat bobbed up and down. "I know that one. Black hole."

Cal replied energetically, "Hey, good call. You folks can jump in to cool off if you want."

Everyone except CeCe, who was applying sunscreen, sprang up and dove off the side. When they had all climbed back in and dried off, she asked Cal, "What does it mean light can't escape?"

"A black hole is a burnt-out star that collapses on itself, becoming denser, with so much gravity that light can't get out. That's why they call it a black hole."

"Oh, that's only a theory. I mean, how could someone know for sure?"

"You'd be surprised what mathematicians and scientists have been able to figure out. But that's not the interesting part. A group of astronomers recently found a black hole graveyard three times the size of our galaxy."

CeCe pushed herself up and sat on the motor housing. "Do tell."

"Now we know the location of hell, where Satan and his fallen angels live. He's the prince of darkness *and* black holes."

The individuals at the dock party weren't particularly good crossword puzzlers, but they were keen observers of people and their quirks. The scuttlebutt had it that something weird was going on between Cal and CeCe. Behind their backs, they were affectionately referred to as Jake Barnes and Lady Ashley, characters in *The Sun Also Rises* by Hemingway. Jake got his manly parts blown off in World War I, which kept him from marrying Lady Ashley.

In search of grist for the mill, the young man in the backseat of Cal's boat, who had waxed his body hair, tried to come up with something outlandish to ask Cal that would get him going. "Do you think Satan is a Republican or Democrat?"

Cal wondered if he was being played. It didn't stop him from pontificating on the subject. "A hundred and fifty million people vote in elections nationally, half for each party. Eighty percent of Republicans believe that Jesus Christ was resurrected from the dead, while 20 percent of Democrats do. I would say Satan is a Democrat."

"Makes sense." The young man couldn't wait to return to the dock to spread that nugget.

Cal grinned and asked, "Would anyone like to ski on the way back?"

The three tagalongs in the backseat raised their hands.

———————————

Lewis Herrington announced a plan in 1909 to create a reservoir by damming up the Dix River, which flowed with unusual force into the Kentucky River at High Bridge, south of Wilmore. He got the bright idea from Daniel Boone, who reported a hundred years earlier that the tributary, immured by palisades, running through first-rate land, always had plenty of water, even during the driest seasons. The project began in 1912, and the land-owners along the banks of the river were forced out. Kentucky Utilities completed the dam and hydroelectric power plant in 1925. The trees and buildings were left standing when the river was flooded, and to this day, stickups gouged the bottoms of boats that blithely hurtled across shallow water.

Herrington Lake, 250 feet deep at the river channel, has a peak summer pool of 740 feet and is routinely drawn down to 725 feet during winter months. If cables tethering docks aren't let out when the water goes down, the buoyant structures end up on the bank, racked and twisted. Spring rains raise the water level again, floating the littoral deadfalls—some big enough to stand on. Party docks, peppering the steep shoreline below the mishmash of year-round homes and slapdash cabins, took a pounding from mammoth waves generated by cruisers lumbering along inexorably. There were no-wake zones of calmer water. Those premier locations had an easier time of it. The consensus among the party crowd was that Calvin Willett owned the finest spread on Herrington Lake, up the long no-wake inlet before the dam.

As if the oscillating water level, tree stumps below the surface, jostling waves, and floating logs weren't enough, there was the problem of alcohol. A dozen big stills cranked out the world's finest bourbon less than fifty miles away. No package stores were allowed near the lake, but all a person needed to do was drive fifteen miles in any direction, to another county, or bring the booze in.

Calvin was intimately introduced to alcohol twenty years ago, after his senior year of high school. He went to keg parties and began drinking beer with his friends. It wasn't until the summer after his first year at Transylvania that he moved on to bourbon. Not being familiar with the doctrine of liquid courage, Calvin thought it a good idea to waterski at night on Herrington Lake.

He misjudged how close the dock was when he dropped the rope. Nearly every bone in his body snapped, and most of his internal organs got busted up. He should have died but somehow lived. A year in the hospital and a taxing rehabilitation put him on his feet again, with a limp, using a cane. At that point, his life took a more productive turn.

Calvin went back home to Harrodsburg and asked his parents if he could have a job in the family garment business. He worked at every position in the place over the next three years. His folks sold him a third of the company at a low price, with the intention of turning the business over to him when they retired.

Once Calvin became general manager, he decided to get a business degree from Centre College in Danville while working forty hours a week. It took him five years to complete the program, and after he earned his sheepskin, a man by the name of Marcel Sutherland came through the door. He wanted to buy the Willett clothing operation for a lot of money.

Sutherland Tailoring had struck it rich selling garments online. Marcel Sutherland discovered an easy way for people to buy clothes that fit. He put booths in cities around the United States where people came to have their bodies scanned, and then he used the measurements to make custom clothes for them in the right sizes. His company had a bevy of designers who continually refreshed the online catalog. A customer bought what they wanted, got measured, and within days, a box showed up on the porch. It was easy to find contract sewing companies, but more difficult to install the necessary software in those operations. Marcel bought Willett's garment business to perfect the electronic process for converting measurements into sewing patterns on the fly. He transferred the technology, once ironed out, to his other vendors, so they could speed up their output.

One-third of the twelve-million-dollar purchase price went to Cal. He used the cash to build a deluxe home and nifty boat dock on Herrington Lake. It didn't take long for nominal acquaintances to wheedle invitations to his parties, and rather quickly, the guests figured out that Calvin Willett was an oddball. He had never forgiven himself for the bout of boozing and skiing that ended in calamity, fueling his admirable abstemious views on drinking, smoking, gluttony, cussing, lying, gambling, and chasing women. Other peculiarities surfaced as well.

Cal decided to lift himself out of the here and now by rolling back the clock to 1967. He believed 1968 ushered in the end of decency and decorum in the United States and began the removal of God from society. He considered the entropy of the wood-boat market and irrelevance of Sinatra's music to be signs that 1967 was the pinnacle of Judeo-Christian life in America, never to be reached again. He liked a quote attributed to Sinatra: "Rock 'n' roll is the most brutal, ugly, desperate, vicious form of expression it has been my misfortune to hear."

After Cal finished building his homestead on Herrington Lake, he enrolled at Asbury Theological Seminary to pursue a Master of Arts in Philosophy and Apologetics. He chose the area of study, completing his degree last Christmas, because it emphasized how to successfully interact with the non-believing world. That's why he had parties on the dock with heathens all around.

And then there was CeCe. How did a decrepit thirty-eight-year-old man land the best-looking woman in the northern hemisphere? Either she liked him and his money, or he was paying for it. Nobody had the courage to float such a rude, suicidal question to her. It was obvious that she spent all her time away from him at the gym and spa. One fact had come to light about CeCe that got passed around as gossip: she was born in Hazard, Kentucky. Genetics like hers weren't plentiful in Appalachia, but the bell curve proved otherwise.

———————

The dock party began breaking up at six thirty that Sunday evening. The sun slid down behind the trees at the top of the hill, making the atmosphere on the water quite pleasant. CeCe wrapped up the leftovers on the bar and said, "I've made up small packages of barbecued pork. Everyone is welcome to take one. Will make a scrumptious sandwich for lunch tomorrow."

When the last of the crowd had climbed the hill and driven away, Cal said to CeCe, "Shall we go for dinner?"

"Not tonight. I've got some things to do this evening. Would that be okay with you?" she asked politely.

"Sure. I offered it in case you had your mind set on going out. The sun has zapped my energy. I'm happy to lay on the couch and doze off watching television."

"Good. I'm sure I'll be hearing from you soon." She bagged the trash, set it on the tram, collected the sheer wrap she'd brought along, and headed up the hill. Cal heard the crunch of driveway gravel as she pulled onto the road to Harrodsburg.

Chapter 2

Marcel Sutherland was a worrier by nature. He had millions in cash and investments in various personal accounts by virtue of profits from his business, yet a sword of Damocles hung over his head.

Two weeks ago, he married Valerie Goddard, whom he met last year when she visited eastern Kentucky from Roswell, New Mexico. She made the trip to investigate an obelisk that purportedly had been brought to earth by a UFO. It turned out to be a hoax. Valerie was out there somewhere, but the sweetest thing the world had ever seen.

The Sutherland wedding ceremony held at Vigneron Winery in Hazard went off without a hitch. Marcel bankrolled the planting of the bucolic hillside vineyard years ago for his younger sister, Maude, before she married a college friend of his, Brock Skinner, who owned half of Sutherland Tailoring.

Brock lived under a lucky star. He inherited a quarter of a million dollars from his grandparents when he enrolled at the University of Kentucky. He impetuously handed the money over to his newfound friend, Marcel, to launch an online clothing business. That's the smartest thing Brock had ever done. Otherwise, he would have drifted into obscurity as a sparring partner for the best heavyweight boxers in the country. He, too, had amassed a pile of cash from the earnings of Sutherland Tailoring for doing very little. Brock had plenty of courage and, at times, helped put starch in Marcel's britches.

"When are the Skinners getting here?" Valerie quizzed her new husband as she watched the sparrows ravage the feeders hanging on shepherd's hooks in the side yard of Marcel's million-dollar palatial ranch house. His place had creature comforts Valerie would have to get used to. She had gone from stony broke in New Mexico to a life of luxury in Kentucky. There'd never been any sword hanging over her head, whether she was rich or poor.

"Seven o'clock. I'll start the grill after they get here," Marcel responded.

A few minutes later, the whine of an expensive Lamborghini grew louder, portending the arrival of their guests. Valerie hurried out the front door to greet them as they stepped out of the car. She spouted, "Don't you feel guilty driving that ostentatious display of wealth?"

Brock had on black shorts and a foppish lime-green Hawaiian shirt. He ran up to his new sister-in-law, gave her a heartfelt embrace, and pecked her on the cheek. "Yes, but I'll get over it." Maude rolled her eyes as she hugged Valerie and handed her the bottle she'd brought from the winery. Brock strode into the house and found his brother-in-law seasoning four beef filets. He said, "It looks like marriage is agreeing with you."

Marcel replied, "What gave it away, the grin on my face? Valerie is an angel. I'm blessed."

"Blessed in more ways than one. You've got your health, a successful, thriving business, and now a beautiful bride," said Brock.

Valerie entered the kitchen, came over to Marcel, and said, "Yet, I've noticed he sometimes borrows trouble, Brock. I just want him to be happy."

Her husband shot a finger at his brother-in-law and chirped loudly, "Hah. Talk about borrowing trouble, you're looking at him right there."

Brock ignored the accusation, asking, "What do you mean, Valerie?"

Marcel interrupted, "I'll tell you about it at dinner. Now, open that wine you brought."

"I think you'll like it," Maude said. "It's the best we've ever produced."

The steaks from the best butcher in town were done to perfection, and the couples decided to eat them in the elegant formal dining room. Conversation during dinner was relaxed and lighthearted. After pushing the plates aside with sighs of fullness, Brock prodded, "So, what's bothering you, Marcel?"

"You know our business has one of the best IT departments in the world. We can hack into just about any database out there."

"And it has come in very handy at times."

Valerie cleared the dishes and rinsed them in the sink before loading the dishwasher. Maude suggested, "Come, Valerie, let's enjoy the sunset while the titans talk business." They poured glasses of wine and slipped out to the patio through the French doors.

Marcel leaned forward and remarked seriously, "There are people out there who can hack our database too."

"I suppose. What would they get?"

"Come now, Brock, think about it. We have the body measurements of thousands of people. I can see it now: a hacker publishing the breast sizes of famous women we've sold clothes to. A class action lawsuit could come from it."

"There's cyber liability insurance for that. I presume we have it."

"Yes. It costs a blooming fortune," Marcel tacked on as he shifted in his seat.

"So, what's the worry?"

"If a breach occurs, our business will be shot to hell. Nobody will trust us with their personal information. No insurance company can fix that."

"I see what you mean." Brock got up from the table and strolled over to look out a window that faced the bird feeders. A cedar waxwing was assiduously extracting seeds from the caged block of suet. "Have you thought of a way to deal with that risk?"

"Yes. Hire the foremost expert in protecting data."

"How would you locate such a person?"

"I got lucky. I've already found him. His name's Frank Romine."

Brock returned to his seat. "What're his credentials?"

"He's a chess grandmaster. Plays in big tournaments for money and is a genius with computers. His hacking prowess is a well-kept secret."

"Are you kidding me? Who turned you on to this guy?"

Marcel straightened up and put his hands on the edge of the table. "A classmate of mine from college came to see me recently. Frank was his roommate. He told me about him confidentially, and that he wanted to move back to Kentucky, his home state. He's been secretly doing high-level hacking for the government and wants to switch to the private sector."

"Why does he want to do that?"

"Because he's afraid he'll be identified by a foreign power, and a hit will be put out on him."

"That's a good reason. The guy must be smart." Brock hooded his eyes.

"Off the charts, I imagine."

"When's he starting?"

"First of September. He's going to put sophisticated computer equipment in a home office and work from there a lot of the time."

"I recommend you have him bonded to make sure you're not missing anything. Now, I say we join the girls out back." Brock got up and led the way. Ideas were bouncing around in his head. Not all of them were good.

To the west, there were high clouds of pure white with gray shadows against the baby-blue sky. The clouds soon turned sunburst orange and then purple as the sky morphed into lighter blue with a yellowish haze. When the sun got near the horizon, Marcel said, "Oh, I forgot to tell you all something. You remember Calvin Willett, the man whose garment business we bought in Harrodsburg a few years ago?"

"I do," Brock replied.

"He heard I just got married and wants the four of us to come to a party at his place on Labor Day."

Maude asked, "Where's that?"

"About ten miles from here, on Herrington Lake."

"I'm game," Valerie threw out.

"If memory serves me, he's a little different," Brock reflected.

"He almost died when he was waterskiing at night and ran into a dock. I'm not sure he's ever mentally gotten over the accident," Marcel reported. "He's a decent bridge player, *and* his partner is a *very* attractive woman."

"Ah, so that's why you want to go to his party. To gawk at her." Valerie got out of her chair and came around behind Marcel and put her hands on his shoulders.

"Hey, now that you mention it, that *is* a good reason to go."

Maude warned, "Watch it, big brother, you just got married."

"What'd you mean when you said he hadn't mentally gotten over the accident?" Brock asked.

"He's got some notion that Satan is pushing God out of American culture, which will soon lead to total depravity in society. He thinks the decline began in 1968." Marcel rotated his hands and pointed at the sky.

"He may be on to something."

Valerie said cheerfully, "I like eccentric people. I find them fascinating."

All eyes went west, and they quit talking to watch the sun drop out of sight. When it did, Brock broke the silence with, "Maude, my dear, let's head for home. Our lonesome dog, Truman, will be wondering where we are. I say we go to the party on Labor Day. I want to see how off-kilter Willett has become."

Marcel said, "Okay, if you'll promise not to cause any trouble."

"Me?" Brock pointed to himself, bugged his eyes, and dropped his mouth open.

———————

Frank Romine, now in his late thirties, grew up on a prosperous cattle farm off Thurman Lane, north of Springfield, Kentucky. He didn't much care for his parents but was eternally grateful to them for the brain he'd been blessed with. His interest in chess began when he received a small board as a Christmas gift from his folks at age eight. They figured he'd master the game lickety-split. They were right. By thirteen, Frank couldn't find anyone who could beat him. That's when he began entering tournaments. His sobriquet was "the black hole" since he always played the black pieces, which were at a disadvantage because they moved second. It cost him some prize money, but he preferred the challenge and thought it would make him a better player.

At eighteen, Romine left home for the University of Kentucky in pursuit of a degree in computer science. He was introduced to the wacky world of algorithms and how to use them to learn all the correct moves in chess. Better yet, he figured out how most software was configured, and became proficient at breaching databases. Over the last twenty years, Frank had stayed one step ahead of new methods used to protect computer systems from being hacked. The federal government followed the breadcrumbs and came calling on Frank, who had been tramping around in secure CIA and NSA databases thought to be impenetrable. They wanted him to use the cover as a chess player while secretly occupying the first chair among government hackers.

Frank achieved grandmaster status at age thirty. His insistence on playing black pieces meant he could never win a world championship, and that was okay with him. He was being paid a fortune to extract information from enemy nations. One day it dawned on him that if he made a mistake and got traced, a hit man from a foreign power could rub him out. His conundrum was the fact that the United States might kill him if he tried to quit. That problem solved itself when another hacker of similar talent came along. Frank worked a deal to go away quietly. No muss, no fuss. After all, if an American chess player of his caliber went missing after a match, there would certainly be an investigation. The government would leave him alone if he kept his nose clean. He could work in the private sector and win a few more chess tournaments by playing the white pieces.

Winning at chess was getting harder by the day. Online cheating plagued the game. Players could have a computer screen on a match, and one next to it on an "engine" signaling the right move to make. That drove pro players to only take part in over-the-board tournaments. All serious competitions had gone back to that, and rapid games were being played using a short timer. Contestants needed to know the right moves and how to make them quickly. Frank spent hundreds of hours memorizing solutions to situations that developed in matches.

———————

CeCe got back to her place at ten o'clock on Sunday evening after completing that errand. She was in bed and asleep by eleven.

At seven thirty on Monday morning, she gulped down a glass of lemon juice and club soda, and then drove to a local gym that had lots of new equipment. She worked out alone for an hour and a half.

Next stop was a spa in Frankfort, where she drank green tea, got a facial and massage, and took a steam shower. She returned home at eleven thirty and fixed a late breakfast of Greek yogurt, fruit, and cold salmon.

CeCe showed up in downtown Louisville at half past one to try on a cocktail dress she ordered from a shop that knew her measurements and could make alterations on the spot. A couple of tweaks were needed, so she slipped next door to the jewelry store in search of earrings that matched her outfit. She found a pair, bought them, and picked up the dress.

The call she was expecting came in shortly before five o'clock. "Shall I pick you up at six?"

"That won't be necessary. I'll drive myself and meet you there at six thirty."

"Okay, if you insist," the man said.

"What time will the event be over?"

"Ten o'clock at the latest."

"Good. I'll see you soon."

CeCe made it to the cocktail lounge on time. The man waiting for her to arrive flashed a warm smile when he saw her, remarking, "You look sensational."

"Thank you." She latched onto his arm as he led the way into the dim blue light of the crowded bar. Every man in the establishment saw her come in and couldn't take their eyes off her. She had never quite gotten used to that but had come to expect it.

"What can I get you to drink?"

"Club soda with lime." She fell in behind him and stood near the bar while he got her drink and one for himself, hoping a lush wouldn't come over to make conversation while she waited.

The man who was escorting her, loudly blurted out, "Oh, there's someone I'd like to have a word with." They worked their way around the perimeter of the room and walked up behind a gentleman who appeared to be about sixty years old. The man tapped the fellow's shoulder, saying when he turned around, "Senator, I want you to meet Celine, a friend of mine."

The senator unprofessionally undressed her with his eyes, and replied salaciously, "Well, hello."

Chapter 3

September first fell on Thursday. A muggy morning drizzle made Marcel's window-laden corner office seem gloomy, suffused with fuzzy light, setting the mood for the subjects to be discussed on Frank Romine's first day. Frank had on a tawny blazer, gold slacks, an ecru shirt, and light-green tie. His thin hair, parted on the left side, was the color of his sports coat. His high forehead and slight build left people with the impression he was some sort of crafty wimp, or only a world-class chess player.

Marcel introduced Brock, who padded over from the window where he'd been looking out. The three of them sat at the hardwood polygon table that had six black chairs around it. Brock began the conversation benignly. "Marcel tells me you know a thing or two about chess."

"I do, among other things."

"Do you consider yourself an introvert?"

"Not really. I'm certainly not the life of the party either. Somewhere in between, I suppose." He crossed his arms, possibly to signal he didn't care for the question. Brock took the gesture to mean Frank thought he was doing Marcel a favor by coming to work at the company. That remained to be seen.

To smooth the waters, Marcel said, "Don't pay attention to Brock's bedside manner. He doesn't mince words."

"I don't mind. I pay more attention to what I see than what I hear."

"I can imagine. So, what do you see in me?" Brock asked.

"Ominous face, powerful shoulders, calloused hands. If I didn't know better, I'd take you for a boxer."

"I am a boxer. What else?"

"Mike Tyson said it best: everybody has a plan until they get punched in the mouth. You like to see how well a person's plan holds together after they've been hit. I may look like a wallflower, but I can take a punch with the best of them." Frank shifted positions and made a tent with his fingers.

"I, for one, appreciate your attitude and style," Brock replied, offering an insincere compliment.

Marcel changed the subject. "So, what do you know about our database?"

"I've already hacked into it. We'll have to put an end to that possibility for others."

"What did you see?"

"It was easy to figure out the body measurements and how they're depicted mathematically. The data needs to be walled off. Do either of you remember what happened to Virgil when he got to the bottom of hell in *Dante's Inferno?*"

Brock volunteered, "He went through the ice and came out the other side to start the journey up to purgatory."

Frank, looking shocked, responded, "I would've bet money that neither of you knew the answer to that question. You're right, of course. I refer to the exit through the ice as the black hole."

"And I've been told that's your moniker in the chess world. What's the significance of a hole in the bottom of hell?"

"It's the way I've been able to make an online database impenetrable. Hackers come through the front door trying to work their way to the bottom. When they get there, I make the gravity so intense, it's impossible for them to get out the way they came in. They get sucked through the bottom and spit out the other side empty-handed, without any data. It's sort of like a man running across a room toward a closed door, and suddenly the door flies open, he runs through it, and a freefall in space is waiting for him on the other side."

"Is that the only way you know of to protect data from being breached?"

"Well, no. You can take information off the server as soon as it comes in and transfer it to an offline system. That's terribly inconvenient and inefficient. I'll set that up if it's what you want."

Marcel put a hand under his chin, rubbed his face, and leaned back. "No. Can you fix everything in our files from your home computer?"

"I can. I'll need the cooperation of your guys running the system here at the company."

"That's easy enough. Have you found a place to live?" Marcel asked.

"Yes. I moved into a luxury apartment near a bourbon distillery not too far north of here where I set up my computers."

Brock said, "Since you're a pro at chess, I'm guessing you know how to play bridge."

"I don't remember every convention, but I can hold my own."

Brock pushed his chair back. "Yeah, I bet you can. Hopefully, we'll get a chance to play."

Marcel stood. "Come on, let's head to human resources and get you signed up for everything. Then we'll go to IT." He stuck his hand out to shake. "Welcome to Sutherland Tailoring."

Frank reciprocated and then took Brock's hand. Looking him in the eye, he said, "I think we're going to get along just fine."

Brock smiled disarmingly. "I never doubted it. Nice to have you aboard."

Forty-five minutes later, Marcel returned to his office after he introduced Frank to a few people and left him in the IT department. Brock was at the window peering out at the claustrophobic weather. He said, "You don't believe that black hole crap Romine was selling, do you?"

"Shouldn't I?"

"He was gaming us. He's not going to share how he does what he does. He won't even let your best IT boys see how things work, and nobody is smart enough to challenge him."

"Are you suggesting I relieve him of his duties?"

"It's too late for that. He's already given the company a proctology exam. He's got our data and could extort us for whatever amount of money he wants."

"You're paranoid." Marcel collapsed in his desk chair. It rolled back against the wall.

"Did you work on getting him bonded like I suggested?" Brock asked.

"No."

"I'd get on that, and if you must pay the premium yourself, do it." He walked out and began the drive back to Hazard.

Just north of the Bluegrass Parkway on Highway 127, Bonds Mill Road ran west up the hill to a well-known bourbon distillery by the name of Four Roses. Past the pumpkin patch, before the railroad tracks, an apartment complex had been built by an intrepid developer on the south side of the road. The owner thought a few adventurous city executives would be interested in renting there to enjoy country living only a short distance from the office. Romine grabbed the last unit available for $3,500 a month. The property had a black-iron fence and stone pillars around the perimeter, strategically placed surveillance cameras, and a sliding gate by the road that controlled who came and went.

There were eight wide-bay garages, four on each side of the two-story structure that had four units on each floor. Frank's apartment was upstairs to the right, facing the front. A concrete pad and swimming pool had been added on the back to embellish the amenities for living there.

Frank walked into his place shortly before noon after meeting Marcel and Brock. He fixed a ham and pickle sandwich, washing it down with sugar-free lemonade. There was noise coming from somewhere in the building, so he stepped out to see what was going on. The door of the unit across the way stood open. He stuck his head in and saw a lovely female unloading groceries. "Hey there, I'm your neighbor. You need any help?"

The woman glanced up and said, "Yeah, that'd be great, go down to my garage and bring up the rest of the food. The trunk is open."

He did as he was directed, returning with three plastic bags hooked over fingers in each hand. "Here you go." He set them on the kitchen counter. "My name's Frank Romine."

"Celine Oliver," she reported.

Frank had seen beautiful women in his day, but none like her. He surveyed what kind of food she'd bought, commenting, "You sure eat healthy. I should get some pointers." Lemons rattled alongside Greek yogurt, breakfast fruit, colorful vegetables, and another bag had lean beef and a variety of frozen fish.

"Helps me keep my girlish figure." She checked to see how he'd react to that statement.

"Looks like it's working."

"I'm used to men staring at me, Frank, so don't be intimidated." She wore a light gray, crinkled-cotton jumper, big-bead black necklace, red heels, and a thin red belt cinching her waist.

Frank tried to remember if he'd seen a figure like hers. "Has anyone ever told you that you look like Brigitte Bardot, only prettier?"

She put her hands on her hips and said, "Let's not get carried away now, Frank."

"Listen to me. I sound like a teenage boy." Checkmate. Frank had been punched in the mouth, and he was glad Brock Skinner wasn't there to see his plan falling apart.

"That happens to me all the time. You'll get over it," she said to disarm him.

"Are you a model?"

Celine finished putting away the food. She replied, "No, I'm an escort."

"You mean like a hooker?" He wanted to take that statement back as soon as he said it.

"There's the teenage boy again. No, I'm not a hooker. I attend social functions with respectable men. I work no earlier than eleven thirty in the morning or later than eleven thirty at night."

"Dare I ask your rate?" He'd already stuck one foot in his mouth. Might as well put the other in there too.

"Three hundred dollars an hour or three thousand dollars for a twelve-hour day. What business are you in?"

"I'm a professional chess player."

"Ooh, I like smart men. What do you do all day?" She was on the cusp of leading him on.

"I sit at the computer studying what to do in chess game situations. Are you working today?"

"No. I just dressed up to go to the store. People gawk at me, so I figured I better look good."

"Well, can I hire you to escort me to a nice steakhouse for dinner this evening?"

"Frank, you've not been vetted as a client of mine, and besides, it's bad policy to fraternize with a neighbor. The answer is no."

"Somehow, I knew you were going to say that. I'm right across the hall if you need anything."

She moved to the door of her apartment and announced, "Thanks for coming over to introduce yourself. I'm sure we'll see each other again."

He threw his hands in the air, smiled, returned to his place, and instantly searched for a picture of Brigitte Bardot on the Internet.

———————

Brock fought through the persistent drizzle on his trip home, arriving at one o'clock. When he marched into the house, Maude saw he was fit to be tied. "What's wrong?"

"Oh, that brother of yours has pulled a stunt that scares me." He threw his Lamborghini keys on the lamp table.

"You, scared? This will be good." She grabbed an elbow and used her hand to prop up her head.

"This guy, Frank Romine, whom he hired to protect the company's data from being breached, is a ringer."

"How do you know that?"

"Because he's already hacked into our database and happened to mention that he had decoded body measurements of our customers, which means he knows how important that information is. He could sell it or use it for blackmail. And then he told us some cock-and-bull story about protecting data. He described a completely ridiculous method for deflecting hackers."

"Are you sure about that?"

"Maude, the guy is a professional chess player. Those people are generally two or three moves ahead of the average bear. He's planning something nefarious. I don't know how to stop him. Well, I do know one way."

"Uh-oh. Does it involve fists or firearms?" Maude tilted her head forward conspicuously.

"I was thinking along the lines of threatening him."

"There must be another way."

"I'm working on it." Brock eased onto the couch like it was a hot seat. The white German shepherd, asleep on his side, looked up blurry eyed, to make sure nothing interesting was going on.

"Does he have a wife, ex-wife, or girlfriend?" Maude came over and sat next to her husband.

He pivoted to face her. "I don't know. What are you thinking?"

"If you could locate his former or current love interest, you might find out about his character from her." She seemed proud of the idea.

"Marcel told me that a friend of his from college was Frank's roommate. Frank probably asked his former roomy if he knew any company that could use his services. The guy must have told him about Sutherland Tailoring and offered to contact Marcel, which he did. That's how we got in this pickle. I could get his name from your brother and talk to him."

"Why don't you just tell Marcel to call him."

"I would, but I'm afraid he doesn't have the finesse to get the information I need."

"How would you handle it?"

"I'd tell the guy we were having a bridge tournament for couples, and before we invited Frank, to avoid putting him on the spot, it would be nice to know if he had a wife or girlfriend who played bridge."

Maude sat up and asked, "Are we having a bridge tournament?"

"I'll suggest it to Calvin Willett when we're at his party. He has a girlfriend who likes to play."

"Yeah, I remember, and according to my brother, she's a looker."

Brock got up and walked around to the other side of the coffee table. "Let's go to the winery so I can get some lunch." Truman understood what that meant. He went and stood by the door.

"Good idea. We're serving grouper sandwiches, cold pearl couscous salad, and succotash."

The three of them got into Maude's SUV to make the short trip to Vigneron Winery, which was behind their log-cabin home, but around the mountain by car.

When they parked at the winery, Truman jumped out of the vehicle and ran into the grapevines, where his job was to chase off the varmints. Brock looked over at Maude and said, "Romine was a high-level government hacker before he came to us. He may have a price on his head."

"Valerie accused Marcel of borrowing trouble. Look who's doing it now."

"Yeah." Brock slammed the door of the SUV and had a frown on his face.

CHAPTER 4

Brock went into Maude's office at the winery and rang up his brother-in-law after he'd finished eating lunch. "Marcel, what was the name of Frank Romine's roommate in college? I want to call him to see if he knows whether Frank has an ex-wife or girlfriend."

"No need to do that. He told me about a girl he's dated on and off for years when I interviewed him. She's a professional chess player who lives in northern Virginia. I believe he said her name was Leslie Blazek."

"Get the IT department to find her cell phone number. Send it to me when you get it."

"If you call her, she'll tell Frank. He's liable to be sore when he finds out," said Marcel.

"I'll convince her not to tell him I called."

"How are you going to do that?"

"Trade secret." Brock cut the line.

The number came across in a text five minutes later. Brock tapped on it. "Is this Leslie Blazek?"

"It is." She sounded put out.

"Hello, Miss Blazek. I'm calling to get some information about Frank Romine. Chess tournament officials are doing background checks on potential invitees. I'm part of an investigative group researching his character. People who know Mr. Romine told us you are acquainted with him."

"What is your name?"

"Brock Skinner. Before you share anything with me about Frank, I would ask that you agree not to tell him that we called you. If you can't do that, then what you tell us will not be considered confidential, and we will not use it in our report. Our sources must be confidential in the event the tournament officials decide not to invite Mr. Romine to play."

"I think you're lying, but what is it you wanted to know?"

"Once again, Miss Blazek, will you agree not to tell him we've called?" Brock figured she wasn't going to hang up on him now.

"Yes, I'll agree to that."

"Good. We want to confirm that Frank Romine has never cheated while playing in an online chess tournament. Do you believe that to be the case?"

"He cheated on me, but Frank would never cheat at chess. He'd rather lose."

"Why do you say that?"

"Because he's the only extraordinary chess player I've met who doesn't get exasperated when he loses. He just goes home and studies more. Eventually, when he's learned enough, and starts playing the whites, he'll be unbeatable."

"This is somewhat personal, but you mentioned he'd cheated on you. Do you consider him to be a dishonest person?"

She huffed at the phone. "Hell no. He was brutally honest about other women. I wanted him to marry me. He, apparently, doesn't want to be tied down. We continue to date, on and off, and I know it isn't going anywhere, but he is fun to be with. He recently moved to Kentucky, so I doubt if I'll be seeing much of him except at tournaments."

"Do you think he's hiding anything in his personal life?"

"I'm not sure I'd call it hiding. He was doing something with his time other than chess. When I asked him about it, he was evasive. I concluded that he was doing computer work for someone under a confidentiality agreement. He seemed to be a whiz at the computer."

"So, you can say that you've never caught him in a lie?"

"No, I haven't. He's not the lying, stealing type. His ego doesn't allow for it. He expects to earn whatever he gets. That's one of the reasons I wanted to marry him."

Brock concluded she was genuinely in love with the man. "Thanks for the candid information, Miss Blazek. It has been immensely helpful. Oh, one more thing, do you play bridge?"

"Yes. What's that got to do with anything?"

"The subject may come up in the future. Enjoy the rest of your day."

Maude stepped into her office and asked, "Well, how did it go?"

"He may not be a crook after all." Brock then told his wife about the conversation, put his hands in his pockets, and shrugged his shoulders. "Doesn't know he was working for the US government. She also said he doesn't get upset when he loses. What does that mean?"

Maude replied, "Sounds like he's on a continuous improvement program, like taking a college entrance exam over and over until he gets a perfect score."

"Could be. He's got the same mindset when it comes to stopping hackers. Just keeps getting better and better at it. He's not a perfectionist though."

"That's for sure. A perfectionist would never take up the game of chess."

Frank spent hours on the computer researching the life of Celine Oliver. She was born at home on property in the woods outside Hazard, Kentucky, thirty-two years ago. She graduated from Berea College with a degree in English. Her high school and college yearbook pictures showed her sporting a short, athletic haircut. Today, her face was fuller, and she had a wavy, mid-length coif. Her looks had improved with age, and her longer hair complemented her face, he thought.

Celine dropped out of sight for five years after college and resurfaced at the address of a house not far from where she now lived. She didn't file anything with the IRS during the time she was missing. At twenty-six, she sent in her first tax return declaring $72,591 in income. Last year's amount was $318,470. The address on the return had been changed to her current residence.

Romine couldn't find where she had a checking account. He wondered how she paid the rent. She had a savings account at a small bank in downtown Harrodsburg with a million dollars in it. He dug up over two years of her credit card statements. Nothing interesting to see there. Her background seemed straightforward enough, Frank surmised, except for the five years she was gone and the million bucks she came into. He didn't yet care to waste time trying to find out where she went.

The knock on the door startled him. "Coming." When he opened it, there stood Celine, wearing the same clothes he'd seen her in earlier that day.

"Since I'm all dressed up, we might as well grab a bite to eat. I told you I wasn't working today, so there's no charge."

"Where shall we go?" Frank decided not to overplay his hand.

"Tony's in Lexington. I'll drive," she said.

"Won't that make me look like a sugar daddy?"

"What's wrong with that? All my clients are sugar daddies."

"Right. You stay here while I change and put on a blazer."

"No, I'll pull my car around. Meet me out front when you're ready."

Frank got in her metallic blue Mercedes and off they went. He thought about saying that he'd never been seen with a woman of her caliber before but didn't want to lapse back into teenage-boy mode. Instead, he asked, "Have you ever played chess?"

"Are you kidding me? With all the effort I put into looking like this?" CeCe raised her eyebrows and gestured her hand down the length of her body. "There's no time for games other than bridge with clients."

"That's a shame."

"I figure I've got eight more years of this life, and when I turn forty, I'll be a perky blonde-haired woman on the skids."

"I wouldn't count on that. More likely you'll have enough money to retire."

"You sound like you know something about my finances."

"I do other things besides study chess moves with those big computers in my apartment." He peered at her sheepishly.

"Uh-oh. I get the feeling you know more about me than I do."

"I should hope not."

She switched topics and said, "Do you have a girlfriend?"

"I used to, sort of," he revealed.

"What kind of BS answer is that? Tell me about her."

"Leslie Blazek. She's a chess player too. I used to live near her in northern Virginia. She likes me more than I like her. I'm ashamed of how I've treated her over the years. I need to apologize for taking her for granted. I'm not in the business of treating anyone badly."

"That's noble of you. If you're trying to convince me that you're a good catch, it won't work. I know more about men than anyone in the Midwest. They're my business. As they say in horse racing, you're trying to move up in class, and you'll soon find out you're in over your head."

"I think I understand."

"Haven't you heard the saying: if you want to be happy for the rest of your life, don't make a pretty woman your wife?"

"I have heard that," Frank replied as though it were a revelation. Celine wheeled her Mercedes up to the valet stand in front of the restaurant. He restrained her when they got to the door, and said, "Now, let me enjoy this. When we walk in there, every man in the place will wish he were me."

"Looks aren't everything, Frank."

"Right. And money can't buy happiness."

She wagged a finger at him and smiled.

Tony himself was seating people. He put them in the corner by the front window. Celine said, "This is kind of fun. I'm with a man, and I don't have to hold my tongue. I can say hurtful things and not get fired."

The noise of the crowd seemed to be increasing with each passing second. "That's refreshing," Frank spoke loudly enough for her to hear. "How many hours do you work in a year?"

"I'll log about twelve hundred this year, roughly twenty-four hours a week." She twisted her body and rolled one shoulder forward.

"Let me see: 300 times 1,200 is 360,000. I guess if you work a full day, there's a bit of a discount, so call it 350,000. That isn't hay.

Not only are you beautiful, you're also a savvy businessperson. You ever worry about one of your clients trying to rape you?"

"Not really. I check people out carefully. I make the rules of the road clear to them." The server came by, and Celine began dictating: "Get him a glass of house Chardonnay. I'll have club soda with lime. We're going to split a Greek salad, and he'll have the sea bass. I would like the yellowfin tuna. Does that suit you?" She looked at Frank imperiously.

"Perfectly." The server backed away without saying a word. "How many clients do you have?"

"Only a few. I have one I spend time with on weekends. He's 50 percent of my revenue."

"Care to share who that is?"

"He calls me CeCe. His name is Calvin Willett. He has a decent spread on Herrington Lake. I like him as a client because he's polite and considerate, and his cushy house is only a short distance from my apartment."

"And you're sure he'll never try to get to second base?"

"Not a chance. Twenty years ago, he was waterskiing on the lake at night and slammed into the dock. He nearly died. He's a little cripple from it, not only his body, but his mind as well."

"Like how?"

"He's sad and depressed underneath. I don't think he's forgiven himself for getting drunk and slamming into a dock. He's retreated to the morality espoused in the Bible, and believes Satan is running amok, destroying America. That's how his sadness and depression come out."

The server brought the drinks and salad. "How did he get the money for a place on the lake?"

"His parents sold their garment business, and he got a share of the proceeds, I think."

"Good for him. Who did they sell the business to?"

"Sutherland Tailoring. Their operation isn't too far south of where we live."

Frank had a small-world moment. He saw no need to tell her he was working for Sutherland. "What about your other clients?"

"A couple of prominent businesspeople and politicians. Enough about me. I think it's fair game to ask how much you make playing chess."

"Plenty. I'm not hurting for cash."

"You didn't answer the question. How much?"

"Half a million a year."

The fish came, and they would have enjoyed the meal more if the place had been quieter.

On the ride home, Celine said, "There's no way a professional chess player making your kind of money moves into an apartment between Lawrenceburg and Harrodsburg, Kentucky. There's another reason you came here. I told you about my life, so you need to spill it."

"I was raised on a farm north of Springfield, which is less than a half hour from where we live. I didn't want to move too close to my parents, but close enough to check on them in their old age. Speaking of being forthright, there's something in your background that doesn't add up. Where did you go for five years after you graduated from college?" That was a zinger. Frank would have been wise to keep that to himself.

Celine had a terrified look on her face. She replied so quietly that he barely heard what she said. "I'm not so sure we're going to be friends." She pulled the Mercedes up to the front of the apartment complex and waited for him to get out.

Frank said, "Thanks for the wonderful time." He reluctantly climbed out of the car. Celine drove into her garage and then headed up the stairs to her place. Frank was standing outside his door fidgeting. "I hope I didn't cross the line."

"I guess if you dish it out, you must take it. If you start digging into where I was those five years, I'll never speak to you again. Kapish?"

"Yeah. Mentioning it was uncalled for. Rude, in fact. It's none of my business. I really did have a wonderful time tonight. Let's not have one stupid thing I said ruin the evening. Sweet dreams." He disappeared into his apartment, determined to discover what she was hiding.

She stood there erroneously feeling like the maven she thought she was when it came to men.

Chapter 5

The Labor Day late morning weather had noticeable flaws with the clouds moving quickly across the sky, and an erratic wind blowing in all directions. The upper-eighties temperature made the breeze an asset. CeCe popped through the front door of the Willett house at ten till twelve. She called out, "Cal, you here?"

"In the kitchen." He stepped around the corner to greet her.

"How many people are you expecting today?" She put the keys to her Mercedes in a bowl on a side table, and her wrap and hat on the couch. The purple, one-piece bathing suit she wore had irregular, diagonal white stripes, somewhat camouflaging her figure. Her hair was in a ponytail.

"Thirty some odd."

"Oh, good. I don't think it's going to rain." She walked to the window to look up at the sky.

"We'll make the best of it. I took the food and drinks to the dock a few minutes ago, so you can relax until people get here."

Ten minutes later, Cal tottered to the front door when he heard a firm rap on it. "Marcel, how good of you to come, and this must be your wife."

"Hi, I'm Valerie. Very nice to meet you." She reminded him of a naïf in need of protection from the hardened party crowd.

"Right through here." The Sutherlands entered, leaving Brock and Maude to be received. "Mr. Skinner. It's been a while. You look well. And who is this lovely lady with you?"

"Calvin, this is my wife, Maude."

"Hello," she said enthusiastically. "Thanks for inviting us."

Cal couldn't help but notice the Skinners were both tall, formidable people, seemingly ready for the Shakespearian stage. "A pleasure. Please come and meet my friend." He swept his hand in a welcoming gesture.

When Valerie and Maude saw CeCe, they glanced at each other without having to say out loud how attractive she was. Pleasant introductions were made followed by a few waggish remarks.

Cal's house had been done in the Tudor motif. The front was red herringbone brick with rows of black windows on either side of a dark-stained, solid poplar door. Inside, the family-room wall facing the lake had tall glass on each side of the fireplace. Straight rods supported diaphanous drapes that were pulled open. The all-white fireplace had a mantel and archway framing the rectangular firebox. Buckskin leather chairs and a couch were on the large, checkered rug that matched the contrasting colors of the brown furniture and white walls.

Brock went to the window and glanced down at the dock. Then he carefully surveyed the room, noticing the landline phone on the table between the two side chairs, and a record player built in the highboy against the wall. He commented, "I love your home, Calvin. What a great place to entertain guests."

"And I enjoy having company. It's twelve o'clock. Let's head down. The rest of the guests know their way." Cal rode the one-person tram while everyone else used the steps. By twelve forty-five, twenty-plus guests were eating, drinking, talking, and laughing on the dock. Cal took his normal seat under the umbrella.

CeCe walked up to Maude and Valerie to make conversation. "In a little while, I'll get Cal to take us skiing. Where do you folks live?"

Valerie went first. "I just married Marcel two weeks ago after living in Roswell, New Mexico, for years. We live near Harrodsburg."

Maude added, "We're from Hazard. I own and run a winery there."

"Oh, really? I was born near Hazard."

Maude's face lit up. "Well, you can come back any time. As a matter of fact, I'm offering you a job right here and now, to be the general manager of a winery. The pay is lousy, and the hours are long, but hey, it's rewarding work."

"I'll take it! No, wait, I don't know anything about running a business. I don't know much about anything other than English literature. Sorry." The three women laughed together.

Valerie asked, "Where do you live?"

"Between Lawrenceburg and Harrodsburg, near Four Roses Distillery."

"Do you work?"

"Part time. I'm an administrative assistant for several politicians and businesspeople. I arrange meetings and do event planning for them."

"How do you know Mr. Willett?"

"I contacted him a couple of years ago and asked if he needed help with his business affairs. His company had been sold, so he asked me to work on philanthropic endeavors. We have become good friends."

Maude said, "My brother, who is Valerie's husband, bought the Willett company. My husband, Brock, and my brother own Sutherland Tailoring."

"Is that so? I've been tempted to buy some clothes from Sutherland."

"Jump right in. There's a booth in Harrodsburg where you can get measured. They fit to a T."

"I think I will."

The women broke up and moved around to talk to other people. Nat King Cole oozed from the speakers like silk pajamas. Brock approached CeCe, saying, "I'm going to ask Calvin if he's in the mood to host a friendly bridge tournament."

"Oh, are you? Be forewarned, he doesn't play for money."

"By the looks of it, he doesn't do several things. The record player and landline phone are kind of indicators."

CeCe noticed Brock was all muscle, the type of man whose adrenalin a person shouldn't arouse. His looks conjured up in her mind a tightly wound roll of barbed wire. She said, "His boat and car are 1967 models. He doesn't have a cell phone, computer, or the Internet. He prefers life as it was back then."

"I've heard that. There's a lot to be said for a simpler life, wouldn't you say?"

"I would indeed. Who did you have in mind to play in a bridge tournament?" CeCe held the front of her floppy hat, which was blowing in the wind, so she could watch his response.

Brock read the hint of suspicion in her expression. "You and Cal, of course. Valerie and Marcel, Maude and me, and a guy by the name of Frank Romine and his girlfriend, Leslie Blazek." He saw her rapid eye movement when he mentioned Romine's name.

"How do you know Frank Romine?" she uttered sotto voce.

"He's a chess player I met recently. Why do you ask?"

"I follow chess as well. I hope Cal likes the idea. I'll see if he'll take us skiing now. When we get back, he'll want to start *The*

New York Times crossword puzzle." She moved off and bent over Willett's shoulder. He got up and walked in the direction of his prized runabout.

The wind and titanic waves caused by too many boats zipping around in the same area made skiing about as treacherous as it gets. No one tried to get up on one ski, being satisfied to shoot back and forth across the choppy wake on two. According to Cal, there was no feeling as good as the tiredness from the exertion of waterskiing, and those who were plopped back in the boat were in a gay and relaxed mood.

Brock threw out a backdoor comment, "I believe this is a 1967 model isn't it, Calvin?"

"Yes. The last time wooden runabouts were widely available."

"What's so special about that year?" The faces in the boat changed into expressions of people watching a movie.

"It was the last year God held Satan back. The devil has been freely roaming about like a roaring lion since then, seeking whom he may devour in our once-great country."

"How did you come by that?" Brock tried to look like he wasn't that interested in the subject.

"I can think of an example: the Beatles released two albums in 1967: *Sgt. Pepper's* and *Magical Mystery Tour.* There was nothing crass about the music. In 1968, they put out *The White Album.* On it were two disturbing songs: *Why Don't We Do It in the Road* and *Helter Skelter.* Charles Manson heard the music, and well, you know what happened."

"I see what you mean. Hey, I wanted to ask if you'd be in favor of hosting a bridge night at your house. I was thinking the six of us here and another couple could fight it out to see who's best. What do you say?"

"That's a fantastic idea. When would you like to do it?" Cal sat up in his seat.

"I'll have to get in touch with the other couple to see when they might be able to play. Can I call you later with some dates?"

"Certainly." He turned to CeCe. "Send him my number when you get a chance. Let's get back to the dock and start in on the crossword."

It took four hours to defeat the puzzle. There was one line left to be filled in. CeCe said, "Great-great-grandfather of Marty McFly. Six letters."

Cal looked around for anyone who knew the answer. "Well?" He raised his arms.

Valerie stepped forward and announced, "Seamus, S-E-A-M-U-S." The crowd hooted and gave her a round of applause.

Marcel came up next to his wife and addressed the host, "On that note, we're going to head for home. Thanks, Calvin, for having us over."

Willett got to his feet, nodded, and smiled. He turned to Brock and said, "You call me about that bridge game."

The four of them offered good-byes and climbed the hill. When they got into Maude's SUV, she told Brock what she was sure would light a fire. "CeCe was born in Hazard, and she now lives near Four Roses Distillery."

Marcel said, "Uh-oh. Frank Romine lives up that way. Wonder if she knows him?"

Brock followed with, "I bet so. When I mentioned him playing bridge with us, her eyes twitched. Who is this CeCe woman anyway?"

"An event planner and meeting coordinator, according to her," Valerie reported.

"My foot. She's got all the markings of a high-class hooker."

"She's too good looking for that," Maude said.

"I'm not so sure Calvin Willett would go for a prostitute," Marcel posited.

"Whatever, he's paying for it. Marcel, I need you to find out everything you can about CeCe. Let me know what her birth certificate says, and I'll try to track down her folks in Hazard if they're still alive."

"What's her real name?"

"I heard her introduce herself to someone on the dock as Celine Oliver," Maude revealed.

"Good. That's a toehold."

Brock said, "I'll talk to Romine to see when he can get Leslie Blazek to come around."

Maude said to Valerie, "Remember when you visited us before you were married, and we went down the rabbit hole trying to solve some silly mystery?"

"I do. It was great fun," she replied.

"Oh, no. We've got another one. I see I'm outnumbered. Just keep this in mind, Valerie: this bare-knuckle husband of mine plays rough at times. Don't be shocked when he rides the outlaw trail."

"What does that mean?"

"Read Louis L'Amour." Maude pointed at Brock. "He's straight out of one of his Westerns."

Marcel laughed heartily and bellowed, "Ride 'em, cowboy!"

Brock glared indignantly at his brother-in-law. "You of all people making fun of me."

"Only for one reason: you can never let anything go."

"You're the one who got us into this, worrying about the database being hacked. Now, I'll be the one who gets us out of it." The crisp, suddenly-quiet atmosphere in the vehicle could be cut with a knife.

"How's this any different than the other times?" Maude asked after the long pause.

———

When the party broke up at dark, the weather had calmed. Cal and CeCe went up to the house where he commented, "People think I'm strange, don't they?" He sat in a chair at the kitchen table and avoided eye contact.

She watched him for a few seconds before speaking. "What people?"

"Everybody."

"I can give it to you straight if you want to hear it, Cal. You know I want the best for you. You're a good person. You've always been nice to me."

"Let's hear it."

"Choosing not to live in the present has people wondering what's in your head. The questions they ask are to figure out what you're thinking. You argue the idea there's no hope for America. You claim Satan's destroying it, leaving people to conclude you are angry and depressed. From there, they suspect you have certain things in your life that are unresolved."

"They're probably right." He hung his head.

"Everybody understands you believe in the morality of the Bible. Just to reassure you, one-third of the eight billion people on this earth are Christian, and they think a lot like you. Christianity is the world's number one religion. Surely, there are some positives you can take from that?"

"But of course."

"And then there's our relationship. Most people don't understand it. They don't know what I'm doing, or what you're doing. You seem to enjoy throwing parties and having people around you who have different values, yet instead of proselytizing them in love, you scare them with gloom and doom. I'm not sure the God of the Bible endorses that. You would know better than me."

He moved into the kitchen and leaned on the counter with straight arms. "You've given me much to think about. I appreciate your frankness." He left the subject behind. "How do you feel about having a bridge tournament?"

"It's a marvelous idea. I'm not sure what Brock's thinking. Would we draw for partners?"

"That's the official way it's done."

"I'd like it better if we played together." She picked up the keys to her car, put on her wrap, and tucked the floppy hat under one arm.

"I'm sure I can arrange that." Cal worked up a frail smile.

"That sounds good. I'll see you soon." She could tell he was hurting. He wanted to know, so she told him. It was for the best, she hoped. Her stomach churned all the way home.

CHAPTER 6

Tuesday morning at seven fifty, Brock's phone dinged. CeCe sent him Calvin's landline number. He called Marcel and asked that HR text him Romine's address. Maude rushed into the kitchen and found her husband finishing his coffee. "Good morning," she said pleasantly. "I'm guessing you're headed somewhere." She filled a cup with water and put it in the microwave to warm.

"To visit Frank Romine, to see if he can get his girlfriend to join us for a bridge game."

"That seems harmless enough." She dropped a tea bag in the cup, gave her husband a kiss, and returned to the bedroom to finish her morning ritual.

Brock pulled away from the house in his Lamborghini at eight thirty. He rang Marcel again and said, "I've got Celine Oliver's cell number here. Run it and see where her place is."

Marcel called back and said, "She lives in the same building as Frank. He's unit seven, and she's in unit eight."

"That's cozy."

He pressed Romine's button when he got to the gate at Bonds Mill Road. "Brock Skinner here." The apartment building looked like it had been flown in from a city. The beige, Flemish bond brickwork gave the structure an artistic flare not often wasted on rental units. The brown roof seemed higher pitched than necessary.

Frank glanced out his front window and saw a fancy car ready to enter the complex. He actuated the gate and waited for the knock on the door. "Greetings. What brings you out?" he asked genially.

"When we met the other day, I suggested we try to arrange a bridge game. The opportunity has presented itself, provided you and your girlfriend are available."

"Have a seat." Brock eased into a black office chair beside Frank's computer as though he was there for a job interview. A CPU tower had been placed sideways under the desk, and two large screens, in a shallow V, faced the room painted a washed-out tomato color. The ensemble of furniture had green fabric with cherry arms and legs. Otherwise, the surroundings were bereft of anything personal. "How do you know about my girlfriend?" Frank asked.

"Marcel told me you shared with him that you had a friend by the name of Leslie Blazek. We're putting together a four-couple bridge night. We have three couples lined up and wanted you and Leslie to be the fourth."

Frank sat in his computer desk chair like he was preparing to play a chess match, disinterested in the conversation. He looked at Brock. "Who are the couples?"

"Marcel and I, our wives, and a guy by the name of Calvin Willett, and his friend. Calvin wants to host the party at his house on Herrington Lake."

"Who is Willett's guest?"

Brock could tell Frank already knew the answer. "Celine Oliver. I believe she lives across the hall. Have you met her?"

"Yes. She's the reincarnation of Brigitte Bardot." He stared at the ceiling, which meant he was holding something back.

Brock said, "I just got introduced to her yesterday for the first time. Dollars to donuts, you've already dug up everything about her online. Care to share what you found?"

"Gentlemen never tell," Frank replied at once, slipping that punch.

"That's too bad. It would have saved Marcel and me the effort of looking her up ourselves."

"A week from Friday, Leslie and I will be playing in a two-day chess tournament in Louisville. It'll be over by three thirty on Saturday. She's staying here with me Thursday through Sunday. I'll see if she wants to play on Saturday night after the chess match."

"Marvelous." Brock handed him a Vigneron Winery ID card that had a handwritten number on it.

"Here's my information." Frank gave Brock an embossed note card in black type featuring the silhouette of a rook. "Can you arrange a lunch so I can meet this chap beforehand?"

"I'm sure he'd go for that. You mentioned *Dante's Inferno* when I met you. Calvin Willett has his own ideas about Satan and hell. You might find them interesting. I'll call him and set something up for later this week." Brock stood and walked to the apartment door. He turned and asked, "How's work going?"

"Good. There are lots of improvements I'm making to the system to secure it. I think you'll be pleased." He got up out of his chair in a way that urged Skinner to move along. "Let me know about lunch."

"Will do." Brock noticed the three cameras mounted on the building and the one next to the gate as he was leaving. They imbued the place with a negative aura.

Marcel was sitting behind his cluttered desk at Sutherland Tailoring when Brock entered his office. "Selling any clothes today?"

"Orders are good this morning considering it's our slow time of the year. Any news about Frank to report?"

"He and Leslie can play bridge a week from Saturday. He wants to meet Willett first though. I'm setting up a lunch date between the three of us for later this week. What have you discovered about Celine Oliver?" Marcel's findings, which he recited in detail, were virtually identical to what Frank had uncovered. Brock asked, "How could somebody drop completely out of sight for five years? That's hard to do."

"The only thing I can figure is she left Appalachia and started using another name."

"Or went to the Philippines or something. Did you pull an address off her birth certificate?"

"It had the street name but no number—Elm Shoal Branch, west of downtown Hazard. I found acreage owned by Rhonda and Perry Oliver near the end of the road, to the east. Here, look at it on Google Earth." There was a gravel road running through the woods to a clearing. One building, which appeared to be a house, had a black roof. A second larger building, twice the size of the house, was off to the left.

"Did you say she reappeared between Lawrenceburg and Frankfort after being gone those five years? Have you checked to see who the house belongs to where she lived?"

"The same guy has owned it for forty years. I called him. He says Celine Oliver rented from him for four years some six years ago. Says it's been rented to someone else the last two years."

"That's probably a dead end. I saw surveillance cameras at the apartment complex where Frank and Celine live. Any way to hack into them?"

"That's a tall order. Frank could probably do it, but I can't ask him."

On the way out the door, Brock said, "See what you can do."

———————

The road back to Hazard took Brock near Herrington Lake, so he decided to place a call to Calvin Willett. "Hey, I stopped over to visit Marcel at Sutherland Tailoring this morning. I wanted you to know I contacted the other couple for our bridge game while I was in the area. They think they can play a week from Saturday. Would six thirty that evening work for you?"

"That's perfect. I'll put out a buffet dinner for us." He sounded enthused.

"I'm on my way home and wondered if I could swing by your place for a few minutes?"

"Sure. Come right on."

"I'll be there shortly."

Celine Oliver opened the door right after Brock pulled into Willett's driveway and got out of his car. He said, "Fancy meeting you here."

She stepped out to greet him. "We're having a light lunch and doing a little more cleanup after yesterday's party. I really enjoyed talking to your wife and sister-in-law. Your wife's a beautiful lady."

"I'm not sure why she said yes when I proposed, but she did." He was starting to like CeCe for no other reason than she seemed comfortable around him, and likely, men in general. She had a warmth that supercharged her looks.

"I can guess why," she said with a smile. "Won't you come in?"

Calvin was unloading the dishwasher. He paused and said, "Well, back so soon? What did you want to see me about?" He put his hands on his hips.

"The guy I asked to join us for bridge wants to meet you before we play. I told him I'd ask if that would be okay with you."

"Sure. What do you suggest?"

"We could get lunch somewhere together later this week."

"Why don't you and him just pick up a pizza and let's have lunch here."

"Suits me. What day works best for you?"

"How about Friday, say, twelve thirty?" Calvin returned to putting dishes away.

"Good. I'll arrange it." Brock went to the window to look out. A heavy-set man in a small fishing boat was near the opposite shoreline. Up the hill, a cattle field with no visible fences featured brown cows grazing on chewed-down grass. The tessellated surface of the lake shimmered from the wind and harsh midday sun. There was an indescribable feeling of foreboding and loneliness to the scene. "I came by in person for another reason."

"What's that?" Cal stopped fooling with the dishes again.

"The guy and his partner are professional chess players. I'm guessing their bridge game is out of our league. I wanted to see what you thought about having them join us."

"They'll still need to get good cards. Are you recommending that we draw for partners?"

"No. I was thinking we limit the bidding to basic conventions."

"Would help level the playing field. I prefer CeCe as my partner. I say we play a friendly game of couples."

Brock turned to Celine. "Does that suit you?"

"Yes. Sounds like fun."

Calvin asked, "What are their names again?" He came out of the kitchen.

"Frank Romine and Leslie Blazek. They're in a chess tournament in Louisville the afternoon of our bridge night. You might want to drive over and watch them play."

"No thanks," Celine replied emphatically. "If I know Cal, he'll want to take advantage of the last few days of the season on the lake."

Cal added heedlessly, "Right. I suspect Mr. Romine will be an interesting person. I look forward to meeting him on Friday."

Celine followed Brock out to his car. She asked, "I know you said you'd met Frank. What was the occasion?"

"I could lie to you, but I'm not going to. Marcel and I hired him to do some work for us at the company. The man's a genius when it comes to computers. He may also be too smart for his own good when it comes to other things. That's confidential, and I trust you'll keep it that way."

"Certainly." She had a troubled look on her face.

"I'm going to go out on a limb here. You look worried. I know you live across the hall from Frank, and I'm sure you've met him. I also know you disappeared for five years after you graduated from college. You're afraid Frank will find out where you were and what you were doing. You're right to be worried. I'm not sure yet if the man is an opportunist or not. I want you to know that you can call on me or Marcel for help if things get rough. I've got a hunch you're going to need some friends."

She was visibly shaken by what Brock said. She couldn't think of anything to say but, "Thank you."

Brock looked at Celine again and saw her natural beauty had contorted into a form of dread he'd never seen before on a woman. He drove away feeling he was abandoning her on the spot. It couldn't be helped.

––––––––––––

It took Romine no time to dig up a phone number for the person who owned the house CeCe lived in when she came out of hiding six years ago. When the man picked up, Frank said, "I'm trying to find a woman who rented from you for a few years. Her name is Celine Oliver."

"What's your interest in her?"

Frank had already rehearsed a plausible story. "Her parents have lost contact with her, and they are concerned about her well-being. They've asked me to help find her."

"I don't know how I can help. She moved out two years ago, and I've not talked to her since."

"Well, I'm kind of working backward. Did you have her fill out an application before she moved in? I'm hoping she listed a prior address on it."

"Let me go look." The man put the phone down momentarily. When he came back on, he said, "The address she listed here is Elm Shoal Branch, Hazard."

"Is there a house number?" Frank remembered that street name from her birth certificate.

"No."

"Did she pay the rent by check?"

"I'm not sure that's any of your business."

Frank tried to twist the request into a harmless pursuit. "The reason I ask is I was hoping to find the name of her bank so I could contact them to see if she put in a change of address."

"They wouldn't give out that information." Frank was worried the man would stop talking. "She paid me in cash. Promptly, on the first day of the month."

"Do you remember if she had any roommates?"

"I don't really know. I never had any reason to check on her. She kept to herself. The place was cleaner when she moved out than when she moved in. One thing I do remember about her, she was *very* attractive."

"Do you know what kind of car she drove?"

"Yes. A white Jeep. She put the license number on the application."

Bingo, Frank thought. "Would you be kind enough to share that with me?" The man read it off. "Is there anything else you can remember that could help me locate her?"

There was silence on the line. The man was tapping computer keys. "I don't know what you're up to, but when you Google 'Celine Oliver address,' it's listed on Bonds Mill Road. If someone else contacts me about her, I'm going to go to the police and give them the numbers that have come up on my phone."

"Numbers?"

"Yes. Your call is the second one I've gotten today asking about Celine Oliver, and no, I will not give you the number of the other caller. Good day, sir." He hung up.

Frank found out the white Jeep CeCe drove for four years was registered to Rhonda Oliver from Hazard. It was traded two years ago for the Mercedes she now owned, registered in her name. Doubtless, Sutherland and Skinner were hot on the trail of Celine's past. He studied his next move, whether to side with her or help his employer.

CHAPTER 7

The heat fever outside broke early on Wednesday, compelling Brock to jog on backroads near his house at six in the morning. He got to the boxing gym downtown by eight and mulled over a plan of action while pounding away on the heavy bag. One of his friends wanted to spar for three five-minute rounds. Brock knocked him flat at the end of the second round. He asked, "Are you okay?" Sweat dripped off his head into the face of the prostrate boxer.

"Yes, my pride's hurt, but I should have known better than to go five minutes with you."

"What doesn't kill you makes you stronger."

"Oh, you're just full of clichés this morning, aren't you?" His friend rolled over, got to his knees, and then to his feet.

After they were through fighting, Brock showered and put on jeans and a loose-fitting black T-shirt. The house was empty when he got home. Maude and Truman had already left for the winery. He went into his office to bring up the Internet. It took him several minutes to find the advertisement for the previously held ten-year reunion of Celine's college class. He called the coordinator, and surprisingly, she answered. Brock asked her, "Is there any way I can get a list of the people in the class who have died?" She gave him a web address where he could access the names.

He took the list and cross-referenced Celine's college yearbook to see if he resembled any of the dead men. There was one former student, Roy Aldiss, whom he could pass for, and to top it off, Roy was in a group picture with her, which meant they knew each other. Nothing came up when Brock Googled the guy's name. Hopefully, the Olivers didn't know Aldiss was deceased.

Maude saw her husband drive into the parking lot at the winery a few minutes before eleven. A fresh temperate breeze had picked up, teasing the tree leaves over the road. She scooted out to greet him. "What can I do for you?"

Her effervescence helped improve Brock's demeanor. He said nonchalantly, "Nothing. I'm going to use the truck to drive over to see Celine's parents. They live on Elm Shoal Branch."

"What do you want to see them for?"

"Try to find out where she disappeared to for five years after graduating from college."

Maude rubbed her forehead and robotically shook her head. "Don't tell me anything more. I don't want to know."

"Okay." Brock walked around to where the truck was parked. He took a screwdriver from the maintenance shed, removed the license plate, put it under the passenger seat, and hid a pistol he'd brought from the house under the driver's seat. Maude waved to him as he drove away.

The two-track gravel road leading back to the Oliver house dodged several large maple trees. They would be turning within weeks, Brock lamented. Once in the clearing, he parked the truck facing the road. He reached under the seat for the gun and tucked it in his belt, down his back. Brock had learned from experience that it wasn't wise to drive onto property in Appalachia unarmed. He noticed the lawn had been mowed too low, creating unsightly brown spots. No landscaping of any kind could be seen.

White vinyl siding cladding the rectangular residence lacked character. Two gabled porches at quarter points were along the front. The oversized black door between the porches, presumably the preferred way into the house, had a small homemade knocker. Brock used it. The woman who appeared when the door cracked open had tired flesh and was a worn-out version of Celine. Her skin was pale from lack of sun, and the whites of her eyes had yellowed. She said, "Yes?"

"I hope you don't mind me calling on you. I'm a friend of Celine's from college. My name's Roy Aldiss."

"What do you want?" She came across as dour, in a strangely familiar way.

"After we graduated, I tried to hook up with her, but couldn't find hide nor hair. I kept trying to look her up for years, without any luck. I thought she was from Hazard, so I asked the police if they knew where any Olivers lived in the area. They gave me your address."

"She lives in Lawrenceburg now. You can get her address by Googling her name." She started to close the door.

"Wait. Where did she go when she graduated from college?"

Rhonda Oliver replied lugubriously, "She came back here and worked in her father's business for several years." She pointed at the green metal building across the field from the house. The homemade sign read: Revilo Precision Parts. What was left of a stone mountain formed half a bowl around one side and the back of the operation. There were seven cars parked next to the long, open wall.

"What business is he in?"

"He has a machine shop that makes small parts for several manufacturers. He built the building right after Celine was born. She started running the office when she got back from college."

Brock scratched his head. "That's funny. I thought she got her degree in English. I figured she'd go to a big city to look for work." Out of the corner of his eye, Brock saw a man walking in his direction from the machine shop. He had the loose-jointed gait of a cowboy and was cradling a double-barrel shotgun.

"Mister, we're not in favor of unwanted guests around here. What does he want, Rhonda?" The man, presumably Perry Oliver, was rough as a cob. His calloused hands were big and strong, as was the rest of him. He trained the shotgun on Brock's head and kept coming closer.

"He's a friend of Celine's. He wants to know where she lives."

A murder of crows cawed as they flew out of a sycamore behind the house. Perry borrowed a glance in their direction just long enough for Brock to latch onto the shotgun and wrench it out of Perry's hands. He removed the shells and returned the gun unceremoniously. "There's no need for gunplay. I'll be on my way."

Addressing his wife, Perry inquired, "What else did he say?" Perry slipped his left hand into his pocket, ostensibly to retrieve more shells.

Skinner showed his pistol and warned, "You don't want to do that. Leave 'em in your pocket."

"What's your game, Mister?"

"I came here to find out where Celine went after she graduated from college. Now that I know how to find her, I guess I'll ask her myself. I don't want any trouble with you folks."

Perry lunged forward and swung the barrel of the shotgun at Brock's head. It missed by an inch. Brock punched him in the side as he spun around. If it didn't break his ribs, they'd surely be sore for weeks. Perry kept coming. Brock threw down the pistol he was holding and dropped the man with a vicious uppercut. Rhonda cried out, "Stop it! You'll hurt him!"

Brock drew a breath, gathered himself, and picked up his pistol. "He had no reason to come at me like that. What's wrong with him?"

Her face screwed into a resentful expression. "It's none of your business. Now, get out of here." She bent down to see if she could wake her husband. He started groaning. He tried to sit up, but his ribs were hurting so bad, he stayed down.

That was the second man Brock had dropped in the first half of the day. He bent over Perry and said, "No hard feelings." He picked up the shotgun, nodded to Rhonda, and jogged toward the truck. Halfway there, he tossed the shotgun into the grass. As he trundled away in the truck, Brock saw the man finally sitting up squinting to see if he could read the license plate, but there wasn't one.

Maude saw her husband returning and thought his trip seemed awfully quick. Dozens of people were in the winery tasting room, so she made her way there to help thin the crowd.

Brock came through the warehouse door, and said, "Let me know when you can take a break."

"I'll meet you in my office in ten minutes." Brock was sitting in the chair next to her desk when she stepped in. She said, "You weren't gone that long."

He didn't respond directly to her comment. "I hesitate to drag you into this mess but suppose it's better you than those characters I don't trust." He flipped his hand in frustration.

"Like whom?"

"Celine Oliver, Frank Romine, and Calvin Willett."

"I take it you talked to Celine's parents?"

"I think so. I'm sure about the woman. Celine favors her mother, who in her day was beautiful. She's been ridden hard and put up wet." Brock had already decided to leave out any mention of the fracas and firearms. "I'm not sure if the man is her father. He could be. What they told me doesn't add up."

"Which is?" Maude sat in her desk chair and leaned back.

"Perry Oliver's business is in a handy metal building next to the house. Celine's mother claimed her daughter came home from college and managed the office for her father's company until she moved to Lawrenceburg."

"When Valerie and I talked to her on Labor Day, she said she knew nothing about business. That would be a lie if she, in fact, did work for her father."

"Somebody's lying, I'm sure of that. Old man Oliver was keenly interested in what I'd asked his wife before he joined our conversation. When I interjected that I was trying to find out what his daughter did after graduating from college, he got belligerent."

"You didn't break his neck or anything, did you?"

"I probably should have. Why would they lie and cover for their daughter? Something's wrong. They're in it deep but will probably never talk."

"Maybe you can get Celine to spill the beans," said Maude.

"If I press her, she'll clam up. I need to find out more about her mother. Marcel should be able to help me with that. She told me her husband built the building for his business shortly after Celine was born. I wonder if those two events are related?"

"I can spin a quick theory for you. What is Celine's mother's name?"

"Rhonda."

"If Rhonda was good looking, she may have gotten pregnant by Mr. No-No, who couldn't afford to be exposed as Celine's father. What's her husband's name?"

"Perry."

"Perry could have gone to Mr. No-No and asked him for a bundle of cash to keep quiet."

"I like that line of thinking. It doesn't lead us to why Celine dropped out of sight for five years."

"True." Maude got up. "I'm going back out to help in the tasting room. You know what I always say when you go down the rabbit hole. At least there are no dead bodies."

"Yet." Brock followed his wife out of the office. He took the best seat available on the veranda and ordered lunch.

The view out over the Appalachian Mountains had never been clearer. Truman appeared from the vineyard and ran over to get a little affection. When Brock was done eating, he retrieved his pistol and drove home.

Marcel recognized the number of his brother-in-law when his phone rang. "I figured I'd hear from you soon enough. I'm not going to delude myself into believing you called to ask how my life is going and to wish me well."

"You paint such an awful picture of me. How is your life going?" He paced around the room, thinking ahead.

"It was going really well until you got all hopped up about Frank Romine and Celine Oliver."

"Yeah, yeah. I'm not that interested in them right now. I made a social call to Celine's parents. Her mother intrigues me. Celine looks like her, and when the woman was younger, she turned a few heads. I need for you to find out about her life."

Marcel grunted. "Oh, that'll be easy."

"And you've got to do it so Frank Romine doesn't catch you digging for the information."

"How am I going to do that?"

"You'll think of something."

"The best way would be for us to hire a private contractor to do the background check."

"Okay but do it fast. Put a rush on it."

"Sure, it's only money. Why are you interested in her?"

"There are at least three people who know where Celine was for five years, and what she was doing. So far, they're not talking. The only way I can think of to find a thread to pull is to investigate her parents' past. Her mother seems like the most logical candidate to check out."

"Okay. I'm on board. I might as well be. You won't have it any other way," said Marcel.

"As I said, you paint such a grim picture of me."

"I think you said awful instead of grim."

"Whatever."

Maude arrived home at six fifteen. Truman cut through the grapevines and was standing by the patio door waiting to be let in. Brock slid the door open and said, "Truman, did you catch any rabbits or snakes today?" The dog didn't appreciate being mocked, so he ignored the banter.

Maude stopped what she was doing in the kitchen and admitted, "I've been ruminating over Celine all afternoon. Why in the world did she just pop up out of nowhere in a place where she has no ties?"

"I've been cogitating on that myself. The best thing I could come up with was that the location is convenient for the places she works." Brock scratched Truman's head to get back in his good graces.

"What exactly is it she does?" Maude had her own suspicions.

"She's an escort without the sex part."

"Kind of what I thought. I wouldn't count out the sex part if she wants something bad enough."

Brock goggled at Maude and grinned. "Of course. I can think of two prospects."

Chapter 8

Frank Romine didn't try to locate who died in Celine's class. He went straight to the yearbook and saw the boy in the picture with her. It only took minutes to attach the name Roy Aldiss to him. There was nothing on the Internet about Roy. Frank determined his parents lived in Richmond. He headed for their house after lunch on Thursday afternoon.

The Aldiss home sat back from the road going east out of town. It was a hundred-year-old red brick two story that had elaborate white cornice work and a slate roof. A wood barn was at the end of the driveway. Railroad tracks in an open field across the street detracted from the sylvan setting of the Aldiss property. Frank rang the bell.

A pleasant-looking woman came to the door. "Hello." She was sixtyish, with short hair and long arms and legs. A white, loose-fitting blouse hung past her elbows. She was wearing tight black slacks that made her seem rather waspish.

"Hi. I'm trying to find Roy Aldiss. Would you be his mother?" he asked pleasantly.

"I am. Roy's not with us anymore." She didn't seem weighed down by that fact.

"You mean he doesn't live here now?"

"No, I mean he's dead. He hung himself in the barn back there eleven years ago." The woman shot a finger over her shoulder, palm up. She had bony hands and pointed fingernails.

"I'm sorry to hear that. What happened?"

She stepped aside and said, "Won't you come in?" Frank noticed the faint smell of patchouli when she closed the front door behind him. "He did it on June thirteenth, right after graduating from college. My husband and I drove over to Pikeville that Saturday to visit my husband's brother. We found Roy when we got back that evening."

"Did he have a girlfriend?"

"I don't think so. We discreetly asked the few friends he had after the funeral. They didn't know of anyone." She sat on the sofa. He took a seat in a wood-frame chair with mohair cushions.

"Did he ever mention a girl by the name of Celine Oliver?"

"Not that I remember."

"Was there any possibility of foul play?"

"No, he was a depressed young man. He had talked about ending it several times. There was no reason to believe someone killed him." No hint of emotion was hooked to her statement. "You know, they say people who commit suicide go to hell." A fleeting tinge of sadness flared in her.

Frank found himself wanting to comfort the woman. "Are you a religious person?"

"Why, certainly." There was indignance in her tone.

"I take it you raised Roy up in the ways of the Lord."

"We did."

"I think there's a good chance you'll see him in heaven. Is your husband at work?"

"He's dead too. He had a heart attack six months ago. He'll be in heaven for sure." That seemed to brighten her mood.

"I'm sorry. Does Berea College know Roy's deceased?"

"A woman with the reunion committee called a couple of years ago and asked what his address was. I told her he had died. She didn't ask how."

Frank stood and moved toward the door. "Well, I need to be running along. Thanks for speaking with me about your son."

"I'm glad you dropped by. I hope you'll come back again. You look a little older than what Roy would be now, but you're still a kid to me." She got up and clasped her hands. Her eyes did not project loneliness, but Frank knew it was back there somewhere. He left without looking back.

Berea College was twenty minutes south, so he dropped into the admissions office to see if, by chance, pictures of graduates were taken receiving their degrees. They were. Frank was given the web address for the file. He found Celine's photo. She had a carefree smile on her face. *One doesn't get a degree in English and transition to an escort in short order without a cataclysmic event,* he thought, *unless her beauty got the best of her.*

———————

Brock was doing a few chores at the winery late Thursday when Maude came looking for him. She said, "Something just occurred to me."

He threw down the hose and wiped his brow. "What's that?"

"What if Frank Romine and Leslie Blazek are grifters? I mean, how do we know they haven't been putting the touch on companies like Marcel's for a long time? Frank could have reached out to his old roommate to find another prosperous business to shake down."

"I thought about that possibility. His college roommate would have probably noticed a streak of dishonesty in the man and wouldn't have recommended him to Marcel if he had one. People do change. However, money has a funny way of eroding integrity."

"When you told me of the conversation you had with Leslie, something about it stunk. Usually, scorned women don't have magnanimous things to say about unaccommodating men. It's also kind of strange that Frank was so quick to volunteer Leslie for a bridge game."

Brock turned the water off at the spigot and smiled. "Have you gone down the rabbit hole?" She stuck her tongue out at him. "Since he wants to meet Calvin beforehand, it's possible he's casing the joint."

"Well, if he is crooked, he'll move heaven and earth to get something on Celine Oliver so he can blackmail her too," Maude said.

"I agree with that. I'm sure he's working some other angle. He'd be too afraid and too smart to go see the Olivers on Elm Shoal Branch like I did."

"That's true. Then we better crank up our efforts. What else can you do to uncover her past?"

"You *have* gone down the rabbit hole." Brock cowered back from her in case she lost her cool. She grinned slyly. He suggested, "I figure it's worthwhile to tail her, to see who her other clients are. Perhaps one of them leads somewhere. Hopefully, a report on Celine's mother will help put things together."

Frank met Brock in a folksy Harrodsburg deli at noon on Friday. They bought a large take-and-bake pizza and drove to Willett's house in separate cars. On the way, Brock called and told Cal to turn on the oven.

When Frank walked in, he surveyed the inside of Cal's house, saying, "Man, I do like these digs. You've got the world by the tail. Is that your 1967 Shelby GT500 in the driveway?"

"Yes, and my 1967 Century Resorter in the boat slip down at the dock. I'm partial to that year."

Frank went to the window to see if the boat was in view. "It's a pleasure meeting you. I grew up in Springfield. Are you from this area?"

"Yes, I was born and raised in Harrodsburg. Twenty years ago, I was skiing at night and slammed into a dock. I almost died. It never shied me away from lake life. I developed this property a few years ago and hope to live awhile longer to enjoy it."

The three men talked for ten minutes about the forthcoming bridge game. When the conversation on the subject died down, Frank asked innocently, "Why are you partial to 1967?"

Cal peered critically at Brock and asked, "Did you put him up to that?"

"No, sir, but I happen to know both of you have interesting views on hell."

Cal answered the question cryptically. "It was the year Edward Hopper died."

"And probably a few million other people," Frank retorted.

"He was an artist. Duke Ellington died in 1974, and Rex Stout in 1975. The end of the greatest era in American life."

"How so?"

"God had shackles on Satan from World War II until 1967. Since 1968, the devil has been killing America. In another ten years, our country will be an irretrievable cesspool."

Frank could smell the pizza cooking. He walked over to the kitchen. "Okay, let's get the premise right. You contend that since there is a God who is good, there must be a devil who is bad, and God is letting him destroy us. I'll string along with that theory. What's your argument?"

"Johnson's Great Society took off in the late sixties. I call it the 'Great Satan.' It encouraged the breakdown of the family and having children out of wedlock. A whole generation of fatherless children were born. And then came abortion on demand, the killing of innocent children. Next was an explosion of pornography, cheapening and debasing life. Something else happened that looked harmless at the time: the invention of the cell phone and personal computer."

Brock said, "A lot of good things have happened in the last fifty years too. Medicine, health, and life expectancy have improved."

Calvin stared at Brock in dismay. "Are you kidding me? Two-thirds of the people out there are obese. They are fat as pigs. Their *god* is their stomach. And look at what they do to themselves. Deuteronomy says to not put tattoo marks on your body. Nearly everybody you see walking down the street has a tattoo. It's a form of self-aggrandizement. That's what Satan is all about. He wants people to be their own gods."

Frank leaned on the wall and said, "Keep going. I want to hear the whole thing before I give you my two cents."

"Look at cell phones. People can't put the damn things down for five minutes. If you try to have a conversation with somebody holding one, and it beeps, they think nothing of ignoring what you're saying to seamlessly go into their own little world. It's downright rude!"

"I'm with you on that one," Brock affirmed.

"Don't get me started on the violence in video games. The worst of it is the Internet and social media ruining the minds of our young people. The kids are depressed, suicidal, and what's the remedy for that? Medication. Drug them up. And the message is to worship the earth instead of God and accept deviant sexual behavior or be branded as a hatemonger. Romans Chapter 1 says that sinful man has exchanged the creator for the created thing. In several places, the Bible calls sodomy, homosexuality, and bestiality sinful and wrong, yet Christians are told to keep their mouths shut."

"Christians don't have to keep quiet, Calvin," Frank interjected.

"But most do. This country now has thirty-five trillion in debt. We have borrowed money to live on since 1967. It's easy to have a good life when you're given things you don't have to pay for. Nixon took us off the gold standard, which means we can print as much money as we want. There will be a day of reckoning. Young people in America have no intention of paying back any debt."

Brock peered through the oven window and saw the pizza was ready. He took potholders and slid it onto a pan. Frank addressed Cal, "Is there more?"

"Yeah, one last thing. Artificial intelligence will be the coup de gras. Satan will be sure robots are programmed to be anti-God. That will be the final frontier."

Cal took the pizza cutter and made small square pieces. Frank said, "I'm not a Bible scholar, but I remember something about a speck in another's eye and log in your own. Having a judgmental nature never carried out anything, and I'm pretty sure God's not in favor of it."

"You're right," Cal admitted, crestfallen.

Frank sat at the kitchen table and slid three pieces of pizza onto a paper plate. "To get a better perspective, you might want to check your history. In 1300, you couldn't go out at night in Italy for fear of being robbed or murdered by a rival political party. The church was corrupt, selling indulgences, and the oppression of poor people was heinous. The same sins of today were high, wide, and handsome back then. Dante wrote about them: lust, gluttony, greed, anger, heresy, violence, fraud, treachery. That about covers it doesn't it?"

"Yes, I suppose it does. It seems my timing is bad. Fleeting good times came before me, and I'm living through bad times, which is the norm, I guess. Trying to harken back to the good times is a fool's errand," Cal remarked sadly.

"Not necessarily. Sometimes it's about what gets you through the day. A loving spirit draws a crowd. What is your aim in this life?" Frank asked.

"Get sinners to see the light by helping them grow in their faith." Willett had fallen off his high-and-mighty perch and was reeling from it. He suddenly turned the tables on Frank. "Do you believe that Jesus Christ was resurrected from the dead?"

Frank acted like an opponent in chess had just sprung a fancy move on him. "Ah. Trying to close the deal, are you? I've considered the question. How about this: God has forgiven you for skiing into a dock twenty years ago. If you'll promise to forgive yourself, I'll let you know my answer."

"You're fast on your feet, Frank. I'll agree to your terms if your answer is yes."

"Then pick up your mat and walk, Calvin Willett. You're healed."

The three men raised their arms and shouted "Hey, hey!"

Once the pizza was gone, Frank felt it best to reveal a fact that would come out sooner or later. "I don't know if you're aware of this, but your friend CeCe lives across the hall from me in my apartment building. I just met her recently. She's quite the lady."

Cal replied, "Boy, is she ever. What can you share with us about your friend, Leslie Blazek?"

"She's smart, gorgeous, and easy to be around. I really don't deserve her as a friend the way I've treated her sometimes."

Cal smiled and said, "Would you like to step into my confessional booth over here?" He pointed at nothing.

Frank covered his mouth, looked away, and said, "Touché."

Chapter 9

When Brock left Willett's house on Herrington Lake at two thirty, he drove the Lamborghini to Sutherland Tailoring with his arm hanging out the window, enjoying the cool air. He got the keys to a fleet car and headed north toward Bonds Mill Road.

If Celine was working that evening, he'd have to wait for her blue Mercedes to roll out of the apartment complex before he could drop in behind it. Brock parked in front of Four Roses Distillery, which was further up the hill, where there was a clear view of the gate. To kill time, he watched high clouds change shape, from one cartoonish animal to another, and then called his wife to report on the lunch conversation and tell her what he was planning.

Celine's car appeared at 6:20 p.m. When she turned on Bonds Mill Road, Frank's vehicle pulled out of his garage and rolled up to the gate. Brock figured he must have headed straight home after the meeting at Calvin's. He waited for Frank to clear the complex before giving chase at a distance.

Beyond I-64, all three cars took the winding road down the hill into downtown Frankfort. Celine parked across from Bootlegger on Main, stepped out of her car, and looked both ways before scampering into the bustling establishment. She was wearing honey-colored slacks, a collared white blouse, and a short, red-brown leather jacket.

Frank drove by the bar and parked at the first available spot on the street. Brock stayed back, pulling in behind Celine's vehicle. He thought the sneaky chess player had planned to meet up with her, but changed his mind when she went in without him. Romine seemed to be doing the same thing Brock was—trying to lay eyes on her client. That posed a mobility problem. He didn't want Frank to see him, so he stayed put.

Brock waited for it to get dark before he got out of his car. He went away from the bar, around the block, to the foot of the narrow stairs leading up to the group of tables facing the river. He crept slowly up the steps, hoping Celine and her friend were not on the veranda. He saw her through the window, sitting at a corner table inside, with her back to the river.

She faced the man who greeted her when she entered the bar. The gentleman sitting between them had the countenance of a pompous lawyer. Frank lurked in the shadows of the vestibule. Celine must've caught a glimpse of him, Brock thought as he himself began to withdraw, to avoid being spotted.

Twenty minutes later, the lawyerly gent came out the door and stepped into a black limousine that had government plates. Brock memorized the number. When the limo drove east, Romine U-turned to follow it.

Celine and her friend went to their own cars. Both drove off to the west. They took the old road to Louisville for several miles before turning north into a small, fenced farm. Brock noted the address as he passed by. There was nothing more he could do that evening, so he retrieved his Lamborghini and started for Hazard. He called Maude to report what had happened, and that he'd be home at midnight. She told him not to wake her when he came in.

———————————

Brock sifted through his email on Saturday morning and opened the report Marcel sent him on Rhonda Oliver. The information was brief. She was born Rhonda Cunningham to parents who somehow avoided notoriety. She attended Perry County Central High School where she was the homecoming queen based on her pulchritude. The king was Clive Natoli, likely a handsome guy himself. Rhonda married Perry Oliver weeks after graduating. Celine came along in the fall.

Brock called Marcel and said, "So, there are two intriguing questions about Rhonda: who is the father of her daughter, and where'd her husband get money to build a house and shop? Maude offered the theory that Perry is not her father, and he blackmailed whoever is."

"Even if that's true, what does it have to do with Celine dropping from sight for five years?"

"There might be some connection. On a longshot, let's see if there's anything out there on Clive Natoli."

"I already checked, figuring you'd ask. He lives on Louisville Road west of Frankfort."

"What's the number of the address?"

"Forty-seven twelve."

"Now we're talking!" Brock blustered. "I followed Celine over to Frankfort last night. She had dinner with two men. One left in a limousine that had government plates, and the other drove out to *that* address on Louisville Road. Celine followed him there. What's our buddy Clive's profession?"

"He's a registered lobbyist working in the Kentucky state government. His father got rich in coal and natural gas, and then became a state senator."

Brock leaned on his desk and switched the phone to his other hand. "The old man could have paid the hush money to avoid the ignominy of having an indiscreet son. I wonder if Celine knows Clive is an acquaintance of her mother?"

"Also, if he is her father, does she know it?" Marcel tacked on. "What're you going to do now?"

"Crack open your newest employee."

"What for?"

"Because he was following Celine last night, and I'm pretty sure she saw him."

Marcel didn't speak for a few seconds. "Well, he must be trying to get something on her."

"There're other possibilities. I'll let you know if I get anything out of him." Brock found Frank's number and was able to reach him. "Are you studying up for your chess tournament?"

"Always. I bet you're calling to see if I'll give you a lesson," said Frank.

"In what? Hacking databases, bridge, chess, or blackmail?" Brock asked whimsically. "Certainly not blackmail. Your mark made you last night in Frankfort. That's a sloppy move for a grifter."

"You get around for a boxer," Frank commented.

"I'm figuring out what you're up to, and more importantly, want to know if you're interested in comparing notes. There's no use playing singles. We'd do better if we played a doubles match."

"I've never played tennis."

"That was a metaphor, admittedly a poor one. Meet me at Copper & Oak in Danville at noon. I'll show you how to hold the racket."

"I've got nothing better to do. Is the food any good?"

"Spectacular."

"Ah, you're a food critic too, along with your many other skills," Frank added speciously.

"And you're smarter than me. I never take an opponent lightly," Brock remarked casually.

"Opponent? I work for your company. I've always been loyal to my employer, to a fault."

"That's what I'm banking on. I'll see you at noon."

The mid-September day was all sun even though the wind blew steadily from the southwest. Everything had dried out from lack of rain. Brock suspected the fall colors wouldn't be all that great this year. He cut across the state, arriving in Danville a few minutes before noon.

Frank stood by the door with his hands in his pockets. He suggested, "Let's eat inside. The wind might mess up my hair."

"We wouldn't want that." The host seated them in seafoam green chairs by the sandblasted, brick wall that had original artwork hanging on it. The young woman covering lunch customers, given her embonpoint, moved gracefully, and featured a terrific smile. She took their orders for the crispy chicken.

Frank said, "Before you turn on the bright light and get out the rubber hose, I'd like you to tell me why you've stuck your nose in this business."

"That's fair enough. My wife says I'm like a cowboy in one of Louis L'Amour's Westerns, riding along, minding my own business, when I stumble onto a farm where cattle rustlers have killed the woman's husband and stolen the cattle. I just can't ride on by."

"And you think I'm a cattle rustler?" Frank asked.

"No, you'd be more like a man who's looking to buy the stolen cattle at a discount. Celine Oliver is an escort. She could have married the richest, handsomest, most successful man in the world, but chose to cheapen herself, hanging out in low places with strange men. Why?"

Frank rearranged his silverware on the table. "I'll admit, that is a head-scratcher. Maybe somebody's got something on her. You think there's a killer and cattle rustler back there?"

"Something or someone made her disappear for five years. I have a glaring personality flaw: I can't let it go. I plan on finding out what's going on before you, her, or that likeable kook, Calvin Willett, gets hurt—unless you're the one trying to profit from the situation."

"I can assure you, I'm not," said Frank.

"Then why were you following her last night?"

"Don't laugh when I tell you this. I'm smitten with Celine and need to make sure she's solid gold before I try to woo her."

"You've got a high opinion of yourself, thinking you can win her affection," said Brock.

"Well, I've got two things going for me, I'm smart and rich. I'm not all that bad looking either."

"Far be it from me to tear the seam off anyone's dream. I'll start. Celine's mother, Rhonda, got pregnant in January, thirty-two years ago. She married Perry Oliver in July, and Celine was born in October. It may be that the homecoming king, Clive Natoli, got her pregnant and his father paid to keep the news of a child quiet. Natoli's old man was a rich politician. Perry Oliver could have used the money to build a house and shop. The Olivers have been stuck in a time warp ever since. That means they aren't involved in any ongoing money-making scheme involving their daughter unless there's something they're patiently waiting to cash in on," Brock explained.

"I can fill in some of the lacunae," Frank said, picking up where Brock left off. "Celine graduated from Berea College in early June eleven years ago. She disappeared soon after that. On the thirteenth of June of that year, Roy Aldiss, a friend of hers, purportedly hung himself, so his mother says. I don't believe it happened like that. Roy knew something about Celine that contributed to his death," Frank declared.

Brock replied, "Enter the killer and cattle rustler. It's hilarious you chased Aldiss down. I visited the Olivers and told them I was him and wanted to reconnect with Celine. I asked her mother where her daughter was five years after graduating. She said Celine worked in her father's shop. That's a lie, which means they know what happened to her. While you were following the guy in the government car last night, I tailed Celine. She went to the house of Clive Natoli, west of Frankfort. He's now a lobbyist."

Frank sat up and said, "If he's her father, what the hell's going on there?"

"We'll have to find out. Did you name the guy you followed?" Brock asked.

"Yes. He's a state senator. It would seem Natoli is lobbying the man for something. Do you think he brought Celine along as eye candy or is there something more?"

"Like, I'll trade you a look under her hood for your vote?" Brock said, shaking off any pretense of Celine being incapable of a louche life. "Who do you suppose Natoli is lobbying for?"

"I'll look it up." Frank took out his phone. He found the list of lobbyists that showed who they worked for and how much they were paid. "Clive Natoli receives forty thousand a year from the Ohio Valley Distillers' Guild. Let me see how many members they have." He found a website for the organization and scrolled down the names. "The distillers are only from the states of Illinois, Indiana, and Ohio. There are about forty companies. That would mean each member is kicking in a thousand dollars a year plus membership dues to influence the Kentucky legislature."

"To what end?"

"I'm not sure it matters, but we should probably try to find out," Frank said.

Crispy chicken sandwiches were politely delivered, and then conversation switched back to Celine. Brock said, "The disappearance of CeCe is when her life took a tawdry turn. Roy Aldiss must be part of it."

"Maybe. Just as importantly, she came out of hiding six years ago, landing in Kentucky's golden triangle between Louisville and Lexington, near Frankfort, the state capital. She may've fallen in with Natoli then in a scheme to influence state senators and representatives."

"There're 138 of them, and many are women."

Frank wiped his hands with his napkin and said, "It would only take a few votes to swing certain bills in the right direction."

Brock pushed his chair back and exhaled in frustration. "Celine and her parents know what we want to find out. They ain't talking. The only other person I can think of who might come across is Clive Natoli. Are you up for a little rough play?"

Frank put his arms on the edge of the table. "What do you have in mind?"

"A little breaking and entering."

"What if he tells Celine?" Frank had correctly figured out the plan without Brock spelling it out. "She might disappear again, for good."

"I can convince him to keep quiet, if I actually get caught or run into him."

"How?"

"Just like I did your friend, Leslie Blazek."

"You talked to her?"

"I did."

"What did she say?"

"That your ego doesn't allow you to lie and cheat."

"But apparently, you believe I'm okay with breaking the law."

Brock waited a few seconds before he answered. "Not necessarily. You would be okay, however, with me finding out what's going on."

Frank chuckled. "You should learn to play chess. You've just backed my king into a corner, and I don't see any move to avoid checkmate."

"I'm not wise or patient enough for that. I *am* happy you've agreed to be my doubles partner. I can see you want me to hold serve."

Brock covered the bill and tip with cash. Frank said, "Just don't hurt yourself. I wouldn't want that on my conscience." They left the restaurant and deliberately headed in opposite directions.

Chapter 10

CeCe banged loudly on Frank's door late Sunday morning. The Chamber of Commerce weather had brought forth one of the last hot days of the year, and every boater in Kentucky knew it. He espied her, and said, "Do you need to borrow an egg or cup of sugar?"

"I don't eat anything with sugar in it besides fruit. Cal called this morning and asked me to bring you along to his dock party. Get your swim trunks on." She was wearing a dull red two-piece that left little to the imagination.

Given the opportunity, men canvas a female body searching for what isn't quite right. The only imperfection Frank could find was a tiny brown mole near her belly button. "Yes, ma'am," he said as he strutted toward the bedroom. "I take it you want to drive again?"

"Naturally. I never go anywhere with strange men without an escape route," she replied.

"Smart move."

"Get a towel in case we decide to go swimming. I'll meet you out front." The diminuendo of her voice signaled she was already on the move. He changed into a green swimsuit, deck shoes, and yellow T-shirt.

CeCe had put on a pink coverup that made her look absurd behind the wheel of the Mercedes. The windows were down.

Frank resigned himself to the fact that his hair would be a mess by the time they arrived at the lake. She wore the expression of a disappointed mother preparing to scold her child. "I saw you at Bootlegger on Main Friday night. Were you following me?"

"What a coincidence. I was going to eat there, saw you, and decided to go elsewhere."

"You're lying. My mother called and said a guy by the name of Roy Aldiss came looking for me. Roy is dead. Were you impersonating him?" A car tailgated them for a while before it swung around and passed by.

"Absolutely not. Who is Roy Aldiss?" For a guy whose former girlfriend said he was incapable of lying, Frank had told two lies in the last thirty seconds.

"He's a guy I knew in college."

"How did he die?" That was lie number three.

"Hung himself."

"Sorry to hear that. Were you close to him?"

"I've never been close to any man. Certain things happened to Roy." Her shudder was akin to a shrug or shiver.

"You seem close to Calvin Willett. He's an interesting character."

"I already told you I like him a lot. He's not hung up on my looks," she said without conviction. "Do you know anything about Brock Skinner?" Brock had told her confidentially that Frank was working for Sutherland Tailoring.

"Not much." Lie four rolled off his tongue. "What's your impression of him?" Frank pried.

"I can only judge by his wife. She's a gem."

They turned off the main road into Willett's driveway. Fifteen cars were parked around the circle in front of the house. The two of them worked their way down the hill, and Cal saw them when they stepped onto the dock. "Hi there, CeCe. Frank, welcome. We're running short on ice. I'm going to ride over to the marina to buy a couple of bags." Cal turned back to Frank and asked, "You want to come along?"

"Sure," he affirmed, stepping nimbly into the back of the boat.

"CeCe, we'll be back shortly." Once up the lake and out of sight, Cal eased the throttle and shut off the engine. He waited for the backwash to settle and then said, "I appreciate what you told me last Friday. I've got a new perspective on being a source of light in this world."

"You look relaxed. That's a good way to win friends and influence people, but I have a feeling there is something else on your mind." Frank put one arm on the back of the seat and his other on the mahogany side deck of the boat.

Cal's relaxed mood firmed. "There is. CeCe has never shared anything personal with me, until recently. She seems worried you're trying to dig up some things in her past. It's got her on pins and needles. I thought I'd get your side of the story."

A rented fun float loaded with corpulent, frog-belly-white folks was approaching from behind. As it veered around and passed by, Cal waved at the crowd onboard. Frank asked, "How long have you known her?"

"Oh, four years or so."

"You'll have to admit, Cal, what she does for a living doesn't square with her looks and brains."

"What's wrong with being a companion for hire?"

"Oh, nothing per se. She really likes you because you're not running any kind of con. If her other clients were as clean as you are, she'd have it made."

"I pay her enough. She doesn't have to work for anyone else."

"That's the rub. She has a customer who I don't believe has given her any choice. He's working some sort of racket, and CeCe is the head of the plow."

Calvin threw his head back and rubbed his eyes. "And you're trying to find out if something in her past is the reason she's hooked up with this fellow?"

"Something like that," Frank replied. He leaned over the side to scoop a handful of water.

"I've never asked her: does she have any other clients besides the fellow you speak of?"

"I doubt it. It looks like he's got a ring through her nose, and she's not straying too far from the barn."

"I wonder why he lets her hang around me?" Cal asked.

"I've been tackling that in my mind. Best I can come up with is he wants to spin the illusion that she isn't his property. Free to do as she pleases. Since she's seen regularly at your parties, no one suspects her of being involved in anything squishy."

Calvin rose and sat on the gunnel. "What exactly do you know about her past?"

"She attended Berea College and graduated eleven years ago with a degree in English. You'd have thought she would have gone to a prosperous place to look for a job, and search for the richest, best-looking, most powerful man she could find. But instead, she dropped from sight for five years. I mean, there's not a trace of her anywhere during that time."

"Why did she do that?"

"She had a male friend who was found dead a week after they graduated from college. I think someone killed him and made it look like he hung himself. I don't know that for sure, but something about his death may have put her in peril, so she disappeared."

"And that's what you're trying to find out? CeCe must think you want to blackmail her if you get the goods on her."

Frank flipped his hand to discount Cal's claim. "That's not the reason. It's the opposite. If somebody has her under his thumb, I'd like to see her get free."

"That's a dangerous game you're playing, Frank. This man you speak of might cut your legs out from under you." Cal dropped back down in the seat and keyed on the engine. "Let's get that ice."

"Cal, I'm asking you to work with me on this. Trust me, I want the best for her, just like you."

"I'll think it over."

"This guy might be her father."

"What?" Cal gave him a three-second glare of disbelief, then turned to look ahead, and pulled the throttle open.

The two bags of ice were taken to the bar when Cal's runabout returned to the dock. He went to sit under the umbrella again, and Frank joined him there. "Let's start working on the crossword puzzle," Cal said, prompting CeCe to pick it up off the table and head to the pontoon. "Frank, you think you can handle *The New York Times* crossword puzzle?"

"Shucks, Mr. Willett, I only made it through the third grade, but I'll give it my best." Everybody started laughing, including Cal.

What sometimes took as long as four hours to complete, the puzzle was knocked out in a little over an hour. CeCe would read the clue, no one in the crowd had a suggestion, so Cal would offer an answer about 20 percent of the time. For the other 80 percent, he gazed at Frank and waited for him to weigh in, which he did on all but one or two of the questions.

CeCe said, "We're down to the last squares. The clue is Miles Archer's son."

Cal panned the crowd and asked, "Who is Miles Archer?"

Frank waited a bit before revealing, "He was Sam Spade's partner in *The Maltese Falcon.*"

"What's his son's name?"

"Lew Archer. L-E-W-A-R-C-H-E-R."

"Who's he?"

"Ross Macdonald's fictional gumshoe. I'm surprised you've not heard of him. He's a pulp fiction version of Edward Hopper's paintings—lonely and isolated in an increasingly impersonal, evil, and complex world. The Archer series was written from the late forties to the early seventies, right in your wheelhouse. There were plenty of bad characters in his dramas."

"How in the hell did you get to be so smart?"

"Listen, look, read, and remember." Frank raised his eyebrows.

"You sound like a robot. Are you sure you're human?" Cal asked, poking a little fun at him.

"The people I play chess against don't think so. They call me the black hole."

CeCe gingerly arose from the pontoon seat where she had been reading the clues and came over next to Frank. "Let's swim across the lake to the other shore."

"Okay." He slipped out of his deck shoes, removed his shirt, and dove off the front of the dock. CeCe was right on his tail. The water was almost too warm on the surface, and flat-out cold six feet down. They took their time after an early flurry of strokes and chatted about inane things all the way over and back. "That was refreshing," Frank commented as he was drying off.

CeCe asked, "Cal, is there a comb on the dock? Mr. Black Hole's coif is a bit disheveled."

"On the top shelf of the first cabinet by the Resorter."

As the afternoon wore on, boats motored up and tied off for a few minutes to see if there was any worthwhile lake gossip to pick up. Cal took everyone out skiing in shifts. While he was gone, a couple of slightly drunk patrons switched the radio to rock music, switching it back when they saw the boat returning to within earshot.

The crowd was gone by dusk. CeCe, Cal, and Frank were up at the house talking about different people who had come to the party. Cal said, "You know, Frank, I've not had a chance to kibitz with someone of your perspicacity for a long time."

"Now, you're using big words on me, Calvin. Are you trying to stump me?"

"No, I gave up on that when I heard you rip through the crossword."

It had cooled enough to open the windows in the main room of the house. The gentle breeze triggered everyone's hunger. CeCe asked, "Are we going to fix a little supper, or should I dump this guy back at his apartment?"

"What do you say, Frank? Would you like to break bread with us? I've got a marvelous salad in the fridge, and we can throw a little broiled salmon on it."

"In for a penny, in for a pound."

"Good. CeCe, I'll fix the fish if you dress the salad and serve it."

"I think I can manage that."

The three of them spent the next hour together. Frank was certain Calvin Willett was a straight shooter, and he kept looking for any sign from Celine Oliver that exposed a rotten part of her. It wasn't there. She was either a sociopath or as innocent as she appeared to be.

As CeCe and Frank were leaving, Cal said, "I'm really looking forward to our big Saturday bridge tournament. CeCe, we'll have to get exceptional cards to beat this muckraker." He pointed in jest at Frank.

"That's the wrong word for me. Brock Skinner is the muckraker of the bunch. I'm a chess player who's known to throw pasteboards around occasionally."

Cal remarked guardedly, "Ah, yes, Mr. Skinner. The man frightens me. I hope he doesn't lose at bridge. He might get physical. He could break someone in half without even trying."

Frank replied, "CeCe seems to think his wife, Maude, is top shelf, ergo, Brock must be a decent human being too. Otherwise, she'd jettison him."

"You keep hanging on to that thought, Mr. Black Hole." Willett grinned.

On the way back to their apartment building, CeCe, in a droll tone, threw out, "I thought you said you didn't know Brock Skinner that well. Sounds like to me you've spent some time with him."

"Enough to know that he's smarter than he looks. I can also say this: everyone who plays bridge this coming Saturday is rooting for you."

"What does that mean?" She seemed uncomfortable with the attention.

"Simply put, good things will happen, if you trust in us."

"My life is great. How could it be any better?" she asked rhetorically.

"If you say so. Oh, by the way, Leslie Blazek is staying at my place from Thursday to Sunday. I'd like for you to meet her." He held a smile for one second.

"I can't wait. If she's as sharp as you are, I'll be in the cheap seats."

"Don't sell yourself short. Beauty is a form of genius, for it needs no explanation."

"Who said that?"

"Oscar Wilde."

"Does that imply I'm a dumb bimbo?"

"You are neither dumb nor a bimbo. In my book, you're sneaking up on perfect in every way."

Her expression was full of insincere distaste. "There's that teenage boy coming out again."

Celine parked in the garage. Frank said, "I couldn't help it. Thanks for a wonderful day. I'll see you when I see you."

Chapter 11

Brock motored quietly up to Marcel's house at 5:40 on Monday morning. He intended to learn more about Natoli before talking face-to-face. Dense cloud cover roiling the atmosphere was the precursor to a windbreaker day. Darkness persisted until seven o'clock that time of year. He got into Marcel's vehicle parked in the driveway, and asked, "Where's that coffee you promised?"

"This is yours." He handed him a stainless-steel traveler. "Do you know where we're going?"

"Yes. Go past his address. There will be a farm road to the north, and one that runs east behind his property. You can let me out there."

The windows in Natoli's house were all dark. Yellow floods at the front corners lit up the rough-cut grass. Spotlights were off out back. When they came to a stop on the road behind the farm, Marcel said, "Call me when you're done."

Brock got out and put on the backpack he'd brought along. There was a thick grove of oak trees on the garage side of the house. He hopped the wood fence and found a place to hide where he could keep an eye out for any vehicle leaving early. His Breitling watch read 6:31.

Emerging daylight brought the farmhouse into full view. Brock noted the speckled gray-brick structure was rectangular with a low-pitch, chalky verdigris roof. A shallow semicircular porch with gigantic, white columns had been scabbed onto the front. Each large white window was adorned with black plank shutters. A second-floor veranda on the back extended out from what looked to be the master bedroom. The windows in the room on the first-floor corner behind the garage were completely blacked out with some sort of opaque material.

A light shone upstairs at eight o'clock. After it went out, one on the first floor came on. It was nearly nine o'clock before Clive Natoli left the property by car. Brock stood and walked through the damp grass toward the front of the house, high stepping with the confidence of a Mormon missionary. He heard the bell chime inside after pushing it with his finger. Nobody came to the door. He waited before defeating the lock and slipping into the entryway. No alarm sounded.

Brock went to the master bedroom to see if a woman's clothes were in the closet. There were none, which meant he lived alone. Next stop, back downstairs, was the office. A PC came to life with a tap on the keyboard. The screen asked for a password. He left the machine alone so as not to leave any trace of being there.

One-third of the main floor consisted of the kitchen, breakfast nook, and dining area. The room behind the garage, with its door off the den, had a lock that couldn't be picked. Three doornails were exposed, so he removed them with the tools he brought along, setting the door aside.

The room was a small theater. A hanging projector faced the white screen on the wall. Black shades covered the windows so completely that light could not enter or escape. Brock scanned the walls carefully. He saw what appeared to be a camera above the screen, and noticed the couch was a sleeper sofa. He played a hunch and began looking for blackmail materials. After scouring the theater room, he rehung the door and meticulously searched every inch of the floors, walls, and ceilings in the house. After two hours, he had about given up when he came upon the false bottom of a narrow, lower kitchen cabinet. He lifted the lid, took the envelope and memory stick that were there, and put them in his backpack.

Brock took out his phone and called Marcel who arrived a half hour later to pick him up where he'd been dropped off. As Marcel turned out onto Louisville Road, Clive Natoli wheeled into his driveway. Brock said, "He must be having lunch at home. We cut it close."

"What else is new. Did you find anything?" Marcel asked.

"An envelope and jump drive."

"That's something. Let's hope he doesn't go looking for them any time soon."

"More importantly, I hope he doesn't know how to find out who stole them," Brock said, with a deadpan expression. "Speaking of lunch, you got anything to eat at your house?"

"Yes."

"You're always thinking ahead."

"Is that a compliment?"

"Why, certainly. Didn't it sound like one?"

"It did. Just wanted to be sure." Marcel rang his wife and asked her to set out sandwich fixings.

Brock fawned effusively over his sister-in-law, Valerie, when he saw her at Sutherland's house. They exchanged pleasantries, and after eating a delicious lunch, Brock retrieved the envelope from his backpack and extracted the letter he'd purloined. It said:

> *Celine,*
>
> *I don't know where you got the book I saw in your room, but I can tell you it's real. If you have the other three, you are*

sitting on a fortune. I'll make you a deal. If you go out with me, I won't tell the police that you're in possession of stolen merchandise.

Roy

Brock made a funny noise and tossed the letter on the table. "This is what got Roy killed. Clive is holding it over Celine's head. I wonder if he intercepted it in Berea or if he got the letter from someone else?"

"What's he talking about the other three?"

"The valuable book referred to must be four volumes."

Valerie spoke up: "*The Birds of America.* It's a four-volume, double-elephant folio of drawings by John James Audubon."

"What's a double-elephant folio?" Marcel asked.

"It defines the size of the sheets in the book. I seem to remember they're twenty-nine inches by thirty-nine inches. I think each of the books weighs over fifty pounds."

"How much are the four volumes worth?" Brock inquired.

"North of ten million."

"Now we're getting somewhere. Enough money to kill for," Brock said with glee. "Get a laptop so we can see what's on the memory stick."

Once downloaded, Marcel played the video file. It started with a frontal nude shot of a girl, not including her face. She turned around to embrace a man. The camera moved up to catch her whole naked backside and the man's face. Once he wrapped his arms around her, the video ended. Marcel asked his wife, "Does that look like Celine?"

"I'm afraid it does."

"What a body. Without a shot of her face, it's impossible to be certain," Brock said.

"I'm guessing the pigeon's a state senator or representative who needed some persuasion on a vote. It appears our friend Clive is a bad apple," Marcel commented.

"What's worse, if it is Celine, and he's her father, he's a pervert. I think we keep this video to ourselves for a while. Marcel, did you happen to check how long Clive's been in his house?"

"Twelve years. It was his father's before he retired as a legislator."

"So, we can't tell how old the video is. It looks like another thing he can blackmail Celine with. I'd like to know why there weren't more videos of other men."

"What about the letter?" Valerie asked.

"I'll talk it over with Frank Romine. Right now, I think he's on the level. He may see something we're missing. Did you ever get him bonded, Marcel?"

"I did. There is nothing in his past that scares an insurance company."

"Good. How about hacking the cameras at his apartment complex?"

"Got that done too. The filming activates with motion. I told IT to change the disc daily."

"Do you think Romine knows we're filming?"

"I suppose so. Does it matter?"

"No. Unless he's a bad guy and is planning to double-cross us."

"That can't be helped," Marcel replied soberly.

Brock called Frank to alert him of an imminent visit, and when he got there, he sat in the same black chair next to the computer. "I just picked up something interesting while out and about." He handed him the letter. "Marcel's wife thinks the book is a valuable Audubon."

Romine sat still and studied the letter for a long time. He shifted and said, "All right. I presume the book is an original *Birds of America*. Someone brought one volume to Celine's room. Roy saw it and took the opportunity to feather his nest, so to speak. Whoever brought the book saw Roy's note and considered him a liability. When they talked to him, he must have mentioned that his folks were over in Pikeville for the day, so they probably choked him to death and made it look like he hung himself. Celine knows about this. Further, whoever had the book kept the note to blackmail her into disappearing for five years. It would have taken two people to kill and hang Aldiss. One of the two might be Natoli, if he's the person who got ahold of this and is still blackmailing Celine. Who's the other person?"

"As you said, Celine knows. You have any ideas on how to play it?"

Frank raised a finger and said, "Let's make a photocopy and send the original to Celine anonymously. We should include our own unsigned note that says we hope it frees her from Clive Natoli."

"What town should the postmark come from?"

Frank asked, "What is the name of the organization Clive represents as a lobbyist? Is it the Ohio Valley Distillers' Guild?"

"Yes, I believe that's right," Brock confirmed.

Frank Googled the name on his oversized computer. "They're headquartered in Madison, Indiana."

"Do you think there's some connection?"

"Natoli is doing something for them. I'd like to know what it is. It's possible one member is the missing piece to the puzzle. That may require wearing out some shoe leather."

"Yeah." Brock shook his head. "Type up a note you want to put in with the letter from Roy and print out an address sticker."

Frank added, "I'll also put a return address from the Distillers' Guild. We might be able to follow her to the missing link." He photocopied the letter and prepared the envelope to be mailed to Celine. "You want me to take it over to Madison?"

"No, I'll do it in the morning. I'd like to drop in on that organization to see if they'll tell me what Natoli's doing for them," Brock said.

A loud knock came on the door. Frank tucked the envelope and photocopy of the letter in the computer desk drawer. He yelled, "Come in."

Celine stood at the threshold. "Brock, I saw you come through the gate. Curiosity got the better of me. What are you doing here?"

Brock directed his full attention to Romine and said, "When Celine asked me how I knew you, Frank, I told her you were doing some work for the company. I presume you didn't intend for that to be a secret."

"Certainly not. We're talking shop, Celine. How are you, on this less-than-fine day?"

"A little confused. I came over because I wanted to ask Brock something, since he's here."

"Shoot."

"Did you go over to my folk's place and tell them you were Roy Aldiss?"

"I did," Brock replied.

"Why'd you do that?" Her tone got snippy.

"To see if your mother would tell me where you went after you graduated from college."

"Why do you need to know that?"

"I don't need to know; I want to know."

"How come?"

"To satisfy myself that you're not on the wrong end of some human trafficking program."

"What do you mean by that?"

"Do I have to explain human trafficking to you?" Brock asked sternly.

"Well, I'm not. So, you can drop it." She looked wounded and scared.

"I would have if your mother hadn't lied to me. You do understand that Frank, Cal, and I are on your team, like caring big brothers, and we think there are people out there somewhere taking advantage of you who may want to hurt you. It's hard for us to stand by and do nothing."

Celine wiped away a tear running down one cheek. "All that stuff is in the past. I don't want to relive any of it. I have a wonderful life now. Please don't screw it up for me."

"Why did you go to Clive Natoli's house last Friday night?"

"He's one of my clients. I insist he pays me in cash. I go there regularly to pick up my money. There is nothing unseemly about it. Does that answer your question?"

"We know he knows your mother. That's where we're hung up. What's going on?"

"Clive is a lobbyist. I go with him to dinners and cocktail parties. He pays me well and treats me like a lady, just like Calvin Willett does. That's all there is to it."

Brock returned to the subject of her parents. "The worst of it is that when I went to see your folks, your dad tried to bash my skull in with a gun barrel. That tells me he's hiding something."

"My father is extremely protective of my mother. Can we drop it now?"

"Yes. Frank and I are giving out free hugs if you need one. Is there anything else you wanted to ask me?" Brock asked.

"No. I feel better now that I know what you're doing. I can tell, though, you're not going to drop it."

Frank said, "You can rest assured we won't cause you any trouble if we learn anything."

Celine's mood improved. She eked out a vulnerable smile, and said, "Brock, have you heard that Leslie Blazek is arriving on Thursday?"

"Is she now? Frank, you have any tips on how we should behave in front of her?"

"Better than I do. I'm surprised she still talks to me."

Celine went on the offensive. "I'm going to grill her about you, Frank. Tit for tat. I want to ask her what you've been doing for the last several years. You have any skeletons in your closet?"

"All you'll get out of me is name, rank, and serial number." Frank glanced at Brock, smirked, and rolled his eyes.

CHAPTER 12

The next morning at breakfast, Maude endured a precise account of what was said, heard, and done by her husband on Monday. She admitted, "I'm ashamed of myself for being interested in this soap opera. We're digging into Celine's past because we don't approve of the choices she's made in her life, all the while trying to find out what she's hiding, which only *we* care about."

"I'm convinced she didn't have a choice. What about the untimely death of Roy Aldiss, the film of her seducing a politician, and Mr. Congeniality, Perry Oliver, who might not be her father?" Brock asked.

"You're not sure it was Celine in that video, and Rudyard Kipling once said: everyone is more or less mad on one point."

"Rudyard, smudyard. Inquiring minds need to know," Brock declared with the intensity of an umpire calling a runner out at home plate.

"You didn't elaborate much on what's in the eye of this storm: *The Birds of America.*"

"I can't disagree with you on that point. I'm driving over to Madison, Indiana, to drop this letter in the mailbox and check out the Ohio Valley Distillers' Guild. Do you want to come?"

"Take Truman with you. He likes road trips." The dog heard his name and entered the kitchen, his nails clicking on the tile floor.

"He'll look silly sitting in the passenger seat of a Lamborghini."

"No sillier than you'll look driving the thing."

"He should stay here to protect you." Brock kissed his wife, picked up the letter and his coffee cup, and hoofed it toward the front door. Truman wasn't quite sure what was going on.

———

Traversing northwest from eastern Kentucky to Madison, Indiana, featured myriad landscapes: tall mountains, deep gorges, rolling hills, and finally, high plains—all breathtaking. On the other side of the bridge, southern Indiana mimicked Kentucky. Brock understood why bluegrass music legend, Bill Monroe, had taken his act north to Nashville, Indiana, in Hoosier National Forest.

A hint of fall was in the air when the Lamborghini roared up to the edge of the last Kentucky mesa a little before noon. Brock headed down to the bridge that dumped northbound traffic near the center of town. The GPS on his phone claimed the office of the Ohio Valley Distillers' Guild was less than a mile west. Taking advantage of how convenient things were in a small town, he parked on the street fifty feet from the door.

The Guild was indubitably a low overhead operation, some twenty-five feet wide and fifty feet deep. The high ceiling room at the back had sixty chairs in it, tucked under two rows of tables. A unisex toilet separated the meeting hall from the one-desk cubicle by the entrance. A spartan plastic chair supplied the chance for a patron to take a load off, which Brock did. The woman at the desk did not seem offended. He asked, "Do you have time to chat with me for a few minutes, or is your lunch hour fast approaching? I don't want to disrupt your schedule."

"I *was* ready to go next door to the cafe for a bite to eat, but it's not often a ruggedly handsome man driving a half-million-dollar car comes to visit me. How can I be of service?"

"I'm hungry myself. How 'bout I buy you lunch?"

"This fairy tale just keeps getting better," she replied in an elegantly cornpone manner.

"Lead the way. What's your name? I'm Brock."

"Pearl." She waited to see if he thought the name was catchy. She was tallish and bowlegged. Her yellow-and-red patterned dress had a peekaboo neckline promoting an ample bosom and freckly complexion.

Once seated in the restaurant, Brock inquired, "Well, Pearl, what do you recommend?" The place was packed with locals acting like family at a holiday meal.

"The chicken salad on a croissant. It's made up daily." Pearl left him little choice. "Do you know how to spell croissant?" she asked.

"No, how?"

"F-A-T-T-E-N-I-N-G. It's all butter. I only allow myself one if I skipped breakfast." The way things were going, Pearl would soon offer Brock a roll in the hay. "Now, what is it you wanted to know about our organization?"

"I'll get right to the point," said Brock.

"I like a man who doesn't fiddle around."

"I just caught wind of Clive Natoli. I understand he's a lobbyist for the Guild. What exactly is he doing on your behalf?"

"Well, to understand that you must know how we're structured. We have forty members, give or take a few, but Nigel Barclay pays the freight. The dues to belong are fifteen hundred a year. That pays my salary and the place we rent. Nigel covers Clive's fee of forty thousand a year by himself."

"Why does he do that?" Brock was pleased she used information to heighten her importance.

"Because he stands to gain the most if Clive is successful."

"At what?"

"Nigel, and family before him, have owned a place called Barclay Farm since 1808. The house is one of the oldest in southern Indiana. The farmland is prime. It's in Charlestown, straight north of Devil's Backbone. Nigel hopes to put a bourbon distillery on the property."

"And Natoli is helping him do that? How did he get hooked up with Barclay?"

Pearl leaned back and wagged her head. "Clive's dad was a Kentucky state senator. Nigel's dad buddied up to him to curry favor. Both those men are dead now."

"What does Barclay want?"

"Well, all our members want what Clive is working on. Kentucky is the only state in the country that has a barrel tax. They count the number of aging barrels of whiskey in the warehouses and slap a tax on the distilleries every year. The millions of dollars they collect pay for schools and social programs and put the distillers at a competitive disadvantage."

"The revenue they take in from the bourbon trail visitors should offset it."

"That's Clive's argument. People building distilleries are telling Kentucky if they don't repeal the tax, they're going to invest in another state such as Illinois, Indiana, or Ohio. That would be good for us, especially for Nigel Barclay. Kentucky doesn't want to lose out on the new distillery business, so a movement to repeal the tax has taken hold. Clive's trying to persuade lawmakers in Kentucky to leave the tax in place."

"But what about the bourbon trail?"

"That's the thing. Barclay Farm is twenty minutes from downtown Louisville. It could siphon off millions of bourbon trail sojourners. There's an investor out there trying to decide whether to build in Indiana or Kentucky. That barrel tax is the tipping point."

Brock made a low whistling sound. "Have you heard how much they plan to spend?"

"Sure. Three-hundred million." Pearl leaned forward, propped her head on her arm, and crafted a magnificent come-hither stare.

"Wow, that's big money." The server brought the chicken salad. It looked and tasted delicious. "What can you tell me about the Barclay family?"

"Nigel's father died eleven or twelve years ago. Clive had just gotten into the lobbying business. The Barclays had two children. Nigel has a younger sister by the name of Jaeger. That's the name of a bird. Old lady Barclay was partial to ornithology." She seemed proud of dropping such a big word into the conversation.

"Did you ever meet the daughter?"

"A couple of times when she was younger. Very cute gal. Her parents were old when they had kids. She stayed with her mother until her mother died six years ago, and then moved away."

"Any idea where she went?"

"No. I'm sure Nigel could tell you." They finished lunch, and she asked Brock a lot of questions. He answered them as evasively as he could, paid the bill, and escorted Pearl back to her forlorn desk. She allowed, "You can come by once a week and buy me lunch. That would make this job worth it."

Brock replied, "I might just do that. By the way, what's your opinion of Nigel Barclay?"

"He's the worst kind of person you could ever meet. He has no regard for people. Don't tell him I said that." The flinty attitude she had while talking about Barclay bled out of her face, replaced by the look of a demure coquette. "Here's my card. Call if you need anything. Get my drift?"

"Yes, I believe I do. Good day, Pearl." Brock dropped the letter addressed to Celine Oliver at the post office and thought it was time to take some chances.

———

Charlestown had a sea of concrete tilt-up warehouses near the beltline, and a bit further north, quaint properties on both sides of the road led up to the Barclay estate west of the highway. A white oval sign with a black rim had a miniature painting of the mint-green house surrounded by drawings of colorful birds. When the light hit the sign just right, the quality of artwork made an undeniable statement about the superior nature of the place.

Brick pillars interrupted a continuous black-wire fence encircling the property. There was a steel plate, left down during the day, which likely got raised at night over the cattle bridge between the pillars, to thwart intruders. Brock took the tree-lined, narrow asphalt pavement back to the turnaround. He parked facing the 200-plus-year-old painted-brick monolith. It was in impeccable condition, as were the grounds. Fireplaces reached high in the air at each end of the house. Five colonial-style windows were equally spaced across the second floor. The porch had a steep gabled roof.

Before Brock could ring the bell, the door eased open, and the man standing there asked, "What can I do for you?" He had on creased camel dress pants, a black blazer with stamped gold buttons, and a starched gray shirt. A mild case of rosacea afflicted his sardonic face, and his short, curly black hair grew too far down on his forehead.

"I'm trying to find Jaeger Barclay. This is her last known address." Brock presumed the chap was the infamous Nigel Barclay.

"Who are you?"

"I work for a law firm. I have a subpoena to serve her ordered by the court."

Nigel put a hand to his chin. "What's it regarding?"

"I'm not at liberty to discuss that with you, sir."

"If you want me to tell you where she is, you will." He acted as though he'd laid four aces.

"It has to do with a man who was killed eleven years ago," Brock revealed.

"What was his name?" Beads of sweat popped out on his chin and brow.

"If she's not here, we'll hire a private investigator to find her," Brock offered, to rattle him.

"She's my younger sister. Left here six years ago after my mother died. She went to South Africa to live with a friend of hers. She may have left there by now. I've not heard from her in several years. I doubt you'll be able to find her."

Brock pulled a Mike Tyson and verbally punched him in the mouth. "Is that your story? Oh, we'll find her, you can take that to the bank. And when we do, I better not learn you've lied to me."

Nigel Barclay scanned him up and down in a frisson of fear. Brock walked to the Lamborghini, reached in the passenger window, and took a roll of duct tape out of the glove compartment. Barclay asked, "What are you doing?"

"I thought about taping your mouth shut, but I'm going to cover my license plate so you can't run it. If I were you, I'd check your insurance."

"Are you threatening me?"

"Certainly not. If I catch you within a mile of your sister, I'll tape your mouth shut for good, and if anything happens to her or any of her friends, you're a dead man. That clear?" He taped over the license number, threw the roll back into his car, and peeled out of there before Barclay had the presence of mind to raise the steel plate at the gate, trap him, and call the police.

Brock took the beltline east over the bridge into Kentucky. Once on I-64, he called Romine. "Celine began impersonating a girl by the name of Jaeger Barclay when she dropped out of sight. Jaeger's father had recently died, and Celine must have gone to live in the Barclay house in Charlestown, Indiana, to take care of Jaeger's mother. I don't know where Jaeger went or what happened to her. Her mother must have thought Celine was her daughter. Jaeger has an older brother by the name of Nigel who's likely behind this skullduggery."

Frank said, "Based on those facts, maybe Nigel killed his own father, and his sister knew it, so he had to kill her too, but not before he had a stand-in for her to avoid any suspicion of foul play. Jaeger probably hinted at some kind of blackmail."

"Celine must look a lot like Jaeger to be able to impersonate her. How would Nigel know about Celine?" Brock backfilled the rest of the information he'd learned about what Clive Natoli was doing, his family's relationship with the Barclay clan, and the grandiose plan for a distillery on the Barclay property.

Frank asked, "Did you find out anything about the Audubon book?"

"I was told that Jaeger's mother loved birds. The sign in front of the estate has birds drawn on it. She probably owned the book. I'm guessing Nigel has it now."

"And it would seem logical that Nigel would be asked to put his property and some of his own money in the distillery deal so he would have sufficient skin in the game. He could get the cash by selling the Audubon."

Brock said, "I've got something you need to see. I'll meet you in Marcel's office at ten o'clock in the morning." He rang his brother-in-law to arrange the Wednesday meeting and tell him what went on over in Indiana. As he got near Hazard, he called his wife to let her know he had plenty to share with her over supper.

When Brock turned off I-75 toward home, a pleasant state trooper pulled him over to ask why he had tape over his license plate. The trooper said, "Most people do it to trick the Ohio River bridge cameras." Brock had unwittingly done that but didn't fess up to it. He got off with a warning.

CHAPTER 13

The three hapless musketeers met at Sutherland Tailoring on Wednesday. Brock gazed out the window, unhappy he was stuck inside. "Frank, do you play golf?"

Romine was wearing a Mediterranean blue golf shirt and gray dress slacks, which weren't flattering colors for his complexion. "It's impossible to be good at everything, Brock. I'm no good at golf. Besides, I work for a living." He glared in Brock's direction.

"Shame. It's perfect weather for it. I'd like to take you to the cleaners." He made a dorky face.

Marcel had on a white dress shirt, an alligator belt, brown slacks, and stylish loafers. He glided along and said, "You don't always have to be the alpha male in the room."

"Sorry. I've been thinking about the situation. Is there any scenario that doesn't involve murder and mayhem?"

"Well, sure," Frank replied. "Nigel Barclay's father could have died of natural causes. Jaeger, his sister, could have left home for any number of reasons, and she may still be alive somewhere. When Nigel wanted to find a person to take Jaeger's place, he somehow targeted Celine for the job. Roy Aldiss could have seen the bird book and written that note to Celine. She could have rebuffed him. Roy's mother said he suffered from depression. He may have hung himself out of despair."

"Who took the bird book to Berea? Why was Celine picked to be the imposter? How did Natoli end up with the note?"

"The more I think about it, the note business and bird book weren't enough to compel Celine to take Jaeger's place. There's something bigger back there that made her do it," Frank suggested.

"Which must go back to how Perry Oliver got the money to build his shop right after Celine was born," Marcel said.

Brock was wearing a pair of navy cargo shorts and a chalk-blue leisure shirt. He wheeled into a seat at the table and stuck his bare legs out. "Nigel wasn't the person to approach Celine. He wouldn't have wanted to get his hands dirty. That would have been left to Natoli."

"No." Frank sat across from Brock, emulating his slouched posture. "Perry Oliver is the one who told Celine something that caused her to act."

Marcel joined the other two at the table. "So, Clive Natoli, whom Celine may or may not have known back then, and Perry Oliver, who may or may not be her father, went to Berea with one volume of the bird book. Perry revealed something to Celine, which gave her no choice but to become Jaeger Barclay."

Brock organized his thinking. "While the three of them were out of her apartment, Roy Aldiss came around and saw the bird book. He wrote the note to Celine and waited to hear from her. She probably ran out to find him after she read it. Natoli came back to the apartment to retrieve the Audubon. She was gone, but the note was there. He took it, and the bird book, and left. Celine found Roy and told him no dice. He went and hung himself."

Frank said, "I still think there's a strong possibility Clive and Perry forced Roy to write that note and then killed him. I'm more interested in why they brought the Audubon to show her."

"That's easy. They told her she'd get a payout from the estate when Mrs. Barclay went toes up. The book's good collateral. That must be how the million dollars landed in her bank account," Brock concluded.

Marcel asked, "Do you think Celine made a deal right then, along the lines of 'I'll do it if you give me a million dollars when she dies'?"

Frank and Brock said emphatically, in unison, "Yes."

Brock stood and reached into his pocket. "And then there's this." He threw the memory stick to Marcel. "Play it for Frank." Once he viewed it, Brock asked, "Is that Celine?"

"No." Frank seemed somewhat disinterested.

"How do you know that?"

"Because Celine's got a small brown mole by her belly button. That girl doesn't."

"You're making more progress wooing Celine than I thought. Who is it then?"

"My guess is it's Jaeger Barclay, and these kinds of shenanigans is why she took off or was killed."

Marcel urged, "Fill that in for me a little more."

"Natoli, or somebody he knew, set these situations up to compromise Kentucky senators and representatives. Nigel Barclay must have had something on his sister, Jaeger, enough for her to take part in stuff like that. He also must have a little something on Celine."

Brock voiced a scenario he liked: "When Nigel's father died, Jaeger intended to break free. Nigel was in a spot."

"That reopens the possibility that Nigel killed his father, Jaeger knew it, and thought her life was in danger," Marcel said.

Frank piped up, "Or Jaeger killed her father and took off. I'm not sure it matters which story is right. We've got to figure out how to get Celine safely away from these miscreants for good."

Brock looked at Frank. "Ask Marcel. That's my specialty."

"Gee, Skinner, I never would have known. I don't recommend roughing them up. They may take it out on Celine."

"I've got a better plan; one you pencil necks would approve of. I'll tell you about it after I gather a few more facts. Marcel, freeze the shot of the guy in the video, crop it, print his face, and get me the keys to one of the fleet cars."

On the way to Frankfort, Brock made a phone call. "Pearl, it's your secret admirer, the man who took you to lunch yesterday." Wednesday midday traffic was light.

"I had a feeling I'd be hearing from you. Let me guess, you're ready to leave your wife for me." She leaned back in her chair and smiled at the phone.

"Nothing quite so drastic. I'm happy to hear you've got such a high opinion of me." He thought she was chumming him but wasn't sure.

"I'll hold on to that possibility. What is it you wanted?" A change in her tone signaled she wasn't born yesterday.

"Do you happen to know the name of the potential investor in the distillery on Barclay Farm?"

"I do."

"Are you in a sharing mood?"

"I could be." She was the cat, Brock the mouse.

"I know better than to bid against myself."

"I'm just playing with you. It's a Wall Street private equity firm by the name of Lolly Gelt."

"That's a funny name."

"Both words are slang for money." She was once again enamored of her own worldliness.

"You don't say. Do you know where they get their capital?"

"Yes. Mostly from colleges and universities. Prominent ones."

"I'm surprised they're allowed to invest in distilleries. How did you come by that information?"

"I processed a bundle of the paperwork. They'd invest in the devil if the return was good enough."

"Do you know who's working on the Barclay distillery deal for them?"

"Yeah, a guy named Willard Lentz. He lives on Old Frankfort Pike just before you get to Three Chimneys Farm."

"Have you ever seen him?"

"Sure, he's been in here a few times over the years."

Brock pulled off to the side of the road. "I'm going to put you on FaceTime. I want to show you a picture of a guy." Pearl popped up on the screen. She studied the face. "Is this Willard Lentz?" Brock asked.

"That's him."

"Pearl, you're one in a million. When's your birthday? I'm going to send you a nice present."

"October thirty-first."

"Coming right up then. It's hell turning thirty, isn't it?"

"You are a cad. When did you say you were going to come around and buy me lunch again?"

"Soon."

"I've got to get back to work." She ended the call abruptly.

Brock took the Versailles exit and veered left toward Lexington. There's no road in the world with greater splendor than Old Frankfort Pike—hundred-year-old deciduous trees, rolling hills, wood fences, thoroughbreds, and stylish barns abound. If it isn't the center of the universe, it's damned close. A mailbox with Lentz etched on it appeared on the left side of the road, amid several famous farms. He parked his car by the garage.

The gambrel-style house had been built out of recycled brick, a good idea that didn't pan out. A brass kick plate on the door made the place look cheap. Brock approached and used his fist to alert those inside of his presence. A thin woman with straight black hair, a deep tan, and false eyelashes greeted him, asking, "Yes?"

"Is Willard Lentz here?" Brock took in her looks.

"He's in his office. Who may I say is calling?"

"I'm an officer of the court. I've got documents to deliver to him." Brock wondered if he would end up in the Frankfort or Versailles jail if he got pinched.

"I'll get him," she said.

It was Willard Lentz, all right. He was considerably older than the headshot from the video. He acted as though people coming to the door delivering papers was a common occurrence, which it likely was in his business. "You have some papers for me?"

"I do." Brock held up the letter-size still of Willard's face.

"What is this?"

"A closeup of you in the act of 'hugging' a naked girl."

"What?"

"Invite me in, and I'll explain." Brock pulled the picture back.

Lentz pivoted and led the way to a room on the front corner of the house that had windows on two walls. He sat down at his desk and told Brock to close the door. "What is it you want?"

"Some information. I've got a video of you getting cozy with a girl in the buff. She's missing and presumed dead. We're trying to find the killer."

"What's your name? Are you with the police?"

Brock ignored the question. "If you tell me about the video, we'll keep it out of circulation, and possibly return it to you when we find out what happened to the girl. You've got three choices: threaten me with a gun, call the police, or tell me what I want to know."

"You sound like some second-rate flatfoot," he said, a slight quiver in his voice.

"Okay. When your investors see the video, your career will go up in smoke."

"It's not my career that worries me, it's my wife. She'd get at least half of the fortune I've built." Willard Lentz was smart enough to know when he'd drawn dead.

"How and when did it happen? I'll be on my way if your story is believable."

"I moved here nearly twelve years ago. I began meeting with people interested in building and opening bourbon distilleries. Bourbon whiskey has been a rocket to the moon, and it ain't never coming back. Our equity firm has experienced premium returns in the business.

"I met with a guy by the name of Nigel Barclay shortly after I came to town. He owns a farm in southern Indiana where he wants to build a distillery and tourist trap. I think it's a home run, but the principals of our fund have been worried about it not being in Kentucky. We've made a lot of other investments in the area, but that one has been on the shelf for a long time."

"Is there renewed interest in the project?"

"Yes. Many investors are placing bets on the other side of the Ohio River because of the barrel tax here in Kentucky. If the tax doesn't get repealed, our fund is going to pull the trigger."

"How does the video figure into it?"

"Nigel suggested I meet Clive Natoli. I went to his house. He wasn't there. A beautiful girl came to the door in a robe. She led me into a room where she slipped out of the robe and grabbed me. I pushed her away and got out of there. I met Natoli later, and he acted like I was weird. I presumed he and Nigel were going to use the setup to keep me motivated to do the deal with them. I've been waiting eleven years to hear something about this, and you're the first person to mention it to me."

"You say you're close to doing the deal?"

"As I said, if Kentucky votes to keep the barrel tax, we'll fund the project."

"How much does Barclay get?"

"He'll donate his farm property and put in ten million of his money for a 10 percent stake."

"The girl who skillfully trapped you is missing. She's Nigel Barclay's younger sister, Jaeger."

"How can that be? I met Jaeger a few times when I visited Nigel at his home after that. She was taking care of her mother who was ill."

"When their mother died, the Jaeger you met disappeared too. She was an imposter. Did she look like the girl that jumped you at Natoli's house?"

Willard spun his chair around and stared out the window. "I'm not sure. You have the video, right?"

"I do. Even if they have another copy, they're not going to use it against you. They can ill afford to draw attention to Nigel's sister and what happened to her."

"Why did the one girl disappear, and another take her place?"

"That, my friend, is what we're trying to get to the bottom of. You should string along until we get some answers. I'll contact you if there is anything you should know about."

"What's your interest in this affair?"

"Frankly, sir, my answer is laughable. I'm trying to help someone who doesn't want my help." Brock asked one last question: "Would Barclay have to wait several years for his investment to pay off?"

"Heavens no. The deal would get bundled in an IPO, and he could sell out for a hundred million in short order."

Brock turned philosophical. "Money's not the root of all evil, it's the love of it, so they say. I'm not so sure about that. People steal, lie, and kill for the money itself, not the love of it."

Frank, Marcel, and Maude were notified of the latest chapter in the Celine Oliver saga. They all scolded Brock for stirring up a hornet's nest. Something bad was going to happen to somebody, and soon, they said.

A boxer's thinking is black and white: kill or be killed. Brock was in no mood to go fifteen rounds.

Chapter 14

Thursday started out cooler than any day since early May. The air was crisp, as were the minds of the Skinners that bright morning. Maude asked her husband, who was milling around in the kitchen, "Are you staying in Hazard today? You've been like a fart in a mitten."

"Only The Shadow knows," he answered sarcastically.

"I've been thinking, Brock. We've got a lot of information. We're smart enough to figure out how it fits together."

"Okay. What's your theory?"

"It starts with the fathers of Celine and Jaeger. We've been thinking either Clive Natoli or Perry Oliver is Celine's father. Both may be blackmailing her. I don't think a biological father of a child would do that. In Jaeger's case, I don't think a biological brother would force his sister, or half-sister, to strip down for blackmail. That would mean Nigel's dad is not Jaeger's biological father, and his mother is not Jaeger's biological mother."

"You know, I married you for your looks and angelic personality. How is it your brain is beautiful too?"

"So, you thought I was dumb when you married me?"

Brock threw his head back and looked at the ceiling. "Why did I say that? I'm such an idiot."

"I married you for the stupid things you say sometimes," she said while he was on his heels.

"That means Jaeger is adopted, and we have no candidates for Celine's father," Brock said.

"Right, but it leads in a direction that makes some sense." Maude began stocking the fridge with club soda cans.

"Like?"

"Eleven years ago, at the beginning of the year, life was a bowl of cherries for these characters. Clive had just gotten into lobbying and had begun advocating for the Barclay family because of the connection his father had with Nigel's father. Celine was about to graduate from college and look for a job. Perry Oliver had a little business in Hazard, and Jaeger Barclay stood to inherit half of the Barclay estate when her parents died. Then things started going wrong."

Brock elaborated, "On his deathbed, Nigel's father told him Jaeger was adopted. Since the old man probably wasn't in favor of turning the family farm into a circus, Nigel came up with a plan. The first thing he did was get rid of his pop by suffocating him with a pillow."

Maude interjected, "Nigel told Jaeger she was adopted and wouldn't inherit anything. He could prove it with a DNA test. Soon thereafter, Willard Lentz came around. Nigel saw a chance to hook him. He told Jaeger if she did this one thing for him, he'd make sure she was listed as an heir. Nigel planned to renege on that promise, so he asked Clive Natoli if he knew anyone who could step into Jaeger's shoes if he made her disappear."

Brock added, "Clive was acquainted with Celine through the Olivers and knew she looked a lot like Jaeger. The only way to get Celine to do it was to have Perry support the idea, which meant Nigel had to come up with a reward for both him and Celine. Perry was offered a handsome cut of the payoff from the new distillery on Barclay Farm. Nigel knew the Audubon book had value, so he suggested Clive and Perry take a volume of it to Berea to show Celine."

Maude brought it home, saying, "Perry and Clive delivered Nigel's offer to pay her the million bucks to impersonate Jaeger until his mother died. Perry might have told Celine that he wasn't her father, and they used Roy Aldiss to seal the deal. When Mrs. Barclay died, Celine got the million and went back to living under her own name. Why she's still beholden to Clive Natoli is where the trail ends."

"What happened to Jaeger Barclay, and did Clive and Nigel have something else on Celine other than the Roy Aldiss note and video of Jaeger? If not, they may go away quietly."

Maude's expression suddenly darkened. She said woodenly, "If Nigel, Clive, and Perry figure out the people around Celine are trying to expose them, they'll want to fix things. We already know they're ruthless."

Brock put it bluntly: "They would have to get rid of me, you, Marcel, Valerie, Calvin Willett, Frank Romine, and Leslie Blazek. It would be a lot easier to make Celine go poof."

"They won't do that. They'll believe we know too much if what we've already found out gets back to them."

Brock grasped a straw: "If we knew Jaeger Barclay was alive and where she was, we could go to the police. In either case, we need to get Celine to tell us what she knows."

––––––––––

Celine bounded down the stairs at noon to retrieve the mail from her box, which was in the hall by the front door. She opened the envelope from the Ohio Valley Distillers' Guild, and when she saw the note written by Roy Aldiss, it brought back bad memories. The second note, wishing her freedom from the grip of Clive Natoli, frustrated her further. She thought about chasing Frank down but let the idea go. As she walked back into her apartment, her phone rang. "Hello, Brock. You need something?"

"Yes. I'm hoping to clean up the business of your five-year vacation before our bridge game. It would help if you'd fill in some blanks."

"What exactly do you think you know?" Her facial expression, which Brock could not see, would have slowed him down.

"After you graduated from college, your dad and Clive Natoli came to see you with an offer you couldn't refuse. They asked you to move to Charlestown, Indiana, to take care of Nigel Barclay's mother until her death. She lasted five years, and Nigel Barclay paid you a million dollars. Did Mrs. Barclay think you were her daughter, and do you know what happened to Jaeger?"

There was silence on the other end of the phone for an uncomfortably long time. Brock didn't fill in the dead space. Finally, she said, "Mrs. Barclay's eyesight was poor. She acted like I was Jaeger, who was gone before I got there. I've never seen or heard from her in my life."

"What do Clive Natoli and Nigel Barclay have on you?"

"Absolutely nothing. I can stop working with Clive anytime I want. I don't because he pays me a ton of money."

"Celine, there's something you're not telling me. We just want to make sure you can live your life freely, without anyone threatening you or controlling what you do."

"Brock, I'm telling you, my father, Clive Natoli, and Nigel Barclay are not interested in what I do and who I do it with. The three of them are trying to get investors to fund a new distillery on Barclay Farm. If that happens, they'll carve a big melon."

"When I saw you last, you said you didn't want to relive the past. What is it you don't want to relive?"

"Roy Aldiss, a college friend of mine, was crazy about me. When I told him I was moving away, he hanged himself. I feel responsible for his death. It makes me sad every time I think about it. And living in that house with that animal, Nigel, was a nightmare."

"Why did you decide to take the job for the million dollars?"

"Hello. Everybody gave her one to two years to live. What recent college graduate makes that kind of money?"

"Did your father tell you anything that made you do it?"

"No," she fired back.

Brock didn't believe her but didn't say so. He called Marcel and Frank to bring them up to speed, and then drove over to the winery to talk to Maude and have lunch. He took a seat on the veranda and said to his wife, "I'm not sure Clive and Perry are blackmailing Celine. If they're not, one of them could be her father. Jaeger's situation is different. We should figure out what happened to her."

Maude said, "Only thing we have is a video. You think Nigel killed Jaeger?"

"If he killed his dad, he killed her. If not, no. I'll have to talk to Clive and Nigel to find out."

"Should we worry about Celine's safety?"

"Maude, I have a way of convincing those men to leave her alone."

"I know you do. I don't like it." She went to the kitchen to get Brock's lunch.

Frank gazed out the window and saw cotton ball clouds high in the blue sky. Leslie Blazek's car was at the gate. He let her through and went down to greet her in front of the building. She parked in a space under a majestic elm tree east of the building. "Frank, how are you?"

"Wonderful. It's great to see you again. Thanks for coming." He kissed her squarely on her lips and gave her a big hug.

Leslie Blazek's persona projected confidence. Glossy, rich brown hair framed her symmetrical face, and a flawless complexion gave her a Hollywood look she used to her advantage. "Boy, Kentucky is beautiful. Now I have an appreciation for why you chose to move here." She gazed upward and protected her eyes from the sun.

"Yes, it's gorgeous country." He clutched her oversized roller bag and led the way up to his apartment. Once she was settled, and they were seated in the front room, he asked, "You on your game?"

"I feel pretty good about it. Is the competition going to be fierce?"

"There are plenty of big names entered. We've beaten most of them at one time or another." He wove his fingers and put them under his chin. "A guy who owns part of the company I work for told me he called you wanting to get some information on me. Did you tell him anything?"

"Not really. I told him you were doing computer work when you lived in Virginia along with studying chess and playing in tournaments. I didn't tell him you were a government hacker."

"It wouldn't have mattered. They already know it."

Leslie, looking pensive, said, "Frank, do you think one of the countries you hacked has identified you and has sent someone to kill you?"

"I have no way of knowing."

"Well, I hate the idea of finding out by you turning up dead."

"What can I do about it?" He stuck his hands out to the side.

"Nothing, I guess," she replied.

"I want to warn you about something else. The girl who lives next door is one of the people we are playing bridge with on Saturday night. A peculiar story has developed around her since I moved here, and the guy who called you, Brock Skinner, is trying to figure out what is going on. I'd like to enlist you to get information from her." Frank spent the next half hour telling Leslie the tale of Celine Oliver. Leslie concluded he was more interested in his neighbor than her.

"What exactly would you like me to find out?"

"Stuff about her mother and father. When you meet her, you'll wonder why she isn't married to the richest man in the state. We can't figure out why she became an escort. With your wits, maybe you can get to the bottom of that."

"Good looking, is she?"

"Yes."

"Is she extremely smart?"

"I'm not sure. She went to college. Enough about her. I haven't seen you in two months. Tell me everything you've been doing," he implored.

"Since you won't marry me, I've been looking for a man," she said, unvarnished.

"Any possibilities?"

"I've kind of determined smart men with a modicum of class are nowhere to be found. I guess there're some around who look like nerds and step on their feet all the time."

"Being smart is a curse, Leslie. It shapes us into becoming elitists. We want to run peoples' lives because we know better. It can also make us think we're smarter than God, which is a dangerous place to be. Satan thinks he's smarter than God. We never want to be that smart."

She leaned back in her chair and let her arms hang down. "See what I mean? I can't talk like this to anyone but you. Tell me again why you won't marry me?" Leslie asked.

"You just described it. You have high expectations. I'm afraid I won't measure up."

"That's crap, and you know it. It's something else. What is it?"

"I don't want any children. You do. Some of the things that interest me, don't interest you, and vice versa. I've been searching spiritually for years, and you seem to have settled the matter for yourself. I don't really care about people. I'm not naturally empathetic. You are. You deserve someone who has treated you better than I have. I'm very sorry about that. I want more than anything in the world for you to be happy in your life."

"Then marry me!"

Frank Romine kept his thoughts to himself. He was interested in Celine Oliver for no rational reason other than her spectacular looks. He liked Leslie Blazek but didn't love her, and the truth be known, she was as beautiful and way smarter than Celine. He said, "Okay, I will." He'd have to figure out how to backtrack on that commitment after the weekend was over.

"What did you say? You will?"

"That's what I said."

"Do you love me?"

"I love you," Frank said, which was another lie from the man whose new fiancée had proclaimed his appreciation for the truth.

Leslie jumped up and cried out, "Now we're getting somewhere! I'm not going to talk about the subject for the next few days, until we're through playing chess and bridge. Is it all right if I give you a big fat kiss?"

"Hey, I wear the pants in this family. Let me do that." Frank got up and moved over to her. In a few minutes, he locked the apartment door from the inside. His phone rang but he didn't answer, as did hers, buzzing on the counter. Frank gathered it was going to be an interesting weekend, more than anyone foresaw.

Chapter 15

Celine heard the timid knock on her apartment door around five o'clock on Thursday afternoon. When she opened it, there stood Miss Blazek. "My goodness, you're a beautiful woman," Celine blurted with a smile on her face.

"Takes one to know one," Leslie rifled back.

"Frank must have a mental disorder."

"Don't all men?"

Celine took a liking to her at once. "Ones I've met do. Come in, and we'll fix something to eat while we chat."

"I don't want to impose."

"Nonsense. I haven't had any girl talk in years."

"In that case, I'll join you." Leslie closed the door after stepping into the apartment. She took in how the place was decorated, hoping to read Celine's personality. Fewer things, better things, seemed to be the theme. The furniture fabric colors were drab gray-and-white patterns. An art glass vase had yellow, red, and purple squares. "Frank has his own plans," she remarked to mask her nosiness.

"Have you been sent over on a reconnaissance mission?"

"I came voluntarily. Nobody tells me what to do," she said, pursing her lips and crossing her arms.

Celine asked, "Can I get you a little white wine?"

"If you're having some."

"Sit down, I'll bring it over." Celine poured two small glasses, and said from the kitchen, "Since neither of us are married. I want to hear about Frank."

Leslie took the wine glass and leaned back in the cushioned seat she sat in. "All through school, I never attracted a guy who was destined to go anywhere, and when I got good at chess, the pickings were even slimmer. I met Frank when we played a chess match. He was smart, good looking, had plenty of money, and high-class manners."

Celine reported, "I've spent some time with him. He strikes me as a boy who never ran with the ribald crowd."

"He wasn't involved in athletics in school. That's generally where boys learn how to behave. His parents thought it was too dangerous."

Celine asked, "Did you like your parents? Have you forgiven them for their shortcomings?"

"No. I was pretty much ignored. How about your parents?"

Celine twisted in her seat and raised her shoulders. "I spent ages zero to eighteen in Hazard, Kentucky. Not an overly exciting place. There was something wrong with my parents' relationship. I picked up more when I went off to Berea College. In the last eleven years, I've learned way too much about this rotten world."

"Did you get along with your dad?" Leslie asked.

Celine's mood became reflective. "He wasn't mean or unpleasant. I never knew him or could figure out what was in his head."

"Any near misses on the man front?"

"There was a nice boy at Berea College who fell for me when I was a student there. I told him I was taking a job in Indiana. He was so distraught, he hanged himself."

"Oh, that sticks with you. I'm sorry to hear that. I'm going to ask straight up: why'd you become an escort?"

"My first job out of college was caring for an elderly woman. I lived in the house with her son. He was horrible. I have a healthy distrust of men. I figured it was a good idea to use my looks and not get stuck with some scoundrel."

"I know what you mean. Frank just said he'd marry me. He doesn't mean it. He's after you. This scenario has happened to me half a dozen times since I've known him."

Celine chuckled. "There are three men in this world whom I'm fond of."

"And they are?" Leslie thought she was getting somewhere.

"My two clients, and a man by the name of Brock Skinner. Clive Natoli, a lobbyist in Frankfort, is very nice, and the gentleman hosting our bridge party, Calvin Willett, is a sweetheart. The other guy, Brock Skinner, who is married to an impressive gal, sincerely cares about my well-being."

"That's a bigger fan club than I have," Leslie reported.

Celine demurred, saying, "Frank's too smart for his own good. He's been digging around in my past, and from what I've seen of him, he'll eventually find out what happened to a girl who went missing. She was the daughter of the elderly woman I cared for. I impersonated her."

"Why'd you do that?"

"Because her creepy brother offered me a million dollars to do it. I took the money."

"Do you know what happened to the girl?" Leslie asked.

"No. I never saw or met her. She might have been killed."

The women chatted more about Frank, Brock, and Calvin Willett. They fixed dinner together and got to laughing at anything mildly funny. Celine was the happiest she'd been in a long time.

Frank saw Leslie step through the door of his apartment after she was done visiting Celine, and commented, "You must've had a nice time."

"I did."

"What did you learn?"

"She's starved for a relationship with a good man, and it ain't you. She's sort of like me."

Frank knew he was walking the plank, so he watched what he said. "I'm sorry if I've hurt you."

Leslie asked, "Who is this girl she impersonated? What happened to her?"

"Jaeger Barclay. That's Brock Skinner's department."

"Celine holds Brock in high regard. I can't wait to meet him."

"He's nothing like me. You'll want him on your team in dodgeball."

Leslie's anger subsided. "Do you think we can beat him and his wife at bridge?"

"Falling off a log."

———

Friday would keep the string going—another dry, sunny, fall day that would make a person feel alive a little longer, until the weather eventually turned bad for the season. Brock got Natoli's phone number and called him at eight o'clock on the dot.

"This is Clive." He had the breezy voice of an experienced salesperson.

"Good morning, sir. A lady by the name of Jaeger Barclay has hired our firm to figure out if a woman who impersonated her absconded with any of her property. She suggested I interview you to get the background of her circumstances." That was a lie, of course, but Brock was getting tired of coming up with scenarios without enough facts to confirm them. It was time to trot out a rubber worm to catch a fish.

"Jaeger? She's surfaced? That's a showstopper. I thought she was dead."

"Could I meet you somewhere this morning to discuss the matter?"

"Sure. Why don't you come to my house? Eleven o'clock is convenient for me." Clive rattled off the address.

"I'll be there," Brock affirmed.

"What's your name?"

"Brock Skinner."

"What's the name of your firm?"

"Willett, Romine, and Skinner."

Clive Googled the firm name and nothing came up. "Do you have a website?"

"No. We work discreetly. We do not advertise our services."

"How does someone hire you?"

"The police send people to us whom they can't help."

"Jaeger's been to the police?" Clive's easygoing manner had sagged.

"I suppose she did. I'll see you at eleven." Brock jumped off before he asked another question.

Morgan Wallen and Chris Stapleton blared from the speakers of the Lamborghini all the way to Frankfort. The fall meet at Keeneland would be opening in a couple of weeks, and anticipatory energy could be felt all around. Brock called Frank before he reached Clive's place, to find out where he was.

"Leslie and I are just now arriving at the hotel. Our first matches are at one o'clock."

"Best of luck to both of you. Call and give me a report when you can."

Brock parked his car fifteen feet from Natoli's front door. Clive let him in and shook his hand.

"Can I get you something to drink?"

Brock had seen Clive with Celine in Bootlegger on Main. Up close he appeared relaxed and benign. "No, thank you."

"Have a seat."

Brock remembered flipping over the couch he was about to sit on in the front room, looking for blackmail materials, which he eventually found in the kitchen. "Nice place you got here." He tried to remember how the kitchen was arranged.

"Thanks. I bought it from my father a dozen years ago."

"Are you married?"

"No." He seemed happy about the fact. "What's this business about Jaeger?"

"When we talked on the phone, I got the impression you were quite certain she was dead."

"Well, a girl who stood to inherit from her parents wouldn't disappear if she were still alive."

Brock derailed that logic, saying, "Unless she wasn't in the will. Miss Barclay intends to go into court and explain how she feared for her life and why she disappeared."

"Good for her."

"Why do you say that?"

"As far as I'm concerned, everybody should get what they deserve," said Clive.

"I understand a girl named Celine Oliver impersonated Jaeger Barclay. What do you know about her?"

"Boy, that's a long story."

Brock leaned to one side and said, "Why don't you start at the beginning."

"I was homecoming king, and her mother was homecoming queen. Her father and I played on the football team together."

"You're talking about high school?"

"Yes. Rhonda got pregnant in January. She married Perry right after we all graduated," Clive explained.

"Perry and Rhonda are the names of Celine's parents, I take it."

"They are."

"What do you know about Celine impersonating Jaeger?"

"My father was a state politician. He got to know the Barclay family from Charlestown, Indiana. I met Nigel Barclay a dozen years ago through my father. He convinced me to work for him as a lobbyist."

"What was he after?" Brock asked.

"He was trying to get an investor to go in on a bourbon distillery on his farm."

"Jaeger Barclay told us that her brother asked her to compromise someone. Was that so he could blackmail the person?"

Clive glanced down and blinked his eyes. "Nigel somehow knew that a camera was set up to film people in this house. He had a key. Nigel's father and my father must have been blackmailing people before I bought the house. When I found out what Nigel and Jaeger had done, I told him I wanted no part of that business, and he wasn't to do anything like that again, or I'd go to the police."

"What happened next?"

"Nigel's father died, and Jaeger disappeared."

"Jaeger has told us that Nigel threatened to kill her. That's why she took off." Brock's yarn kept getting longer and more elaborate. "She also told us she found out Celine was impersonating her. Were you part of that?"

"I was. Greed got the best of me. Nigel shared that Jaeger had taken off. He wanted me to find someone to take her place. He said he'd cut me in on the distillery deal. I knew Celine through Perry and Rhonda and thought she'd be a good choice. I'm still waiting for my payoff."

"What did you do?"

"I told Nigel I knew the perfect candidate, but he'd have to pay her and her dad off. He gave Perry a piece of the distillery deal like he'd done with me and said he'd pay his daughter cash if she'd care for his mother until she died."

"That was a million dollars I believe. Did Celine want any collateral to make sure he would pay when the time came?" Brock asked.

"Nigel figured she'd want something, so he sent Perry and me over there with one volume of a valuable Audubon book. She gave it to Perry to keep until she got the money. Something else disturbing happened when we went to Berea to talk to her. There was a boy, Roy Aldiss, who tried to blackmail her into dating him. He wrote her a note to that effect, and when she told him she was taking a job in Indiana, he hanged himself. I took the note. I still have it."

Brock hoped Clive wouldn't get the itch to retrieve the note from its former hiding place. "How valuable is the Audubon book?"

"Worth fifteen million, I'd say. Nigel will sell it when it's time to invest in his distillery."

"Jaeger told our firm that the representative for the potential investor in the distillery is the man she and Nigel set up to blackmail. I think she said his name is Willard Lentz."

"That's right."

"Is the deal ever going to go?"

"Soon. I'm lobbying for that outcome. Otherwise, I'll never get a payoff."

"One last question: when we researched Celine's parents, her father came into some money right after Celine was born. Do you know anything about that?"

Clive cackled. "Yeah, when I asked Perry where he got the money, he half-seriously said he got it from the father of his daughter."

"Frankly, Clive, I was wondering if you were her father." Brock gave him the fisheye.

"I wish I would have had sex with Rhonda. She was one good-looking woman. Not as beautiful as Celine, but damn close."

"Do you have any contact with Celine these days?" Brock knew he did and wanted him to admit it.

"I do. She goes with me when I'm lobbying Kentucky senators and representatives. She's a classy person. Such a delight to be around. I pay her well for her companionship. When Nigel's mother died, I helped her find a house to rent near Frankfort. She was only a few minutes away from Lexington and Louisville, where I would meet legislators often."

"Do you know if she had a roommate?"

"I don't think she did. There were other women there occasionally. I never met them."

Brock stood and said, "Thank you, Clive. The information you gave me is quite helpful."

"How does Jaeger look these days? I remember her as a pretty girl."

"She's been through a lot. I'm not sure you'd recognize her." Brock played that angle in case he needed to produce someone claiming to be Jaeger.

Clive winced. "That's a shame. No telling what Nigel will do if he finds out she's alive."

Brook had a menacing look on his face, which scared the wits out of Natoli. "If he knows what's good for him, he'll stay away from her. I'd recommend that you not tell him she's still alive."

"I'd already come to that conclusion." He opened the front door and invited Brock to leave.

Chapter 16

The syndicated chess tournament prize money was set at
$160,000 for the winner, $80,000 for second place, $40,000 for
third place, and $20,000 for fourth place. Sixty-four contestants
had been invited to play, and the card was loaded. It would take
at least five wins over six games to win money.

Round One on Friday went from one until three, Round Two
from three thirty to five, and Round Three from five thirty to six
thirty. Round Four on Saturday was set for one until one thirty,
Round Five from two to two thirty, and the final round
scheduled for three o'clock. The whole affair would be done by
three thirty including pictures, and the prize money given out at
once. If Leslie and/or Frank made it to the final round, they'd be
back at his apartment by five o'clock, in time to drive to Willett's
for a relaxing game of bridge.

At six thirty on Friday evening, Frank rang Brock to report that
he and Leslie had won all three of their matches.

"You're hoping for a showdown tomorrow, I take it," Brock said.

"That would be nice. We'd sneak out of there with nearly a
quarter of a million dollars."

"Our bridge game will be a big letdown if that happens."

"Not if we have a side bet that Calvin doesn't know about."

"I'm up for that. Will you take ten-to-one odds?"

"How much were you thinking?" Frank asked.

"Oh, it would just be for bragging rights. I'd say my hundred for your thousand?"

"How about your ten thousand for my hundred thousand?"

"Dang it, Frank, if I lost that much, Maude would make me sleep outside in a tent."

"Scared money never wins."

"Yeah, and scared men who don't bet never lose," Brock quipped.

"Okay, your hundred to my thousand it is."

"Good luck tomorrow."

"Celine told Leslie where a good dress shop was in downtown Louisville. She's going to go there in the morning to see what she can find."

"Oh, so you want everybody to dress up for Calvin's party?"

Leslie came on: "No. I wouldn't want to be upstaged by your wife and Celine."

———————

CeCe slipped on hot mitts in Cal's kitchen, preparing to put a piece of fish in the oven. She remarked, "I spent time with Leslie yesterday. She's the best. Good looking and extremely smart. I don't understand why Frank doesn't throw a net over her."

"My guess is he doesn't think he'll live very long."

"You know, I asked him once why he moved here from Virginia. He gave me some phony excuse that he wanted to be close to his parents in their old age."

"Did you ask Leslie about that?"

"No. I should have. Where do you want to eat?"

"Let's go out on the back porch."

With the noise of boat traffic reverberating off the shoreline across the lake, they enjoyed the tuna steaks on a bed of greens, and after scrubbing the kitchen until it shined, Celine took off. She heard people talking in Frank's apartment when she arrived home and was about to step into her place. She knocked on his door.

"Come in."

"I heard voices. Thought I'd butt in."

"Please join us. Would you girls mind if I took your picture together? I want to be able to prove that I hang around with the smartest, most beautiful women in the whole, wide world."

Leslie said, "Frank, you're so full of it."

"Both of you must have won at chess today," Celine threw out.

"We did. What have you been doing?" Frank asked.

"I've been at Cal's making sure we have everything ready for the bridge party."

"We're looking forward to it. Don't tell him, but Brock and I have a side bet on our game."

"Keep that quiet. I don't want you to ruin the evening." Celine paced around the room and put a hand on her forehead. "There's another reason I stopped by. I've got a feeling you're in some kind of trouble, Frank, and I want to know what it is." She stared at him, forcing a response.

He looked at Leslie and said, "You want to tell her?"

"For the last several years, Frank worked as a hacker for the federal government. He has stolen secrets from our enemies, and we're worried he's been marked by a hostile foreign country."

"Are you saying he's in danger of being killed?" CeCe asked.

"That's about the size of it," Frank confirmed.

"Sort of makes my five-year stretch at Barclay Farm rather insignificant."

Leslie added, "And the worst of it is there's no resolving the matter."

"I can think of one way . . . disappear. I'm an expert at that. I did it for five years."

Frank went to his apartment door and leaned on it. "I'm starting to warm up to that idea."

―――――――――

The forecast for Saturday included cloudy skies, wind, and rain. A shelf of clouds had formed by eight o'clock, but the wind and rain had not made their grand entrance. The Skinners left for the winery early to get a jump on the chores for the day. They'd be pulling out at three o'clock, three hours before the winery closed.

Leslie was standing outside the dress shop in Louisville at nine, waiting for people who worked there to unlock the door. She tried on several dresses and bought the two she liked, and then met Frank for lunch at 11:30 at a Mexican restaurant near the hotel. He said, "Did you find anything?"

"I did. A couple of nice things."

"You'll have to model them for me later." Frank was trying to put her in a good mood before an intense, lightning round of chess.

They both won their next two matches.

Leslie Blazek and Frank Romine were announced at three o'clock as the two finalists. The crowd and fallen contestants gathered around to watch the last match. Frank insisted Leslie play the white pieces, so she ran an Orthoschnapp Gambit in the Steiner Variation of a French Defense Opening and beat him. He shook her hand professionally and followed her to the award stand. On the way, she asked, "Did you let me win?"

"You know me better than that. Since we're in separate cars, the code to get through the gate at the apartment is 9-1-8-2 in case you get there first." They left the hotel parking lot separately a little after four.

Leslie arrived before he did. She knocked on Celine's door and told her, "I won. I beat Frank in the final match."

"Congratulations. How much did you win?"

"A hundred and sixty thousand." Her face lit up as she said the amount.

"Girl, you're flying high now."

"Thanks. We can ride together to Cal's as soon as he gets here, and we change. I found two lovely dresses at that shop you suggested I visit."

Celine replied, "Good. Come over and get me when it's time to go."

Leslie went from the bedroom to the bathroom several times getting ready, and Frank never appeared. She tried his cell and got no answer. The tracking device on his phone showed he was in the apartment building. She went down to his garage. The car was there but no sign of him. She opened the driver's door. His phone was lying on the passenger seat. She ran back upstairs and knocked on Celine's door. "What is it?"

"Frank's car is in the garage, but he's gone. What should we do?" It was ten minutes after five.

"I've got Brock's number. I'll call him." After he picked up, she spoke in a harrowing voice: "Leslie and I have been waiting for Frank to come in from the chess tournament. His car is in the garage, and he's not here."

Maude heard what she said to Brock and exhaled in disgust. He said, "Okay. We're on our way. Was the garage door up or down?"

"Up," Leslie said.

"Maude and I should be there in forty minutes. Celine, call Calvin and tell him that Frank may have been kidnapped, and to keep quiet about it until I can figure out what's going on. What's the code to get through the gate?"

"9-1-8-2."

Brock called Marcel and told him what happened. "Go to your office and get the camera disc for what went on at Frank's apartment today and bring it to his place." He gave him the gate code.

The Skinners arrived and ran up the steps. The door was ajar, so they entered his apartment. Celine and Leslie were nonplussed, sitting together on the couch. Brock said, "Take me down to his car." After looking the situation over, he was convinced it would be easy to sneak up behind someone. Brock took the phone off the passenger seat and said, "I take it this is his?" Leslie nodded in agreement.

Marcel and Valerie arrived a few minutes later carrying a laptop. He picked up the action at the front gate from noon on. Several cars with Kentucky plates went in and out until 4:12. That's when a vehicle with Indiana plates came through. Leslie arrived at 4:46, and Frank's car pulled in at 4:53. The Indiana car went back out at 4:58. Brock said, "He must be in the trunk of that car. Marcel, run those plates."

It took him forty-five seconds to find whom it was registered to. "It belongs to Clifty Car Rental located in Madison, Indiana."

Brock asked Celine, "Did you talk to anyone in your apartment about your personal situation recently."

"Well, yes. Leslie came over, and we talked about everything."

"All right. You need to turn your apartment upside down and find the bugging devices. There are probably at least two, maybe more.

Disconnect them and save them for me. I'm going to drive to Madison to see if I can find Frank. Whoever's behind this is playing for keeps, and Frank won't be the only target." Brock ran out.

The five left behind scurried across the hall to start digging. It took them an hour to find the four bugs that had been planted. Celine dropped them in a bag and gave the bag to Maude. She said, "I'm going to call Cal again to see if we can come by after all. He's got food he prepared, and I would like to let him know what's going on so he can keep an eye out."

"Good idea," Maude said.

When they got to Herrington Lake, Calvin was glad to see them. Six of the eight bridge players were there, so he suggested, "After we eat, we might as well play cards for a couple of hours until we hear from Brock."

Clifty Car Rental was headquartered in a repurposed gas station one street north of the main drag in Madison, Indiana. The cars for rent were packed on the lot like sardines. It was nearly seven when Brock banged on the office door. The poorly groomed man behind the desk, who didn't look up, hollered, "We're closed."

"It's an emergency. A matter of life and death."

The man gave in and came to the door. "What do you want?" He had a short fuse and wore it on his face. His leonine head had too many bumps and scars to count.

"Has the car with this plate number been returned?" Brock handed him a crumpled note with the letters and digits on it.

"It hasn't been rented for several days. It's sitting right over there." He pointed at a black Ford sedan.

Brock worked his way to the back of the car. "Someone has removed the license plate."

"Damn it, it'll cost us a hundred bucks to get a replacement. What do you know about this?" the man asked.

"A car with the plate was seen in Kentucky where it shouldn't have been. A person of interest is in the car and could be in danger. You don't have a surveillance camera for this lot, do you?"

"Hell, man, we can't afford that." He was beginning to resent the aggravation of the situation.

Brock got in his car and shot back over the Ohio River Bridge. He called Marcel when he got into Kentucky. "Where are you?"

"Brock, I've put you on speakerphone. We're at Calvin Willett's house. Did you catch the car?"

"Someone stole the license plate off a rental. No telling which direction they went. Leslie, if you can hear me, does Frank have a prize money check on him?"

"Yes. Eighty thousand."

"If he's still alive, the people who took him might have him cash it. What's the bank's name it's drawn on?"

"Esse Bank and Trust."

"Never heard of it. Do they have any branches?"

Marcel looked it up on his phone. "Apparently, they only have the one location, which is in downtown Louisville."

"We should alert them about the situation on Monday morning. I thought of something else: if some foreign country has taken him, they may like to get their hands on his computer. I want to get the CPU out of his apartment. I'll stop by there and get it on the way to meeting up with you all at Calvin's house."

Leslie asked, "How are you going to get in? I locked the door. He gave me a key."

"I'll pick it."

Brock parked in Willett's driveway a little after nine o'clock. He went into the house and asked Marcel to come out and open his trunk. They transferred Frank's computer out of Brock's car, so Marcel could take it to the office on Monday.

After they went back in the house, Cal said, "There's plenty of food here. Get yourself a bite to eat. We've been playing cards to stay busy."

Valerie asked, "What's going on, Brock?"

"There are three possibilities: foreign assassins came to kill him, he wanted to drop out of sight, or somebody's trying to stop him from uncovering something in Celine's past."

"Like what?"

"I'm working on it. I have a few pieces of the puzzle. There's a lot I don't know yet. The fact that Celine's place was bugged means she's in it up to her neck."

"Should we call the police?"

"I don't think so. If he wanted to disappear, he doesn't want the police looking for him. If they came to kill him, he's already dead. I will try to find him if he's still alive."

Leslie mentioned, "He did say he was warming up to the idea of disappearing."

Chapter 17

Brock got a plate of the food Calvin had laid out for the bridge party. He sat at the kitchen table and said to Celine, "You need to tell me about your parents and Nigel Barclay."

"What do you want to know?"

"Is there any reason to believe that Perry Oliver isn't your father?" Brock gave her a quick peek.

"He acted as if he wasn't while I was growing up. He treated me like a guest in the house."

"What about your mother? What was she like?"

"A broken woman. I don't think she's left the house in over thirty years. It's like something bad happened to her and she doesn't want to venture out into the world again. She's been good to me, though. I know she loves me." Celine's eyes went back in time.

"Are you aware that Perry came into some money shortly after you were born? Did you ever hear where he may have gotten it?" Brock asked.

"When I learned about that, I asked my mother. She said he inherited it. I didn't believe her."

Brock stopped talking to shovel in a little food. Then he asked, "What was Nigel Barclay like?"

"Difficult. Clive helped me move into the Barclay house when I left Berea. Nigel's mother was wonderful. She didn't deserve a rotten son like Nigel."

"What's wrong with him?"

"Rude, belligerent, uncaring, abusive, and worst of all, treated his mother horribly at the end of her life."

"How so?"

"Kept telling her he thought it was unfair that she loved her daughter, Jaeger, more than him. He said a lot of other hateful things to her. She died of a broken heart."

"I'm starting to believe that Mrs. Barclay knew you weren't her daughter. Otherwise, she would have told you more family secrets. Does Nigel Barclay have a job or a business?"

Celine's face slowly tightened. "You kidding me? Barclays have never worked. Magnesite was found on the property years ago. They get a check from a mining company once a year. The last one I saw before Mrs. Barclay died was a quarter of a million. I got the impression from her that the yield from the mine had been declining for years."

"What did you do during those five years when you weren't caring for the woman?"

"I planned what I wanted my life to be like after she was gone. I told Clive what I was thinking. He wanted me to help him in his lobbying business. I worked nonstop on fitness, nutrition, and my looks."

"Do you think Nigel could have killed his father?"

"I don't think so."

"Why do you say that?"

"Because if he had, he'd have killed his mother too. Besides being mean to her, he made sure she was attended to by doctors. He took good care of her physically. I think he was covering his tracks. The doctors could testify in Nigel's favor if need be."

"Do you know if she inherited the farm from her husband, and did Nigel inherit it from her?"

"I'm sure of it. Nigel made me sign a document that said by taking the million dollars, I waived any claims against him and the estate. After she died, I returned the Audubon book, and Nigel gave me a certified check. I deposited it in a Harrodsburg bank. Clive helped me find a place to rent near Frankfort."

Calvin spoke up, "Well, I'm sure glad we met. You've been a great blessing to me in my life." He suddenly looked embarrassed over what he'd just said.

"Do you think there's a chance Jaeger was adopted?" Brock asked.

"I don't know. The only thing I can tell you is that Mrs. Barclay said Nigel would get what was coming to him after she died. I thought then that she had given everything to Jaeger."

"Do you think Nigel could be the person who kidnapped or killed Frank?"

"Not a chance. He's not that industrious."

———————

The Skinners stayed at the Sutherland house that evening and left for Hazard on Sunday morning. As they passed by Berea heading south on I-75, Maude commented, "Seems like Nigel got onto the distillery idea when he became aware the magnesite money was going to eventually run out."

"Looks that way."

"We've cast just about everyone in this saga as a bad person at one time or another, but when you've dug deeper, none have ended up being that bad. We're running out of candidates. All you've got left are Nigel Barclay and Perry Oliver."

"I hope Frank Romine isn't dead. I want to hear what Nigel Barclay has to say first and will leave Perry Oliver for last. He acts guilty, and likely has all the answers."

Truman had slept on the back porch and wagged his tail when his "mom and dad" arrived home midday on Sunday. "Yes, we're happy to see you too," Brock told the dog. Maude decided she wanted to go to the winery to make sure everything was running smoothly. "Do you want me to ride over with you?" Brock asked.

"Sure," she said. "What are you going to do tomorrow?"

"Go to that bank in Louisville and over to see Nigel Barclay if I can catch him."

———

Brock was standing at the entrance to Esse Bank and Trust on Monday morning at nine o'clock. He went in and was directed to the person in charge, a man of forty who had chosen not to retire an ill-fitting suit that was too small. He had a round head, short neck, and complexion that signaled he might be in poor health. Brock wondered if nepotism was prevalent at the bank, and hoped the man's ticker didn't give out while they were talking.

"What can I do for you, sir?"

"Your bank issued a certified check for eighty thousand dollars to Frank Romine on Saturday afternoon for coming in second in a chess tournament. Mr. Romine didn't arrive at the function where he was expected on Saturday night. I wanted to alert you to that fact in case someone other than Frank Romine has ideas of getting ahold of his money."

The manager became wide-eyed, leaned forward, and propped his short forearms on the desk. "You don't mess around with pleasantries, do you?"

"I'm sorry. Let me start again. I've noticed this isn't a retail bank. What do you folks specialize in?"

"We cater to Kentucky and southern Indiana clients in the distilling, horse racing, and farming industries. We also do transactions for venture capitalists investing in those businesses."

"Ever hear of a fund by the name of Lolly Gelt?"

"I have."

"What do you know about them?"

"Sir, that would be indiscreet of me to share what I know."

Brock leaned back in his chair and replied, "Yes, I guess it would be. How did your bank get involved in the chess tournament?"

"Frankly, I don't know. We've been handling the funding for years. Regarding your original point about Frank Romine, I was the one who gave him his winnings at the tournament. Something odd happened."

"What was that?"

"When I handed him the certified check, he asked If I'd do him a favor. I told him, within reason, I would. He took the check, put it in an envelope that he pulled out of his blazer, and asked me if I'd stick a stamp on the envelope and drop it in the mailbox. I said I would—and did that evening."

"Who was it addressed to?"

"I don't think it would be proper for me to tell you. I can say Mr. Romine seemed distracted. He kept glancing at the crowd as though he was fearful of someone. I surmised that for safety reasons, he didn't want to have the check on him when he left the hotel."

"Just one more question and I'll be out of your hair: are you acquainted with the Barclay family? They've owned a farm in Charlestown, Indiana, for over two hundred years."

"Yes, I believe I once met Hogan Barclay. I think he died, gosh, maybe a dozen years ago."

Brock got up from his chair and said, "Thanks for seeing me."

"My pleasure. If I may ask, what business are you in?" His unhealthy pallor disappeared when he turned salesperson.

"Garments. What is the minimum account value you prefer handling for your customers?"

"We generally start at a million."

"If I open an account for that much or more, would you reveal the address on that envelope?"

"I'll call your bluff. You bring in that million, and I'll tell you."

———

That Monday was windy and cloudy, more like a spring than fall day. Brock's car got blown around as he drove into Indiana, over to the Barclay farm in Charlestown. He got through the gate and parked as close to the front door of the house as he could. This visit, he had to ring the doorbell to attract attention. It took Nigel a long time to answer the call. "It's you again. What is it you want now?"

"We're getting close to finding your sister. We've also learned that you're planning to build a bourbon distillery on this farm. I want to get some information from you."

"Based on the way you threatened me the last time you were here, I'm more inclined to call the police than anything else."

Brock knew he'd get busted one of these times. He hoped it wasn't this time. "Go ahead. They can listen to what this is about. It may not help your cause though."

"You might as well come in. I want to get to the bottom of your story, so you'll go away." He turned and walked back into the house. Brock followed and swung the door closed.

The floors and walls in old brick homes were usually creaky and crooked. Brock noticed that was not the case at the Barclay house. It had been impeccably repaired and kept up over the years. The stairs were in the main hall, and the parlor was to the right. It had a fireplace, yellow walls, and bird pictures hanging everywhere. The seating had been covered in a gray-and-red patterned cloth, in contrast to the deep, dark wooden floors. Nigel sat on the couch. Brock took the chair closest to the entrance to the room. Nigel said, "Fire away."

"The last time I was here, I told you I had a subpoena for your sister related to the killing of Roy Aldiss, which happened in Richmond, Kentucky, eleven years ago. I will not hold on to that pretense anymore. You know about his death. I also know Celine Oliver impersonated your sister after she went missing. I'm trying to find out what happened to your father and sister. Recently, a friend of mine, Frank Romine, has disappeared. I'm also looking for him."

"Well, I've got nothing to hide when it comes to my father, or my sister."

"Before, you told me your sister had moved to South Africa. If you'll admit that was a lie, we can get somewhere with this conversation," said Brock.

Nigel threw his arms out to the side. "Oh, your lie to me is all right, but mine to you is out of bounds."

Brock pushed back: "Okay, we're even now. Let's start with Jaeger. Why did she disappear?"

"It happened after my father died. She took off. I was afraid that with her disappearance, people might think I got rid of her, if you know what I mean. That's why I hired Celine to impersonate Jaeger and care for my mother until she died."

"Was Jaeger adopted by chance?"

"No. My father had DNA tests done on me and her to prove we were his children."

"What kind of person is your sister?"

"Scary. Cold-blooded. She was as anxious as me to get the distillery deal."

"The way you describe your sister is how some folks have characterized you. How did you get Jaeger to trap Willard Lentz?"

"It was her idea! She told me Dad, in cahoots with Clive Natoli's father, used to film politicians in the Natoli house to blackmail them. She was the one who lured in Willard Lentz. I don't think anything ever came of it."

"So, Jaeger inherited half the farm, right?"

"That's the funny thing. When the lawyers read the will, she wasn't mentioned. My mother left it all to me. When she was alive, I complained to her how disappointed I was that she favored Jaeger. Maybe she was making it up to me."

"Or maybe she saw Jaeger as who you say she is—a sociopath. What happened to your father? How did he die?"

"In his sleep of natural causes, I suppose."

"That sounds a little fishy. Could there be any other explanation?"

Nigel stood, went over to the fireplace, and put his hands in his pockets. "Yeah, Jaeger killed him. She probably figured if my mother died first, he'd cut her out of his will."

"Why would he do that?"

"When it came to my sister, my parents were always taking sides, using her as a pawn. My father came to resent her, and she turned mean as a snake. The more he turned against Jaeger, the more my mother favored her over me."

"What will Jaeger do when we find her, and she comes out in the open?"

Nigel kicked the fireplace hearth and a look of pain crossed his face before he added, "Knowing her, she'll contest the will and want half of the farm."

Brock added, "And half of everything else, including the Audubon book. I presume you plan to sell it for seed money in the distillery deal."

"And if she prevails, the worst that could happen would be she gets half of my piece."

Brock rose, preparing to leave. "From what I hear, that would be half of a hundred million. You could get along okay on that."

CHAPTER 18

Brock made it to Romine's apartment by early afternoon. He told Leslie about the envelope. "So, that's what he was doing. I noticed something was going on between him and the guy handing him his check. Who do you suppose he mailed it to?"

"You, me, or Celine. Do you know where his mailbox key is?"

Leslie yanked open the drawer in Frank's computer desk. "Here it is."

"Let me have it. I'll check the box." There was nothing there. He gave the key to Leslie, who put it back in the drawer. "When are you returning home?"

"I'll drive out of here in the morning. Would you be kind enough to let me know what you learn about Frank after I'm gone?"

"Certainly. I'll keep checking his mailbox to see if the money comes here. He may have included a note."

Brock went next door and worked the same routine on Celine. No check there either. He left for Hazard in time to make it home for supper and called Maude on the way to tell her about his day.

Over their evening meal on the patio, Brock said, "I'm giving up on this stupid thing. Nobody seems to be unhappy. Why am I trying to manufacture mischief where there doesn't appear to be any?"

"Because that's what you like to do. Don't sell yourself short. Jaeger Barclay is a wild card. She may pop up somewhere and be able to tie this mess together. What about those bugs we found at Celine's? Don't you want to find out who put them there and why?"

"I'm only worried about Frank Romine right now. I've got to find him first."

———

Tuesday morning, on the floor of the Kentucky legislature, an hour was dedicated to discussing whether there was enough interest in repealing the barrel tax to put it to a vote. There wasn't. Clive Natoli, with a smile on his face, stepped outside to call Nigel Barclay. "Hey, they're not going to do it. Why don't you call Lentz and see if he's ready to do the deal?" The traffic noise amped up the excitement in his voice.

"Fantastic! I will. Thanks." Nigel dialed Willard Lentz and said, "The barrel tax is staying. Can we close the deal now?"

"Ah, good news. Yes, we can. First thing we must do is capitalize the company. You'll get 10 percent of the ownership in exchange for deeding over the farm, excluding your house, and putting up ten million dollars. Lolly Gelt will put in ten million initially along with a $260,000,000 letter of credit. Once the permits clear, we can start construction. After that, your shares can be put in an IPO, which could happen by next spring. Congratulations!"

"When will you have the paperwork ready for me to sign?"

"In a week or so. I'll call you. Get your cash ready."

Nigel called Perry Oliver. "I know you thought this day would never come. The distillery is moving ahead. It'll be official in a week or so."

"When will I get my payoff?"

"Next spring when I roll my share into an IPO. You and Clive are each in for 5 percent of what I get."

"When I get my money, I'm selling this place and taking Rhonda out of here."

"Good for you. I thought you'd want to hear the news."

"Yeah." He hung up.

Midday Tuesday, Brock got the mail from the box by the road in front of his log cabin. The envelope he was hoping for had the eighty-thousand-dollar check and a note wrapped around it.

Brock,

Get a deposit ticket from my apartment and deposit the endorsed check in my account. I'm disappearing because I saw a man here who I'm sure is planning to kill me. He's from a country I stole secrets from. I'll meet you on October 1st at noon at the place we had lunch together in Danville. Well, unless he's successful. If I don't show up, go to the police with this note. Tell Leslie, Celine, and Calvin to keep quiet.

Frank

He gave the note to Maude. "I guess there's some hope in this," she offered after reading it.

"I know from what the guy at Esse Bank told me that it's authentic, not a red herring."

"But you're forgetting one thing: he was hauled away from his apartment at five o'clock on Saturday by a car that had stolen plates. How do you explain that?"

"I can't. It's probable that he has been taken."

Maude wove her hands behind her head. "Or he got home, saw the person waiting for him, ran through the building out the back door into the woods. I guess we'll have to wait a couple of weeks to find out if he's alive or not."

Brock rang Celine and told her about receiving the check with the note. "Cal and I are going out on his boat this afternoon. Do you want me to tell him what's going on?" she asked.

"That would be good."

Brock reached Leslie in her car as she was driving back home to Virginia. He decided to wait a bit before telling her about the envelope from Frank. He first wanted to get information from her. "Do you remember anyone at the tournament Frank saw in the crowd whom he may have been fearful of?"

"There was one guy, yes."

"Call up the tournament officials and see if they can send you any shots of the crowd. It would be great if you can pick him out."

"I can do that."

Celine got to Calvin's place at three o'clock. The weather was like a yellow rose that had been in the vase for several days and, from far away, seemed alive and well. Up close, there was evidence it was desiccated, nearing collapse. That's why Calvin wanted to get out on the water again before the bloom was off the rose.

They eschewed swim trunks, figuring swimming would not be in the plan. The lake midweek, late in the season, was calm and empty. The throttle could be pulled wide open to skitter over the mostly smooth water at speeds that would otherwise mess up the spine. They did just that, finally slowing near the dam. Cal keyed off the engine and put his legs up on the front seat to relax. CeCe was in the back seat doing the same thing. She told Cal what Brock had said when he called her.

"I certainly hope he hasn't been killed. That would be horrible." Cal was at eye level with the flat top of the motor housing. He noticed a grease smudge on the chrome latch. Something was wrong. No one was allowed to touch the boat, but clearly, someone with greasy hands had. Cal hoisted himself up and stepped around behind the engine to raise the top panel. He looked down at the well, below the motor. A large bundle of explosives was strapped where the gas line came in. He screamed, "CeCe, there's a bomb in here!"

"What?" She became temporarily disoriented. When she got up to see for herself, she barked, "Let's jump and swim for shore."

They got about eighty feet from the boat when it exploded. The sound reverberated off the dam wall as wood planks and shards blew out like fireworks on the Fourth of July. Things that didn't float, like the engine, headed straight for the bottom of the lake, 250 feet down. They both dove under the surface to avoid getting hit on the head by debris falling back to earth. Calvin gasped when he popped back up out of the water. "What the hell?"

A boat not far away heard the explosion and headed straight for the wreckage. The driver saw the two people in the water waving. He curved around them, hit reverse, and keyed off the inboard—outdrive. "What happened?" the man yelled. His wife or girlfriend leaned over the side toward them, pointing to the ladder on the back deck.

Cal said quietly to CeCe, "Let me handle this." They climbed aboard and accepted towels to dry off with.

"That was a hell of an explosion," the man said emphatically as he stood and pushed a captain's hat back on his head. He had a muscular build and deep tan.

Cal quickly perfected his story before he was asked any questions. "I smelled gas and opened the motor housing. The gas was already on fire. I didn't think I had enough time to use the fire extinguisher, so we dove into the water. The gas tank must have exploded."

The woman said, "Thank goodness you're all right." Her eyes were dull as though she was either dumb or drunk.

"Yes, by the grace of God," Calvin replied.

"Is there anything in the wreckage you want to salvage?" the man asked.

"No. If you would be kind enough to take us to my dock, I'd appreciate it. It's less than a mile up the cove." He pointed toward his home with a chop of his arm.

"Certainly. We'd be happy to."

They puttered along, not talking much. Cal handed both towels back to the woman when they stepped onto the dock, and he thanked them effusively for their help. He glared at CeCe and said, "Let's head up the hill. I want to call Brock and tell him what's happened. Somebody's trying to kill us."

Calvin and CeCe showered in a hurry and changed clothes. He called a Conservation Officer to report the accident, and then his insurance agent. When he got Brock on the line, Calvin said, "CeCe and I almost got killed. We were out in the boat. Someone put dynamite under the motor. I found it just before it went off."

"I suggest you don't tell anybody about the bomb."

"I haven't. The people who picked us up saw we didn't have swimsuits on. I told them a gas fire had started, and I didn't have time to extinguish it. We jumped overboard."

"You're in a spot now. When you file a report with the police, they're going to want to know the details of what happened. You better tell them the truth, I guess."

"I already called them. They'll be here in a few minutes. What should I say when they ask me who might have put the explosives there?"

"The truth. You have no idea. Let them know that if anyone other than the police ask what happened, you'll tell them the gas leak story to keep people from sticking their noses into a police investigation. They'll also want to talk to Celine. Tell her to play dumb and not mention any names."

"Okay. Who do you think did this?" Cal asked.

"Your guess is as good as mine. It's hard to know if both of you were targeted, or just Celine. Whoever bugged her apartment is afraid she knows something damaging to somebody somewhere. I'll find out what it is and put a stop to it."

Brock drove to the winery to break the news to Maude. She knew her husband was back in it with a vengeance. "Where are you going?" she asked as he walked away toward the warehouse door.

"To see Perry Oliver."

It was a few minutes after six o'clock when Brock rushed the winery truck up to the front of the Oliver house. If the door was locked, he was going to kick it in. He had a pistol and a shotgun on him when he turned the knob. The door swung open. He saw the Olivers sitting at the kitchen table. Perry backed away but didn't try to make a move. "You better be prepared to use that gun, Mister."

"I am but hear me out. Someone just tried to kill Celine a couple of hours ago. I don't think either of you would be in favor of that. I'm worried for her safety. I need to find out who wants her dead and why."

"Who the hell are you?" Perry asked.

"Brock Skinner. I met your daughter through friends of mine, and I learned some things about her that don't make any sense. I'm sure you have all the answers, and it's time you explain to me what's going on."

Perry looked confident when he said, "I'll take that gun away from you before you get a shot off. Then I'll beat you to death. After that, I'll take you into the woods and bury you where no one will ever find you. If you're smart, you'll march right out of here and never come back."

"Go ahead and try it. I'll throw the gun down and give you a worse beating than I did the last time. Either way, I'm not going to back off until I get answers from you or somebody else."

Perry looked at him askance and said, "There's just enough doubt in my mind to believe you. Let's take this conversation outside." He turned to Rhonda and said, "I'll be back in a few minutes."

Brock backed up to let Perry go out the front door. When they reached the yard, Brock ordered, "Stand over there." The sun was at nine o'clock, Perry at ten o'clock, and the front door to the house at three o'clock. That way, Brock could cut him off if he tried to run back inside, and If Rhonda pulled anything, it could be seen. "Depending on what you have to say, it may be that you and I are on the same team in this matter. I'm hoping that's the case."

"You mentioned someone tried to kill Celine. Why don't you talk about that first."

CHAPTER 19

"She was out in a boat on Herrington Lake with a friend of hers, and the boat blew up. He saw the bomb before it went off. They dove in the water."

Perry added, "And that would be Calvin Willett. He's Celine's other client in her escort business."

"Right."

"Why were you digging around in her affairs before someone tried to kill her?"

"I was afraid she was being blackmailed over something."

Perry turned to look at the sun, which was getting ready to drop below the tree line. He put his hand on his forehead to shield his eyes. "Go ahead, tell me what you know. If there is anything I can add, I will."

"I'll start at the beginning. Rhonda Cunningham and Clive Natoli were high school homecoming king and queen. You were friends with Clive. Rhonda got pregnant with Celine. It was a traumatic experience. You married her but you're not Celine's father. You know who is, and you made him pay to keep quiet."

Perry crossed his arms. "That's a close enough rendition. What else?"

"Who is Celine's father?"

"I can't tell you that. I was paid money to never reveal it."

"Your buddy, Clive, got in the lobbying business because his father was a politician. He introduced Clive to the Barclay family in Indiana. They want to build a distillery on their farm. Nigel Barclay told Clive that he'd pay a handsome fee if an investor was found. That depended on whether the barrel tax in Kentucky was repealed or not.

"Nigel's father died eleven years ago and his sister, Jaeger, vanished. Nigel was fearful he'd be blamed for the death of his father and disappearance of his sister. He asked Clive to find someone to take her place so that no one would suspect anything. Clive thought Celine would be a good candidate. You told Celine that she could squeeze a lot of money out of Barclay, and you worked a deal for yourself."

"There's not much I can add to that either."

"Oh, but there is. What happened to Celine's boyfriend, Roy Aldiss?"

"He hung himself."

"I don't believe it."

"I can tell you that Clive and I had nothing to do with his death. If there was foul play, it was someone else."

Brock said, "You know what I think? He was the first person killed by whoever is behind this business."

"What business?"

"The death of Roy Aldiss, the death of Nigel's dad, Hogan Barclay, the death or disappearance of Jaeger Barclay, attempted killing of Celine and Calvin Willett, and the disappearance of Frank Romine."

"Who's Frank Romine?"

"Celine's neighbor. He was a friend of hers and just turned up missing."

"You surely don't believe I'm involved in any of this, because I'm not."

Brock walked closer to the house. "It's either you, Clive Natoli, Nigel Barclay, or some combination thereof."

"Nope. You've got it wrong. The three of us are trying to get rich on the distillery deal."

"What do you know about Nigel's father and Clive's father blackmailing Kentucky politicians by filming them in compromising situations at Natoli's house?"

"Clive was upset about it when he found out. Hogan Barclay was a creep, a lowlife. He wasn't interested in building a distillery on his farm; he just wanted to see naked women seducing politicians. I was told he used an intermediary to blackmail them for cash."

"Who was that?"

"I don't know. Maybe Nigel does."

"How did Clive find out about it?"

"I'm not sure," Perry replied, unconvincingly.

"I think you know but aren't telling. I've got to find out if Jaeger Barclay is dead or alive. You have any information that could help me?"

"No. I've had enough of this. You need to move along."

Brock made eye contact with Perry and said, "Just know this: I'm going to find out who Celine's father is, even if I have to test the DNA of everybody in the county."

"Good luck on that. You thought we might be on the same team. As far as I'm concerned, we are unless you screw up the distillery deal. If you do that, I'll be coming for you."

"I'll be ready." Brock looked over in the direction of Perry's business. "What do you make in there?"

"None of your business."

"You ever make any bugging devices? You might as well tell me if you do. I'll find out soon enough."

"No. Small metal parts. No electronics, why?"

"Whoever's behind this has been bugging Celine's apartment. I hope it isn't you." Brock got in the truck and drove out.

Perry Oliver went back into the house. Rhonda was sitting there, despondent. He would be counting the days until he got his money, and they could get out of there.

Brock reported to Maude when he arrived home, "Either one of them is lying, or we're missing something." Truman came over and looked up at him. "What, buddy? You have something to say?"

––––––––––

Wednesday started good weatherwise, and only got better as the morning wore on. Brock was at the winery when Leslie Blazek called. "Did you get any pictures of the crowd?" he asked her.

"I did. But the person I was searching for wasn't in any of them."

"That's too bad. I have some news for you. I received *the* letter from Frank yesterday. He confirmed he dropped out of sight because of someone he saw at the chess tournament. That squares with what we thought. I'll meet up with him in a couple of weeks to see what he's planning to do."

"That's encouraging."

"Hey, we never talked much about you winning the chess tournament. Pretty impressive."

"Not really. Frank knew how to defend against the gambit I played on him. He let me win."

"You know what they say: a win is a win, no matter how you get it."

She exhaled. "Brock, I know I haven't known you long, but judging by your wife, I feel I can talk openly to you about things. Would that make you uncomfortable?"

"Depends on what's on your mind. Why don't you try me?"

"I might as well be blunt: I think Kentucky is beautiful, and I'd like to move there. What do you say about that?"

Brock spun around in the warehouse and gazed up into the air. "When we first talked, you told me Frank didn't like you as much as you like him. I really don't know what I'm talking about, but it would seem you would have to stop seeing Frank. That's if he ever comes back. How good would moving here be under those circumstances?"

"Ouch, that hurt. I would like to find a man and get married. I must break it off with him. I know that."

"What if he tells you he's madly in love with you and begs you to marry him?"

"I guess I'll have to tell him no." Leslie tried to stand her ground.

"Really? You could do that?"

"I doubt it, but it sounded like the right thing to say."

"Leslie, since we're sharing, I'll tell you what's in my head. I hope you won't think less of me."

"Shoot."

"My wife, Maude, is the love of my life. I don't know why she loves me, but she does. When I see other wonderful women, I root for them to be happy. My business partner, Marcel, just married a girl who is as quirky as they come, but I love her to death. I think they're happy as a couple. They make Maude and me smile when we're with them. I feel the same way about you. You're drop-dead gorgeous, smart, and fun to be around. I don't know what's wrong with Frank. If you came to Kentucky, you'd have to run in circles where a good man could be found. I'd be devastated if you settled for someone second-rate."

"Where is it that good men can be found?"

"Middle to higher-level social circles in Lexington and Louisville. You'll need a friend to break into that group."

"And do you have those connections?" she asked.

"Yes, because I'm wealthy. Money has its advantages. If you tell anyone we've had this discussion, I'll disavow any knowledge of it. You know, there are a lot of things that need to be right in a relationship. Having opposing worldviews can be a problem. The Bible calls it being unequally yoked."

"I'm with you on that. Frank said something strange to me the other day. He said being smart is a curse. It makes a person believe they know better than God."

"Satan's like that. From him and those he's ensnared, even light cannot escape."

Leslie kept talking on. "I spent some time with Celine. Not being close to her father has hurt her relationships with men."

"For starters, she doesn't know who her father is. I'm hell-bent on figuring that out."

"She's extremely good looking," Leslie threw out.

"You give her a run for her money."

"A married man shouldn't talk to a single woman like that. She might get the wrong idea."

"Okay. I'll take that back. Yes, other than my wife, she's the best-looking woman I've ever seen."

"You see what's wrong with me, Brock? I say the wrong thing sometimes."

"No, you don't. I've got to get off here. My wife will be wondering what I'm doing. I'll call you if we hear anything about Frank." He ended the call, looked at the phone, and smiled.

Marcel and Valerie showed up for supper at the Skinner log cabin at six o'clock. Maude had just gotten in from the winery. Brock poured four glasses of white wine and led the way out to the patio. He went back inside to get light jackets for everyone since the warmth of the day was dissipating fast. Brock said, "I got an interesting call from Leslie Blazek today. She said she'd like to move to Kentucky."

Valerie had a comment on that: "Uh-oh. She's one of *those* women."

"What kind is that?" Marcel asked.

"Too smart. No common sense. Goes after the wrong man."

Brock reflected comically to himself how one of the world's flakiest women, albeit lovable, was talking common sense. He stared at Maude and waited for her to "shoot the gap" like a thoroughbred in a race. She didn't disappoint him. "Valerie, I dare say, it's only by God's grace that a woman finds a good man. They are complicated creatures, and there's usually something about them that takes getting used to."

Marcel piped up, "See, Valerie, why I'm such a good man? My sister, even though she's a little younger, made me into the person I am."

Brock put his hand up. "Will you all excuse me, I think I'm going to be sick." Everyone laughed, and the conversation picked up even more steam. After twenty minutes of snappy palaver, they moved inside to make an Italian salad, which would go well with the lasagna baking in the oven.

Brock commented, "You know, Celine said something interesting the other day. She said Mrs. Barclay told her Nigel would get the surprise of his life after she was dead."

Maude remarked, "The only thing that would be considered a major surprise to Nigel Barclay would be a reversal of his financial fortune."

"Okay, let's run with that."

Marcel offered, "The only clod in the financial churn would be if his distillery deal got derailed."

Valerie suggested, "It could be something like an environmental spill or a defect in the title of the farm. You said it had been in the family for over two hundred years. Maybe the title isn't clear."

"I doubt Nigel would have missed that," Brock supposed. "Nigel told me he was surprised his mother cut Jaeger out of the will. He even suggested if she reappeared, she might want to contest it."

"That kind of tells us that Nigel didn't kill her. He wouldn't have offered such a scenario if it wasn't a real possibility," Maude said.

"Nigel also painted Jaeger as rotten. There must be a way to find out if she's still alive," Brock pleaded.

Marcel suggested, "Let me see if there's any trace of her over the last eleven years. Maybe she slipped up somewhere, and we can find her."

The salad and lasagna were spectacular. The four of them played bridge for three hours afterward. The Sutherlands decided to stay in Hazard for the night since it had gotten late.

Marcel said, "What about Calvin Willett's situation? The person who rigged up a bomb in his boat would have to be mechanically inclined, probably a man."

"I think we should ask him for a list of people who come to his dock parties and check their backgrounds. Somebody may have been paid a handsome sum to do the dirty deed."

Maude didn't care much for the idea. "I'm not sure about that."

"We don't have much to go on," Valerie said. "You might as well ask for pictures of the dock party crowd. Maybe a photo will lead somewhere."

"Is Calvin Willett all there?" Marcel asked.

"I'm afraid he is. He's just ahead of the rest of us. He sees where this world is going, and it's scary. We don't happen to feel it because we have money. We're insulated from the bad things out there."

"I'm not sure I like being characterized like that," Marcel grumbled.

Everyone turned in for the night. Valerie was noodling on why Jaeger would have disappeared. Marcel got hung up on what Nigel's surprise might be. Brock tried to figure out who Celine's father was. Maude wanted to know which of them was most likely to be lying, and how they could be caught.

Chapter 20

After a hearty breakfast of bacon and eggs the next morning, the Sutherlands headed for home. Brock hovered by the coffeepot and asked Maude, "Where are those bugs you found in Celine's apartment?"

"In the drawer right in front of you."

The listening devices were small discs with two short lead wires. "I take it they were hardwired?"

"Yes. We found them in the smoke detectors."

"These are microphones that broadcast signals. There must be a receiver nearby."

Brock called a security shop in Lexington and read off the make and model of the bugs to the technical guy, who reported, "You can only get that brand from Sigea Spy here in town."

"How far do you think the signal reaches?"

"I don't know. Try calling them."

The guru at Sigea Spy was even less communicative than the first guy. "How far away can the signal be picked up?" Brock asked.

"A thousand meters," the guy replied.

"What's the setup on the other end?"

"A nearby computer connected to a remote one."

"Thanks." He explained to Maude, "There was a computer in the area receiving signals, sending them to another location."

"If it's not in one of the apartments, whoever planted the bugs probably removed it."

"I guess I better check to see if anyone saw anything."

An hour and a half later, Brock turned onto Bonds Mill Road and figured out what was within a thousand meters of Celine's place. The Kentucky-style curio and craft shop across the road, by the looks of it, sold anything it could seasonally. The building was gray, reclaimed barn siding, and it had a galvanized roof to keep the water out. The woman proprietor employed two strongback country boys. "See anything you like?" she said in a chipper voice. The sunlight made everything a radiant orange— hay bales, calico corn, pumpkins, and gourds.

"How much for the whole place, building and all?"

"Oh, I'd take fifty thousand and hand you the keys." She reminded Brock of the Cheshire cat.

"That's too cheap. The land's worth twice that amount. I wouldn't feel right taking advantage of you."

"Is that a long-winded way of telling me you don't want to buy it?" Her repartee called his bluff.

"Yes. What I really need to know is whether any utility technicians have been around recently to work on the power."

She took a closer look at Brock, to figure out if he was on the up and up. "There was a guy who came by a couple of days ago."

"What exactly did he do?"

"He went inside, disconnected some sort of electrical equipment, and took off. I thought something was fishy, so I read his license plate. It was from Kentucky." She wrote the numbers and letters on a piece of paper and handed it to him.

"Thanks."

"What was he doing?" she probed.

"Spying on someone who lives in that apartment complex over there." Brock pointed across the road.

"Isn't that against the law?"

"Yes. That's why I'm here."

"You look like you could use a few gourds for the house. Give me fifty smackeroos and pick out what you want." She smiled, and he handed her a hundred-dollar bill and left without any gourds.

Brock called his brother-in-law and asked him to see who the plate was registered to. Thad Cameron's address on the title put his location northwest of downtown Midway. The trip took twenty minutes.

The property had a rusted, mangled wire fence that ran the length of the lot frontage. The combo house and garage sat perched on a narrow flat spot below the road. Sheets of fake brick-veneer siding on the walls had begun to curl at the edges. Three abandoned cars were lined up to the left, perpendicular to the house. A van with the correct plates was parked on the right side of the driveway, facing the garage.

Brock left the Lamborghini off to the side of the main road and walked down the hill. A guy was in the garage working on what looked like an electric motor. "Are you Thad Cameron?"

"I am." He was skinny, long boned, without an ounce of fat. One of his front teeth, presumably dead, had turned chalky gray-brown.

"A friend of a friend told me you could put bugs in a house for me."

"Your house?" Thad glanced up quickly.

"No, the house of the rotten bastard who's servicing my wife when I'm not around." Brock thought the man had the demeanor of a mechanical or electrical genius.

"That's not legal."

"I guess that means your fee will be higher."

"I can't help you, buddy." Thad kept working with his hands.

"That's surprising. You hardwired mics to the smoke alarms in the apartment of the girl I'm seeing on the side."

"I don't know what you're talking about."

"And you strapped a bomb onto the bottom of a boat motor of a guy I know."

"What are you, the police or something? I didn't do any of those things." Thad dropped the wrench he was holding and came out of the garage. He sized Skinner up and decided not to tangle with him.

"Okay. I must have the wrong man." Brock winked sarcastically and started back up the hill to his car. "You enjoy your last day of freedom," he said over his shoulder.

"Hold on a second. You came here for some information. What do you want to know?"

"Who hired you for those jobs?"

"I'm not saying I did them. I'm certainly not going to take the rap. Somebody, who didn't give a name, came by to talk."

"What did the person look like?"

"I can't help you there. I don't remember."

"There's only one way you can keep from getting busted: find out who hired you and call me with their name. I'll even pay for it. You get me what I need, I'll keep your name out of it. Here's my number." He handed him a calling card with nothing on it but an untraceable cell phone number. Thad returned to his workbench and ignored Brock as he scaled the hill and drove off.

The first call Brock made on the way home was to Calvin Willett. "I just found the guy who got paid to strap a bomb in your boat.

Whoever's been listening in on Celine's conversations is running scared. He's trying to exterminate you, Celine, and Frank. I'm going to call Celine and insist she move in with you until this thing is over. I'm also going to hire a security guard to watch your place."

"You planning to tell the police who this person is?" Cal asked.

"Been weighing that. I'll tell them soon enough." Brock knew he was taking chances with people's lives.

"What's this all about?"

"Money, I think. I'm working on it as hard as I know how. In the meantime, I want you and Celine to stay safe."

"I second that. This person will come after you too. Don't let your guard down."

"Yeah. Good advice."

Car traffic on the interstate was moving along at twenty miles over the speed limit. Brock called Marcel and filled him in on the latest news. He went on to say, "I'm having second thoughts about what happened to Frank. I'm beginning to believe he was taken when he walked out of the hotel in Louisville. I don't think Frank would have driven into a trap at his apartment."

"What went down instead?"

"It had to be a two-man play. The bad guy came up behind Frank with chloroform while Thad Cameron distracted him. They put him in the trunk of the car with the rental plates. Cameron drove that car to Frank's apartment ahead of the bad guy who drove Frank's car and parked it in his garage. He got in with Cameron and lay down in the back seat. The three of them were in the car with the rental plates when they left the apartment—Cameron driving, Frank knocked out in the trunk."

"If it happened like that, they probably killed him."

"If they did, he's most likely at the bottom of Herrington Lake, near where Calvin's boat blew up. There's only one way Frank could have escaped alive: he woke up in the trunk, pulled the emergency release, and jumped out."

"Not totally implausible," Marcel commented. "I've been digging for anything on Jaeger Barclay. I found her Indiana license issued fourteen years ago. She never renewed it. The address on it is Barclay Farm. I can see why they drafted Celine to replace her. They look a lot alike. The different haircut throws you off."

"What was her birthdate on the license?"

"August twenty-ninth. I hacked into the database of the hospital where she was born to make sure the date is correct."

"That makes her five weeks older than Celine. Anything else?"

"Yes. On June thirteenth eleven years ago, I saw an item on Mrs. Barclay's credit card statement where someone bought gas in Richmond."

"Uh-oh. That would have been Jaeger Barclay. She must have borrowed her mother's card. What was she doing over there the day Roy Aldiss died?"

Marcel replied, "The bigger question is whether she met Celine or not?"

"Or had something to do with Roy's death," Brock continued.

"Also, there's a charge for a flight from Cincinnati to Grand Cayman. She was originally scheduled to fly out on May twenty-sixth, but it was changed to June fifteenth."

Brock reflected, "So, that's where she disappeared to. Did she come back?"

"If she did, she's not going by the name Jaeger Barclay. There's not a trace of her since that flight."

"When was that ticket purchased?"

"May twentieth," Marcel reported.

"That means Jaeger disappeared after the ticket was purchased but stayed around to go to Berea or Richmond."

"How would she have known to go where Celine, Perry, and Clive were on the thirteenth of June?"

"There's one possibility: Mrs. Barclay got in touch with Jaeger right before she was to fly out and alerted her to Nigel's plan to find a replacement. It's starting to look like Jaeger and her mother were working together on some sort of scheme that is yet to play out."

"What do you mean?"

"Remember Celine saying Mrs. Barclay told her Nigel would get the surprise of his life after she was dead? That surprise is yet to come. Mrs. Barclay figured Nigel might kill his sister, so she recommended to Jaeger that she get lost, at least temporarily."

"And reappear at the opportune time?" Marcel asked.

"Yes. When did Hogan Barclay die?"

"Derby Day, May fifth. He was buried on the ninth."

Brock reviewed the timeline in his head. "All right. Between the ninth and twenty-sixth of May, Jaeger and her mother hatched a plan for her disappearance, and Jaeger found out about Celine being selected as her stand-in. She went to Richmond or Berea for some reason right before she flew off to Grand Cayman."

Brock ended the call with Marcel and started one up with Celine. He told her about Thad Cameron. She agreed to move in with Calvin Willett for a while. He also revealed, "Jaeger flew to Grand Cayman on June fifteenth eleven years ago. There's no record of her back in the country since then. I'm betting she's still alive. I'm going to find her so we can end this madness."

Celine reported, "Clive called me today and said the distillery on the Barclay property is going ahead. It'll be announced this weekend. He seemed very happy."

"I'm guessing."

"I hope Frank's alive. I feel I've brought trouble to both him and Calvin, and possibly you."

———————————

Calvin sent a van and two men over to Celine's apartment on Saturday morning, the twenty-fourth of September, to move into his house what she would need to live comfortably. The spare bedroom had its own walk-in closet and elegant bathroom right outside the door. Celine didn't want anyone to know it, but she'd give up her apartment in a heartbeat to embrace the lifestyle at his place.

Calvin waited for her to settle in before he sprang an idea on her. "CeCe, would you be in favor of a road trip to Holland, Michigan?"

"I hear it's delightful there in the fall. What did you have in mind?" she asked.

"I want to search for a wood boat to replace the one we lost."

"I can help you with that." She took her laptop from the bedroom and opened the Internet browser. "I know you don't care for technology. You'll set aside that bias when I show you lots of pictures of boats that are for sale."

He sat beside her and perused the two dozen runabouts that were advertised. "I can't believe how cheap some of them are."

"They're considered vintage relics that require too much maintenance, and they aren't as comfortable or as fast as new boats. They don't have all the latest features either, like today's cars compared to that hotrod you have out in the driveway."

"Are you trying to dissuade me from getting another wood boat?"

She had him going now. "Not necessarily. I'll make a deal with you. Let's go to Michigan and see what we find, and then test drive a new Correct Craft Nautique."

"Deal."

"I can't wait to see your face when you shove down the throttle of a boat that's quieter and has twice the power of a Century Resorter."

Cal said, "I hope this isn't a trend. Next, you'll be wanting me to get a cell phone and cable TV."

"You never know." She rubbed his back, shut down her laptop, and became saturnine. "I hope Brock can find out who's behind this mess."

"I'm sure he will. Until then, we've got security out there to keep us safe. Shall we fix dinner?"

"Good idea." CeCe opened the refrigerator. "Cal, I hate to bring this up, but I'm going to have to go to the grocery store to stock up on better food for us."

Cal stood and asked, "Is this what it's like being married?"

"To me, it would be."

"CeCe, you're one of a kind. I say, do whatever makes you happy. I'll go along with it."

They spent a relaxed evening together on the back porch as they often did, overlooking the dock. The sounds of grasshoppers and crickets grew louder as the daylight stalled out. The whine of two fishing boats moving to new spots interrupted their conversation. Cal spoke about artificial intelligence, keeping his comments positive. She talked of fashion, colors, literature, and the personalities of men. Cal said warmly, "CeCe, you are an absolute delight. I'm so happy we met."

"You'll be even happier when you drop your fanny into the cushy seat of a new Correct Craft."

He said oafishly, "If you say so. Let's clean up the kitchen and hit the hay."

"On that suggestion, I have no rebuttal." She grabbed the empty plates and went into the house.

They were both asleep five minutes after their heads hit the pillow.

178

Chapter 21

Nigel Barclay knew everyone thought he was callous and uncaring. Compared to his father Hogan, who had been a world-class sleaze, Nigel thought of himself as a bouquet of sweet-smelling flowers. He wasn't stupid or unskilled. Quite the contrary. His ideas were big, bold, and clever. He'd been working on the distillery design for ten years, and the *Courier Journal* broke the plan with a feature article on Sunday, which included a handsome rendering Nigel sent the publication of his dream.

Foremost in his mind was getting rich off the idea. Millions in a bank in this life came right from Satan's playbook. If his bankrupt soul had enough money, he wouldn't need God. Nigel thirsted for a life where he didn't need anything or anybody. He developed that mental condition by growing up with a twisted sister. She crossed the wires in his head, burning out many of the circuits of compassion most nice people had.

Nigel was three years old when Jaeger came into the house. He had no memory of her until he turned five and she two. He tried to love her, but she gave him no quarter. The family dynamic put him on an island, the one he'd been on his whole life. Mrs. Barclay, knowing the rotten nature of her husband, conscripted Jaeger to combat Hogan and her son, whom she assumed would also end up bad. The two women were against Nigel, and teaming up with his dad wasn't a possibility. He had to go it alone.

The vision behind the distillery wasn't particularly original. Variations on the theme had been built by several developers over the last fifteen years. Barclay Farm Distillery intended to differentiate itself by location and size. Three hundred million would fund a Taj Mahal bourbon experience and being on the Indiana beltline around Louisville put it in a position to dragnet vacationers coming south.

An accelerated construction schedule pointed toward getting juice off the new still in fifteen months. The whiskey would sleep in barrels for six years before it got dumped and put into the bottle. The chances of the bourbon being worth what they intended to sell it for were slim. One way to keep the first seven years from being a money pit for investors was to have someone else make whiskey, which could be put in the bottle on day one. Ninety percent of the bourbon out there tasted bad, and nobody really cared. According to author and salesperson Elmer Wheeler, it's about the sizzle, not the steak.

The dark side of the bourbon industry that no one talked about was what went in the bottle. Insiders only drank brown liquor from distilleries that had invested millions of dollars in equipment, to control the quality of the product. Those would be the majestic old stills that've been around for a long time. Barclay intended to spring for the best quality equipment available, and then he'd disparage bootstrappers, of which there were many, including his friends at the Ohio Valley Distillers' Guild.

Nigel went off to Hanover College after graduating from high school, and Mrs. Barclay and Jaeger made peace with Hogan. They learned he was blackmailing Kentucky politicians, so Jaeger, fully developed and crazy good looking at age fifteen, offered to be the cat's paw. After several years of home movies shot at Natoli's place, Jaeger leaked to her brother what she had been doing, which gave her the idea to entrap Willard Lentz. Hogan was found dead shortly thereafter, and Jaeger disappeared. Nigel suspected his sister of killing their father and making up evidence that he was the one behind the Lentz affair. Nigel wanted Jaeger to stay gone, and to keep anyone from looking for her, he scrambled to find a stand in. He was naïve enough to believe his mother wouldn't know the difference. She played along.

According to Brock Skinner, Jaeger had been found, or will be soon. That was a problem.

———

Maude read the article about Barclay Farm Distillery on Sunday afternoon while she sat in her office at the winery. The calm weather had attracted a good number of visitors to the advertised wine tastings. Brock checked to make sure stock at the tasting-room bar was plentiful before he joined his wife. She said, "Our pal Nigel's hit the big time."

"Sort of. He's got to sell the Audubon. I'd like to know how he's going to do that."

"I bet he's got a private buyer already lined up."

"I think I'll ask him."

Maude looked up at her husband introspectively. "Why do you care?"

"Maybe I can buy the book from him at a fire sale price."

"Why do you want to do that, to flip it for a profit?"

"Maybe." He sat on the couch across from her desk, took out his phone, and made a call. "Leslie? Brock. How are you? Would you be kind enough to send me the pictures you have of the crowd at the chess tournament? I'd like to see if I recognize anybody." He gave her the email address to use and rang up Willett next. "Cal, I need you to do me a favor. Call your friends and ask them if they have any pictures of the people who attend your dock parties. Specifically, I'm looking to make sure everyone who recently came around is well-known to the crowd and was invited to your house. If you find anyone who you're not sure about, I'd like to see a photo of them. Celine has a laptop where a picture can be sent to me."

"Okay," he said. "It'll give us something to do this afternoon."

"Thanks."

"Hey, I wanted to tell you, CeCe and I are going to drive up to Michigan tomorrow to look at boats for sale."

"Be careful. Make sure no one follows you besides the guy I put on your door last night." He asked to speak to Celine to give her his email address.

When he hung up, Maude said, "You're going to need a lot of luck."

Cal and CeCe enjoyed organizing the contacts and getting in touch with the partygoers. It gave him a chance to put names to faces and learn a little about each of the people who were regulars. It brought back memories of the dozens of boat trips he'd made out on the lake with friends. If he were to buy a brand-new boat, the crowd would have something to flap their gums about.

Brock went back to the house to print out the pictures Leslie had sent him. Thad Cameron was in several of them, confirming he was part of the kidnapping of Romine. Brock got tired of waiting for anything to come across from Celine, so he had Truman join him on a run through the backwoods. A few of the leaves on the weaker trees had begun turning red and yellow as fall was coming on.

At five o'clock, a picture came in of an attractive girl on the arm of a guy standing on the dock. The email from Celine said, "The boy keeps Cal's car and boat clean and serviced. He's a regular at the parties. Claims the girl approached him at a gas station and asked what he was doing Sunday two weeks before Labor Day. He told her he was going to the lake, and she pretty much invited herself along. Thought it might be the beginning of a good thing. He hasn't seen or heard from her since." Brock shuffled through the pictures from Leslie, looking to see if the mystery girl was in any of them. She was, but never next to Cameron.

"Leslie, it's Brock again. Did the people who came to the chess tournament sign in to see the matches?"

"I think so."

"There's a girl in some of the pictures. She may be involved in Frank's kidnapping. How can I get a list of the attendees?"

"Well, one of the officials at the tournament thinks a lot of me. I could try to call and talk him out of the list."

"Do you have a number for him?"

"I do."

"Work your charm. I'll be standing next to the computer tapping my foot."

When he got the list from Leslie, the first thing he noticed was that Thad Cameron's name wasn't on it. He must've used a fake ID. It appeared that the person who typed the list had taken the addresses of the attendees off their IDs. Brock sent the list and picture of the girl to Marcel and asked him to call.

"What do you want me to do with these?" Marcel asked.

"Find the name of the girl on the list."

"Okay. Done."

"That was fast. Who is it?" Brock thought his brother-in-law was being sarcastic.

"Rhonda Hogan."

"How do you know that?"

"Because her listed address is where Celine Oliver lived when she came out of hiding."

Brock, exasperated, said, "I didn't see that name. What in the hell is going on?"

"You better ask Celine."

"See if you can find out the backstory on her."

Brock got Celine on the line and asked, "Do you know the girl whose picture you sent me?"

"I don't think so."

"You were on the dock two weeks before Labor Day. She was there."

"I don't remember seeing her."

"Her name is Rhonda Hogan. She lives in the house you lived in before you moved to Bonds Mill Road."

"Wait. Now that you mention it, I think I met her a couple of years ago at the gym I went to. She asked where I lived, and I told her I was going to move to an apartment. She must have slipped in behind me to rent the house. You said her name is Rhonda Hogan? That's suspicious. It's a combination of my mother and Nigel's father. What gives?"

"I'm guessing she's Jaeger Barclay," Brock surmised.

"Why don't you go see her and find out?"

"I will, first thing in the morning."

Brock heard Maude's vehicle pull in close to the house and saw on the stove clock that she had arrived right on time. He fixed a Greek salad with grilled lamb on it while he caught her up on the Rhonda Hogan sighting, and then told her what he planned to do on Monday. Truman rested his head on Maude's leg. He was either lonesome or begging for food. She said, "Go pester your dad. Do you think she's Jaeger Barclay?" Truman moved over to Brock.

"Maude, this thing gets more complicated by the day. She's somebody important. One thing is for sure: she's a bad egg. She was at the chess tournament along with Cameron. That can't be a coincidence. She probably came to the dock party to check the layout for him."

"She must know what happened to Frank."

"Yes, she does."

Marcel called Brock after dark to report on Rhonda Hogan. "I found her banking information. A couple of years ago, she got a wire from a bank in Grand Cayman to open the account. Nothing else I found looked suspicious."

"She's got to be Jaeger Barclay. Why did she change her name?"

"To avoid being hunted down and killed by her brother?"

"That makes some sense. The fact she knows Thad Cameron suggests she's in on the attempted killing of Calvin Willett and Celine."

"And Frank," Marcel uttered.

"Yes. The first order of business is to confirm who she really is."

"Is there an easy way to do that?"

"DNA. Nigel told me he and Jaeger were tested by Hogan to confirm they were his blood relatives."

"So, you think you can talk her into getting tested?"

"I do."

"There's something else going on, Brock."

"Did you see the article in the *Courier Journal* about the Barclay Farm Distillery?"

"I did."

"It would seem logical that she's going to cut herself in on the deal somehow," Brock said. "Is there any way you can get a copy of Mrs. Barclay's will leaving everything to Nigel?"

"I will see if I can hack into Indiana court records from six years ago. If so, I'll call you back."

It only took Marcel twenty minutes to download a copy of the will. "It's a one pager. A law firm attested it."

"Send it to me. What's the date on it?"

"May thirteenth."

"Hogan Barclay dies on May fifth eleven years ago, he's buried on May ninth, Mrs. Barclay amends her will leaving everything to Nigel on May thirteenth, Jaeger buys a plane ticket for Grand Cayman on May twentieth, to fly out on the twenty-sixth. She changes the flight to June fifteenth, and is in Richmond on June thirteenth, the day Roy Aldiss was killed. She stays in Grand Cayman nine years, comes back under the name Rhonda Hogan, and rents the house Celine Oliver vacates."

Marcel asked, "Why in the world would Mrs. Barclay cut Jaeger out of her will?"

"I don't know. There must be more to it. Who hired Thad Cameron to bug Celine's apartment, kidnap Frank, and try to kill Calvin and Celine?"

"It could be Jaeger, but I didn't find where she paid Cameron anything out of her bank account. There's someone else behind this. Could it be Clive Natoli or Perry Oliver?"

"Perry stays close to home. Clive doesn't have the countenance of a thug."

"But you do, Brock. Maybe it's you."

"Ha-ha." Brock hung up on him.

CHAPTER 22

Brock jimmied Frank Romine's apartment door a little before eight o'clock on Monday morning. He still had the eighty-thousand-dollar check and found a deposit slip for it. A blanket of clouds had formed a high deck in the chalky sky that was getting lighter by the minute. The outside air was comfortably warm and still. Brock retrieved the mail in Frank's box, set it on his computer desk, locked the apartment, and took off for Rhonda Hogan's place.

The 1950's vintage house, a hundred yards off the main road, was on a lot carved out of a weedy cattle pasture bordering the property on three sides. It was likely where the owners of the farm lived until they built a larger place. The tidy abode had a black hip roof, white brick, and one-car garage. Celine Oliver had lived there for four years and moved out two years back. A fetching young woman opened the door when summoned. Brock asked her, "Are you Rhonda Hogan?"

"Yes." Her innate confidence was an imaginary nimbus around her attractive face.

"My name's Brock Skinner. Are you also Jaeger Barclay?"

"What gave you that idea?"

"She flew to Grand Cayman eleven years ago, reappeared two years ago, and opened a bank account with money from the Caymans. You're the right age and have the right looks."

"I guess you'd better come in." The living room had expensive furnishings, out of character for the location and style of the house. A phallic watercolor of a didgeridoo, painted to look like a coral snake, hung on the robin-egg wall above the divan. A purple area rug covered most of the old-fashioned, blond hardwood floor. "Have a seat. There's coffee in the pot. Can I get you a cup?"

"No, thanks." Brock conjured up in his mind a scenario where she poisoned him, and he awoke in heaven.

"Have a seat. Why are you looking for Jaeger Barclay?" Rhonda asked.

"You know the answer to that question."

"Why don't you enlighten me." Rhonda sat in a side chair, not seemingly in a hurry to hear what he was going to say. She resembled Celine, only thinner and harder in the face.

"To be honest, I'm fearful of you. Why're you using the name Rhonda Hogan? That's a bullhorn for trouble," Brock said.

"What's wrong with it?" She shifted her eyes and feigned indignance.

"It's the first names of Celine Oliver's mother and your father. That's no coincidence."

"Speaking hypothetically, what's the big deal with Jaeger Barclay?"

"Money and revenge. I have no problem with the money. The revenge involves a lot of killing and death. I'm not going to stand for that."

"I can assure you: I have never been involved in the killing of anybody."

"So, it's the money you're after. I'm sure you've heard your brother will be inking the deal for a distillery on Barclay Farm in a few days. What's your angle?"

She got up with a start and said, "It was nice of you to stop by, Mr. Skinner."

"If you are Jaeger, you'll need to prove your identity before you can get a piece of the action."

"How does a person go about doing that?" she asked.

"DNA. You'll have to go to a lab, present a valid ID, get fingerprinted, and have a genetic profile worked up. The chain of custody must be verified. If it matches the one your father had done of you years ago—game on."

"That's an interesting approach."

Brock got to his feet and remarked, "I might as well cut to the chase. You get me your genetic profile. I'll take it to your brother. Then you can let me in on what surprise you and your mother cooked up for him back when she was alive."

Rhonda said, "I hear those tests take three or four days to get the results back. Why don't you swing by here again Friday after lunch? I might have something for you then."

"I'll do that. Oh, one more thing: you've been spotted in pictures at a recent chess tournament in Louisville. Thad Cameron was also there. That's an unusual coincidence."

"Who's he?"

"Come now, Rhonda. You've got to give information if you expect to get any in return."

Brock arrived at Barclay Farm in less than an hour. Nigel still had a euphoric hangover from the big distillery deal being announced over the weekend. His mood darkened when he saw the Lamborghini rush up like a thirty-three record on forty-five. When Brock got to the door, Nigel asked, "Does anyone ever enjoy seeing you coming?"

"My wife and dog. Beyond that, generally not. I can be a fun-loving guy if the stars are aligned, which isn't very often."

"What bad news are you spreading today?"

"Are you going to invite me in?"

Nigel resolved that a tetchy attitude on his part would be counterproductive, so he turned on the charm. "Why not? Soon, I'll be telling everyone you're my best friend." He took Brock to the backside of the house, into the redone kitchen replete with marble counters, a porcelain sink, Subzero refrigerator, and Viking stove. The room smelled antiseptic, almost too clean.

"I've just spoken to your sister. She didn't ask me to say hi."

"Where is she?" Nigel looked as if he'd just eaten something sour.

"In Kentucky."

"How do you know it's her?"

"I don't. That's why I came to see you." Brock leaned back on the edge of the countertop. "I think you said your father had DNA tests done on you and Jaeger to make sure you were blood relatives. Do you have a copy of her genetic profile?"

"I think so. I'll have to find it among the papers in the filing cabinet. Can I get you anything to drink?"

"I'm good. I insisted she get a test so I could authenticate her identity. She agreed, which leads me to believe it's her."

"If I find the DNA profile, I won't let you take it. You'll have to bring hers here. We can compare them together."

"Nigel, now that we're buddies, I'd like to hear a little more about Jaeger. I've concocted a few scenarios about her disappearance, and frankly, I think they're all wrong. I'm missing some important facts. Can you think of anything that could clear up why she took off?"

"According to what she told me, my father was filming her seducing Kentucky politicians, and then blackmailing them. Jaeger eventually got sideways with Dad. Told him to go to hell. She came to me with the idea of filming Willard Lentz. I couldn't figure out why she did that."

"And you don't think it was to compromise him and force him to finance the distillery?"

"Well, yeah, but she wouldn't have vanished then. You would have thought she'd have stayed around to take care of Mother and try to convince her to cut me out of her will, so she'd get the benefit of the new distillery herself."

Brock leaned off the counter and said, "I think she took care of that before decamping. Celine shared with me that your mother told her you'd get the surprise of your life after she died."

Nigel replied, "That was six years ago."

"And there was no reason to stir up anything until the distillery deal got closer."

"What's she going to do?"

"After the DNA test, we'll find out. Jaeger's using the name Rhonda Hogan. Means she intended to attract attention."

"I guess. There's nothing I can do to stop her."

Brock spun around and said, "Nothing legal that is. You could have her killed, and if you do, I'll make you pay."

"I don't have the courage to kill anybody or have anyone killed."

"That's what Celine said. Why does she have such a dim view of you?"

"Because I treated her like crap. I treat everybody that way. I shouldn't. A psychiatrist would say I have low self-esteem."

"You could always apologize, ask for forgiveness."

Nigel abruptly walked out of the kitchen. Brock stayed where he was. "Are you coming?" Nigel yelled.

"Where are we going?"

"I want to show you something."

Brock followed him up the stairs to the room over the kitchen. The four volumes of *The Birds of America* were stacked on each other in a tinted Plexiglass case. He wasn't surprised at the size of the books based on how Valerie had described them. They were right out of a Henri Rousseau painting, not to scale with everything else around them. "Audubon. What do you think the set is worth?"

"Some people say fifteen million. Others believe it will only bring eleven million at auction."

"I take it you're going to sell the set to raise capital for the distillery?"

"Yes." He put a hand on top of the Plexiglass case as though he wanted to caress it.

"I'll give you ten million for it," Brock threw out.

Nigel stared at him in disbelief. "You don't look like you have that kind of money. On the other hand, you are driving an expensive car."

"I've got the money. Say the word, and I'll bring you ten million in gold coins."

Nigel led the way back downstairs. "If I can't get a higher price, I might take you up on that." He moved to the front door, expecting Skinner was out of things to discuss.

"Another tidbit that may interest you: Jaeger flew to Grand Cayman eleven years ago."

"You think she went there by herself?"

"I don't know. One more thing: I recommend you have the house swept for bugs. It may be that someone is listening in on your plans. It's possible a killing spree is underway, and I don't want you to end up in the obituaries, now that we're such good friends." Brock offered his hand to Nigel as he walked out the door.

Brock was no psychologist or psychiatrist. He did, however, have a penchant for getting at what made people tick. When it came to Frank Romine and Nigel Barclay, their white whales were in plain sight. For Frank, it was the raw beauty of a woman, and Nigel, the feel of cash money.

Calvin Willett, on the other hand, was a formula missing an ingredient. If a dose of something got added to him, he'd turn into Love Potion Number Nine.

Celine Oliver and Jaeger Barclay were damaged goods because of their emotional solitary confinement. It was almost impossible to reprogram those defects later in life. If Celine dropped her guard, God could do it. Brock thought Jaeger might be too far gone, and that Satan owned her. The girl he met, using the name Rhonda Hogan, didn't appear hopeless. The jury had yet to give a verdict.

Brock liked Leslie Blazek the best. Her conundrum would be easy to explain if her pheromones, or body odor, were off-putting, but they weren't. She deserved a good man. The right fit for her would be Calvin Willett. That wasn't in the cards. Frank would be a terrible fit for Celine Oliver. His attributes would only warp her further by stunting her emotional growth. Those were the things Brock thought about but knew he could never honestly say to anyone other than his wife, which was probably for the best.

———

There was time for Brock to run by Thad Cameron's place before returning to Hazard. He put his car in the same ruts off to the side of the road when he pulled up in front of the house. The vehicle being worked on in the garage had its hood up, and a portable radio blared a country song that echoed around like the speaker at the county fair. Brock worked his way down the hill, and when he got around to the front bumper, he noticed legs sticking out from underneath. They weren't moving. The car seemed too low to the ground. That was because the hydraulic jack had been depressurized, crushing the chest of Cameron. Brock turned and ran back up to his car. He was down the road, away from the house in a matter of seconds. He looked in the mirror to make sure no one was following him. Normally, he called the police. He knew he'd be stuck at the station for three days explaining everything if he called it in. If anyone saw him drive up and pull out in a hurry, the decision to run would be a bad one.

Brock arrived at the winery before it closed, figuring Maude would still be there. Truman saw him park and get out of the car. He ran over to follow Brock wherever he was headed. They ended up in Maude's office where she was finishing some paperwork. "Should I ask how your day has been?"

"Thad Cameron is dead."

"What?"

"Somebody dropped the front end of a car on his chest."

"Who would do something like that?"

"A person who uses people, and then discards them. Frankly, Maude, I worry about the safety of everybody involved in this affair."

"Should you go to the police?"

"Probably." He debriefed her on what happened in the last twelve hours.

A few minutes after six, Maude locked the winery and drove home. Brock followed her in his car while Truman cut through the grapevines and was waiting to be let in the house when the

Skinners got there. She stuck the chicken cordon bleu she'd made up earlier in the day in the oven to cook. "Frank's missing. There's nothing we can do about him. Hopefully, he reappears."

Brock said nervously, "I worry now about Nigel Barclay, Clive Natoli, and Perry Oliver. I wouldn't be shocked if one or all of them turned up missing or dead."

"What about Celine and Calvin?"

"They took off for Holland, Michigan, this afternoon. He wants to look at boats for sale."

"From what you've told me, it sounds as though Jaeger Barclay, a.k.a. Rhonda Hogan, is the black hole from which no light can escape."

"Yeah. She didn't seem that menacing when I talked to her. I don't think she's a lone wolf."

"That brings us back to Nigel, Clive, and Perry."

Brock put his hands in the air. Truman stared at him, trying to figure out what was going on. "I just don't see the connection, yet."

Chapter 23

"Why'd you pick the place we're going for supper? That's my job," CeCe asked.

"Because the owner of a boat we're going to see tomorrow recommended the place. I called and asked about their steaks." Cal checked to see if she showed any interest in the subject.

"What about them?"

"They have a Kobe beef filet and steamed vegetables."

"Nice." CeCe was looking out the window, studying the Dutchified arrondissements of Holland. "This is a clean town." She had on high-waisted blue jeans, a low-cut black singlet, and a short, mauve, embroidered jacket with handmade blue buttons.

"Certainly is. Do you want to check into the hotel first, or go straight to the restaurant?"

"Let's eat now and walk it off while it's still light."

Cal parked on the street across from Yukon Savory Grill. When they got seated, he commented, "This is a great city to visit because the traffic is manageable. I hope the food is good."

"Me too. I'm hungry."

They enjoyed a tasty meal and ran out of things to talk about by the time the server brought decaf tea. Cal revived the conversation by mentioning her neighbor. "I get the impression Frank Romine is sweet on you."

"He is, or was if he's dead. Most men are. The ones who aren't are using me."

"That's a cynical point of view."

She put her hand on his and smiled. "Cal, you're an anomaly. You're sweet on me, *and* you're using me too."

He leaned to the side in his chair. "Can you think of a better word than *use?*"

"Of course. How about you're sweet on me and you get enjoyment from my company."

"By golly, every bit true. One last little tweak: I get enjoyment out of our friendship."

"You've got me there," CeCe said.

"Have you ever considered getting married?" Cal asked.

That was a curve ball. "I don't trust men. If I did, I would."

"I take it you don't trust Frank Romine."

"Especially him. I got to know his girlfriend, Leslie Blazek. She has everything in the world going for her, yet he's blasé toward her. There's something terribly wrong with him."

"Well, I wouldn't say terribly wrong. He's nuts about you. That's a point in his favor."

"Would you like to get married, Cal?"

"No."

"You want to expound on that?"

"I would be a project," he admitted.

"What if I asked you to marry me?"

He was caught flatfooted. "Here's my diplomatic answer: you are the only woman I would ever consider spending the rest of my life with."

She laughed loudly, and everyone in the restaurant heard her. "Cal, I think I've got it wrong; I'm the one using you." She blushed, something Cal had never seen of her before.

"You probably don't know this, but there was an expression on the edge of silver coins in the eighteenth century that read: to be esteemed, be useful."

"Let's take a walk, my esteemed friend." As they were strolling out, every man in the place did a double take. She saw them gawking. When they got outside, she said, "Did you see how all the men in there were leering at me?"

"That, CeCe, is the dumbest question I've ever heard. Since the minute I met you, every man with average to good eyesight hasn't been able to take their eyes off you."

Street performers were spaced out every half block. Three handsome, twenty-year-old college students attracted the most attention. One guy was strumming an electric guitar the size of a dulcimer, another plucked a tiny bass, and a surfer boy pounded on the bottoms of drywall buckets. The trio played their version of "Uptown Funk" by Bruno Mars. Cal, not familiar with modern music, found the tune catchy. The vignette was a harbinger of things to come, but he didn't know it.

The hotel catered to the young crowd. Everything about it unnerved Cal. He tried to figure out what all the gadgets were in his room, and how to work the shower. The artwork had an edge to it. He began to have second thoughts about venturing away from his comfortable home and 1967 lifestyle. Unable to fall asleep, he perused a magazine touting things to do in Holland. He heard a knock on the door. It was CeCe. She said, "Do you mind if I join you?"

"Mi casa, su casa," he replied without hesitation.

———————

Cal had arranged to see two wooden boats the next morning, both 1967 Century Resorters. He asked the owners to put them in Lake Macatawa and drive them to the Boatwerks dock, so he could test drive each. The first was scheduled to arrive at ten o'clock and the second at eleven. The calm weather made for smooth water, perfect conditions to run a watercraft at top speed. CeCe pointed at the first vessel as it approached, commenting, "That looks just like the one you had."

"It's almost identical." Cal talked to the owner for fifteen minutes, discussing the history of the runabout, before taking it out for a spin. CeCe climbed in with him for a test drive. The machine felt much like his old one. When they returned to the dock, he said to the owner, "Nice boat. What's your best price for it?"

"It's advertised for twenty thousand. You can haul it away right now if you write me a check for eighteen thousand."

"That's a fair price. I'm looking at one other model. I'll decide right after we have lunch."

The second version that pulled up to the dock at eleven looked quite a bit different. There was a slight taper in the tail, the metal trim on the side was fancier, and the interior upholstery had been done in a rolled-and-tucked metallic green material. It was quieter and faster on the water, at a walkaway price of twenty-two thousand.

After the second boat puttered away from the dock, Cal asked, "You want to have lunch here and talk about it?"

CeCe wasn't paying attention to him. Her eyes were squinting, looking out over the water. She said, "What is that?" The boat she caught sight of was heading straight toward them. When it got close enough, she said with fervor, "It's a Ski Nautique. Now, that's a boat."

Cal eyeballed the thing and said, "It's orange and white. Looks like a creamsicle."

"Thing of beauty, isn't it?" CeCe shuffled out to the edge of the dock.

The driver of the Nautique got up on his knees in the seat, and yelled, "Hey, I heard you people were looking for a nice pleasure craft. Can I come in?" He didn't wait for permission, easing the boat up to the dock. When he saw CeCe up close, he grinned from ear to ear. "Come aboard. I want you to try this baby out. I deal in boats in these parts. I just got this piece of heaven from the factory a couple of days ago. Since the season is over, I'm really motivated to sell it." CeCe jumped in, turned to Cal, and beckoned him to do the same. After he did, the man behind the wheel said, "Here, you drive."

Cal sank down in the comfortable seat, surveyed the instrumentation, and used his right arm to push away from the dock. The interior was a combination of white fiberglass, white padded waterproof fabric, and brown flooring. He started the engine and could barely hear it idling. Out on the lake, Cal pushed the throttle all the way down. At that moment, he had second thoughts about living in 1967. He already knew what CeCe would have to say about the boat—buy it!

Upon disembarking, Cal uttered, "I'm afraid to ask the price."

The man replied, "Retail is a hundred grand. I'll take ninety thousand on the spot."

Cal peered at CeCe. She was thrilled like a kid in a candy store. He gazed up at the sparse cloud cover and said laconically, "But it's orange and white."

"They call it Crush Orange to be exact. You'll be the only guy on your lake with one." The man trying to close the deal shifted his weight from one foot to the other.

CeCe started laughing. "You'll keep them guessing with this missile parked at the dock."

Cal reluctantly took a folded piece of paper out of his pants pocket. "Okay. Here's a copy of my driver's license, which has my name and address on it. Make out a bill of sale for eighty-five thousand, haul the boat and trailer to my house, and I'll write you a check."

"I'm not sure I'll take that for it."

Cal put out his arm and said, "Come on, CeCe, let's get some lunch." They began walking away.

"Come back. We've got a deal. You want to write me that check now?"

"We'll be eating next door here. You run and get the bill of sale. When you bring it back, I'll give you the check."

"Will do."

Cal offered to shake. "Do you promise we're going to like the boat?"

"Absolutely." He took Cal's hand and shook it vigorously.

When they were seated in the restaurant, Cal saw the light fall across CeCe's smile. She looked as happy as he'd ever seen her. He was happy too.

"You're now going to be BMOC at Herrington Lake," she said pleasantly.

"I thought I was already," he retorted high-handedly.

The man delivered the bill of sale just as they were finishing lunch. He said, "A driver is leaving in a few minutes to deliver the boat to your house. It'll be there about the time you get home."

The orange Nautique in Cal's driveway late Tuesday should have been delivered to the carnival, he thought as he wheeled in next to it. "This Sunday is October second. I wonder what the weather will be like?" The man guarding the house drove by slowly. Cal waved to him.

Celine used her phone to check the forecast. "Partly cloudy. High of seventy-seven."

"Good. Let's call our friends and have a party. The water will be warm enough for skiing. If not, we'll put on wetsuit tops. I can't wait to hear what folks will have to say about the boat. What should we name it?"

"The guy mentioned the paint color is Crush Orange. Why not flip it and call it Orange Crush?"

"Not original enough. How about Clockwork Orange?"

"That's even less original," Celine scolded.

"How about Orange Velvet?"

She threw her hands in the air. "That's it."

They made tuna fish sandwiches for supper and got the cards out afterward for a few hands of gin. Cal carefully broached the subject they had discussed the night before. "You know, married people do better if they have the same concept of God. What do you think the meaning or purpose of life is?"

She stopped shuffling the cards and drummed her fingers on the table. "We are to serve Him and love our neighbors as ourselves." She nodded as though that was the final word.

"I agree. How do you think we're doing?" Cal asked.

"Miserably. I look at my life and how woefully short I've fallen. I've wasted the gifts God gave me. I've used my looks for money and have done little else."

"I'm not much better. I know what to do but have stood on the sidelines with my eyes closed to the sinful world we live in today. Paul says in Romans: what a wretched man I am. But there is no condemnation for those in Christ Jesus."

"What do you think Judgment Day will be like?" CeCe asked.

"It depends on which door you go through. Door number one is for unrepentant sinners. They'll have to give an account of the things they've done in their lives, all of which were filthy rags. That will be a terrifying moment. Door number two is for righteous believers. It will be like an award ceremony where trophies are given out to each person according to their acts of service in this life."

"You mean I won't be punished for the bad things I've done?" She dealt the cards after Cal cut them.

"When you ask God to forgive your sins, He remembers them no more." Cal arranged his hand and threw out the first discard.

"That's reassuring. You know, Cal, I'm almost to the point where I trust you. That would make you the first man to achieve that status." She took his discard and threw down a different card.

"That's nice of you to say that. I'll never betray your trust in me."

They played several games, chatting about this and that. Celine came out on top in the end. She said, "I got good cards."

"And you played them skillfully. Are you going to visit your other client this week?"

"Yes. He's asked me to go with him to a dinner party on Friday night in Frankfort. There will be lots of politicians there. He told me about the distillery that's going to be built on the Barclay Farm where I lived for five years. If he gets a big payoff from the deal, he'll probably retire from the lobbying business."

"Would that mean you'd lose him as a client?"

"Probably so. That wouldn't bother me. Just means I could spend more time with you."

Cal went into the kitchen for a glass of water. "I'm worried about Frank Romine, and the person or people who tried to kill us."

"Me too. Brock Skinner won't give up until he gets to the bottom of it."

"What about Skinner? Do you trust him?"

"I do, as a matter of fact. Ha, I forgot about him. I guess I trust two men now."

"Enough of that business. I say we put the new boat in the water in the morning and take it for a ride to the other end of the lake, to see how we like it."

"That sounds marvelous. You're going to love it. Don't you have to apply for a title?"

"Yes. We'll do that too."

CHAPTER 24

Brock rang Calvin Willett first thing on Wednesday morning. The sunbeam coming through the office window of the log cabin shined on the dusty bookshelf in the corner. Brock mopped it with his finger and checked to see how much dust he'd collected. "Hey, do you remember me telling you about the guy I chased down who I'm sure put the bomb in your boat?"

"You said his name was Thad Cameron."

"Right. I just saw a news flash. He was found dead by a UPS driver trying to deliver a package to his house. A hydraulic jack malfunctioned, and he was crushed by the car he was under."

"Malfunctioned?" Cal asked for clarification.

"That's the party line. I don't believe it. Whoever is trying to kill you, or Celine, must have erased him to cover his tracks."

"So, you're sure the person trying to kill us is still out there?"

"I am," Brock affirmed.

"That's rather inconvenient. I recently bought a new boat in Michigan and want to have a party on Sunday to show it off and take people skiing."

"I'll only allow that if Maude and I are invited. I'll want to bring my German shepherd."

"Sure."

"Good. If I get a chance, I'll drop in on you this afternoon." Brock ended the call and left the house to join Maude at the winery. When he found her, he pleaded, "You've got to help me figure out why someone bugged Celine's apartment and is trying to kill her."

"It must be Jaeger Barclay. She's afraid Celine knows something that could derail her plans."

"What plans?"

"You're the one who told me Jaeger's mother had a surprise for Nigel after her death," Maude declared.

"Celine would help Jaeger's case since she was the one who heard about the surprise from Mrs. Barclay. If Jaeger's behind this, she has someone helping her."

"Who would that be?"

"Hell, I don't know. I'm going to put the squeeze on Clive Natoli. Whatever he's keeping to himself, I'll get it out of him."

Maude turned into a stern statue. "Just don't hurt him, Brock."

"Yeah." He shrugged his shoulders in anger.

Cal had been studying the manual that came with his new boat all morning. After he called his insurance agent, he said to CeCe, "I see where we can apply for a title and registration numbers online. Can you help me?"

"Yes." She went to the licensing website, scanned in the bill of sale, filled everything out, made a payment with Cal's credit card, and then wrote down the new registration numbers.

"I'll run to a hardware store to get the stick-on letters." When he got back, she helped him find where to mount them, spaced properly, in a straight line. The guy who kept Cal's boat brought a truck over to haul it to the launch. They topped off the gas tank at the marina before heading toward the long end of the lake. Cal said, "This thing is as smooth as a baby's butt."

"I told you," CeCe exulted.

Beyond the no-wake zone, he poured on the gas. The hull shot forward with zero vibration. The trip to the Danville end of the lake was a good twenty miles, if you took the direct route. Cal did curlicues and yawed hard into several twists and turns to get the feel of piloting the ski boat safely. The lake shallowed, and the shore flattened as they approached the headwaters. He keyed off the engine and announced to CeCe, "I love it. You want to drive?"

"Step aside, mate," she replied playfully.

They got back home a short hour later. The guy who helped him with the boat was waiting on the dock when they pulled in. He asked, "Well?"

"Spectacular. Let's adjust the lift so the rails seat properly when it's raised out of the water."

CeCe went up the hill and fixed lunch for the three of them.

––––––––––––

Clive Natoli opened the front door of his house at twelve thirty on Wednesday afternoon to find Skinner standing there. He had reluctantly agreed to give Brock the back half of his lunch hour. Both men had already eaten, so they wouldn't be breaking bread together over a relaxing meal. "Come in," Natoli said robotically as he turned away. He walked briskly through the house, and they eventually ended up sitting on brown, crushed-velvet chairs in Clive's office.

"I hear the distillery on Barclay Farm is moving ahead. That should've put you in a good mood, but I see it hasn't," Brock offered.

"It's you who took the grin off my face. You remind me of the grim reaper." Clive had dropped his otherwise breezy and congenial demeanor.

"Why do you say that? Because I won't leave you alone? I know you're hiding something from me. If I find out you haven't told me what you know, things will get rough for you."

"On what subject?" Clive asked feverishly.

"Celine Oliver."

"What about her?"

"Who's her father?" Brock was bearing down, and Clive began to fear him.

Natoli put his hands out to the side, stared up at the ceiling, and exhaled like a deflating balloon. "Thirty-two years and nine months ago, Rhonda and I drove to this house from Hazard right after New Year's, before we were to start back to school for the last half of our senior year. We were friends, and she wanted to take a trip somewhere. Visiting my father was the only thing I could think of that wouldn't cost money. My mother had recently died of cancer. I thought he might appreciate seeing the two of us."

"What happened?"

"Hogan Barclay was here visiting my father. He spoke to Rhonda and said he wanted to show her something. She followed him into the theater room, he locked the door behind her, and he raped her. When they came out, she was disheveled and disoriented. She looked like a zombie. I grabbed Hogan and punched him. My father restrained me while Hogan got out of there."

"Did you take her to the hospital to confirm the rape?"

"No. She refused to go. She implored me to take her home."

"Why didn't you go over to the Barclay place and shoot the son of a bitch right between the eyes?"

"I should have, but we didn't know she was pregnant right away. There was plenty of time to deal with him. Perry Oliver, who was sweet on Rhonda, said he'd marry her after her pregnancy came to light. We figured we could shake Hogan down if we kept quiet about the baby. He gave each of us a quarter of a million dollars to keep our mouths shut about the rape."

"Okay, that's how Perry got the money to build his shop. That means Hogan Barclay got his wife pregnant with Jaeger around Thanksgiving, and five weeks later, after the first of the year, he scored again with Rhonda. The man was busy."

Clive leaned forward and put his arms out to the side. "The man was an asshole."

"Why'd your father like him?"

"He didn't. Barclay was blackmailing him. I don't know what my father did. Barclay forced my dad to let him use this house to film politicians in compromising situations."

Brock stood and said, "And Hogan started using his own daughter, Jaeger, as bait as soon as she was old enough. I think she killed him for revenge and that's the reason she disappeared."

Clive got to his feet. "But why has she surfaced again? You said you've seen her?"

"I have. She came back from Grand Cayman and moved into the house Celine lived in until two years ago. I stumbled onto her by accident. She's going by the name Rhonda Hogan."

"That's strange. What's she planning to do?"

"Prove her identity, and then somehow stake a claim on the Barclay property."

"How's she going to do that?"

"That remains to be seen," Brock replied as he walked over to a window to look out.

"When Jaeger took off, we told Celine she could get rich quick by stepping into her shoes. She resembles Jaeger so much, no one would be able to tell she wasn't the genuine article."

Brock retorted, "You already told me that. Are you planning to see Celine anytime soon?"

"Yes. She's going to a cocktail party with me on Friday night in Frankfort."

"Am I right in saying you've never told Celine who her father is?"

"Correct."

"Please don't do it now. I'm shadowing Jaeger and want to see if I can keep her from disrupting the distillery deal. If she does, it could be bad news for you and Perry. Frankly, I'd like Perry and Rhonda to get their payoff so he could take her away from Hazard. She has suffered enough."

"I agree."

"There's more. Someone bugged Celine's apartment and tried to kill her and her other client."

"Calvin Willett?"

"Yes. I'm not totally convinced this someone isn't trying to kill you, Nigel, and Perry. Celine's neighbor has also disappeared. I'm telling you this, so you'll watch your step."

"Thanks. The logical culprit would be Jaeger, but she couldn't create such havoc by herself."

"That's what I think too." Brock moved toward the front door. "I'll call you if anything goes on you should know about."

Brock arrived at the Lentz residence twenty minutes later. This time, Willard opened the door instead of his wife. "Ah, it's you again. Any news to share?"

"I was going to ask you the same thing. I've heard the Barclay Farm Distillery is a go."

"It is in fact. We're signing the deal next Wednesday at the office of Ohio Valley Distillers' Guild in Madison. Nigel is bringing the title to the farm and ten million bucks, and Lolly Gelt is putting in ten million and two hundred sixty million in a letter of credit."

"I came here to tell you we've found Nigel's sister, Jaeger, and she's alive. There's a chance she will try to gum things up."

"Let's hope not. We've been trying to get this project over the hump for twelve years. Thanks for the update."

Brock went to Sutherland Tailoring next to debrief his brother-in-law. Marcel recited, "So, you are going to take Jaeger's DNA profile over to her brother's house to compare it to the one her father had done years ago. If they're a match, you expect Jaeger to turn over her ace in the hole?"

"That's about the size of it. When I go to Nigel's, I'm going to take ten million in gold to buy the Audubon, if he hasn't already sold it."

"Why are you going to do that?"

"Because if the deal goes through, I'm betting Nigel will want to buy it back from me in a year for eleven million. He'll figure he can get more than that from somebody else or he may want it back. He'd only be pawning it to me."

"And if he doesn't want to buy it back?"

"I'll put the four volumes on the coffee table at home and leaf through them in the winter, next to the fire."

"You are a complete and utter nut."

"Thank you. It takes special talent to be like this."

Brock's last stop was Calvin Willett's place. He wanted to see the new boat. Celine came to the door wearing tight white shorts and a navy-blue T-shirt. She said, "Hello. Any news about Frank Romine?"

"No. I'm still trying to run him down."

"Cal's down on the dock admiring the new inboard."

"You mean new, as in brand-new?"

"I do." Her eyes twinkled.

"That must mean you've broken his 1967 hypnotic trance. Has he also recognized how beautiful you are? I mean as a person."

"That, he's always known," she assured him.

"Yes, I suspect he has. I think I'll run down the hill to say hi and look at your new toy, I mean his new toy."

"Ha-ha, very funny. Brock, is this thing going to be over soon?"

"It will. By a week from Sunday, everything'll be a distant memory," he assured her.

"How do you know?"

"Because the stars are starting to align."

"What happens then?"

Brock put his hands behind his head. "I turn into a happy-go-lucky fellow without a care in the world. People accept me more when I'm like that, especially Maude."

"You wouldn't want to disappoint her, now, would you?"

"No. Please watch yourself, Celine, until the coast, or should I say lakefront, is clear."

"Will do. Brace yourself. It's bright orange."

Calvin saw Brock working his way toward the gangway over to the dock. He yelled, "Ah, I see curiosity got the best of you. I suppose CeCe told you she talked me into buying this beauty. I'm likely to never live it down."

"I'll tell you a little story. I used to drive an old muscle car, Cal, and when I got my Lamborghini, I learned what I had been missing. What a fool I was holding on to the past."

"What do you think about the orange?" He smiled, knowing Brock didn't have the heart to say anything bad about it.

"I love that color. You'll understand what I mean when you see my dog. He's a white German shepherd with orange markings. I've got an idea: we can get him an advertising contract with the manufacturer. His name's Truman. I can see it now: Truman regally perched on the driver's seat of a new, orange runabout, with his tongue hanging out, looking ever so cool."

Cal walked over near Brock and looked into his eyes. "Are you okay? You sound silly. I've never seen you this way."

"This is the way I get when things are beginning to make sense. I take it your trip to Michigan was a rousing success?"

"Well, if you call being a hundred grand lighter in the wallet a rousing success, I guess you could say that."

Brock laughed and responded with, "You can't take it with you, Calvin. I don't know about the boat though. You might be able to take that. I'm sure there are lakes in heaven."

Cal put his hand on Brock's forehead. "That's funny, you don't seem to have a fever. Sunday, I'll take you skiing. Maybe you'll snap out of whatever is ailing you."

Brock became serious. "Until then, be careful." He scaled the hill and took off for home.

CHAPTER 25

A gentle rain shower snuck in right after eight o'clock on that gloomy Thursday morning. There was no wind to speak of, and the spritzing called for intermittent swipes of the windshield wipers. Nigel arrived at the art dealer's establishment in Louisville as soon as it opened.

The gallery, in an antebellum, four-story downtown brick building, had a high ceiling consisting of rough-hewn wood of the floor above, and white sheetrock walls that only went up nine feet. Scraped brick had been tuck-pointed to keep the place from looking like it might collapse. The artwork, mostly cheap stuff, wasn't how they made their money. They put buyers and sellers of expensive art together and took a fee for their troubles.

Nigel went through the ornate brass door on the back wall of the gallery and sat down in the cypress-paneled office of the proprietor. He said peevishly, "My *Birds of America* are the finest originals in existence. I sent pictures of pages in all four books. Have you found an interested buyer?"

"Yes, several. None are interested at your minimum of eleven million dollars." The vainglorious proprietor looked past his glasses and down his nose at Nigel, making him feel as though his asking price was too high.

"How much are they willing to pay?"

The art dealer jiggled his necktie knot and said, "Ten million seems to be the high-water mark. If you want to get more, we'll have to up the advertising and wait until the right buyer comes along." It was a sure thing that a buyer was already out there willing to pay the eleven million. In fact, it was also a sure thing that the buyer had told the art dealer to beat the seller down, and every dollar below eleven million would be shared between them.

"I can't wait that long. I need the money by next Tuesday. What do you suggest I do?"

"Borrow against it or take the ten million. Your net would be nine point eight million after my two-hundred-thousand-dollar fee."

"See if you can get a net amount of ten million. I'll call you tomorrow." Nigel left disappointed.

The art dealer put his arms on his desk and did the math in his head. Ten million for Barclay, ten million five hundred thousand from the buyer, and five hundred thousand for the house. *Not a bad day's work*, he thought.

Due to the persistent, aggravating drizzle, the crowd visiting Maude's winery could be described as paltry. She decided to go into the dank warehouse to have a word with her husband. When Maude found him, she said, "I've been thinking more about who had Celine's place bugged and why they did it. What if they were only interested in hurting people around her as punishment for something?"

"Okay. Run with it."

"Jaeger was in Richmond eleven years ago. What if she killed Aldiss just to spite Celine?"

"She would've needed help. If she bugged Celine's apartment to find out who else to kill, Frank Romine and Calvin Willett would be high on the list. But as far as I can tell, she hasn't tried to put Clive Natoli out of commission."

Maude raised a finger. "That's because he's helping her brother, Nigel, close the distillery deal, which she plans to profit from. Wouldn't surprise me if she tries to bring Clive and Nigel down on the backside of this affair."

Brock put his head back and widened his eyes. "I might get behind that. I've also been thinking: if Romine is still alive, he'll have no choice but to change his identity and disappear for good."

"I suppose that's true," Maude agreed. "When are you supposed to meet him again?"

"Saturday in Danville. I'm going to see Jaeger and Nigel tomorrow. I'll need to borrow your SUV to haul something."

"What's that?"

"*The Birds of America.*"

"So, you think he's going to sell it to you?"

"I do. I'm taking off. Got an errand to run." He kissed her on the cheek and shot out the back.

Brock went to a department store that had metal luggage and bought six stainless-steel, ribbed cases with wheels. When he got to the bank, he spoke to the woman guarding the safe deposit boxes. Her parents hadn't seen fit to have her rogue teeth fixed when she was younger. Other than her snaggle-tooth smile, she was quite attractive. She knew Brock well and knew he had a ton of gold in several of the boxes. It took him a half hour to pack the five thousand coins in the six cases, each weighing about sixty-five pounds.

The final day of September marked the end of the third quarter, and the date seemed more noteworthy when it fell on Friday. Business pundits reported what the stock market had done in the last three months, which was usually insignificant compared to the results of a typical fourth quarter. Bad weather, around the corner in October, would dampen investor sentiment as the specter of winter became real, driving away hope for good financial fortunes and quality of life in Appalachia through the end of the year and into the next.

Rhonda Hogan was sitting primly in a folding chair in her driveway when Brock arrived at noon. The SUV rode low due to the weight of the gold in the back. The sun didn't seem as fierce as it had been only a few days ago. She stood, took him by the arm, and led him into the house. She said, "I take it you're married?"

"Yes, why?"

"What a shame. You're one big hunk of a man. There is nothing but beach bums and fat cats in Grand Cayman. You have a tinge of beach bum in you. Just the right amount." She stroked his arms and backed away.

Brock concluded she was damned good looking. "It's always better to be liked than disliked," he replied to close the subject.

Rhonda went into the kitchen to grab two manilla folders. She returned and told Brock to take a seat before she sat down herself. "Here is the DNA profile I had done. Bring it back after you've verified who I am." She gave him one of the folders.

He scanned it and said, "Okay. This should prove you're Jaeger Barclay. I'd like you to clear up a few things for me, if you don't mind."

"What is it you want to know?"

"Why'd you take your clothes off in front of men at Natoli's house when you were young?"

"Because my rotten father made me. I was hoping he'd get caught and protective child services would take me away."

"Why didn't you just run away?"

"And go where? I was afraid he'd find me and kill me. I didn't want to leave my mother alone with him anyway."

Brock shifted in his seat, rubbed his brow, and glanced down. "Okay. Did you kill your father?"

"I did not. If I did, do you think I would tell you?"

"You were over in Richmond, Kentucky, on June thirteenth, a couple of days before you flew off to Grand Cayman eleven years ago. What were you doing there?"

"I don't remember any such trip," she said flippantly.

"You're lying. You had already gone into hiding. I think you went there to kill Roy Aldiss, a friend of Celine Oliver. Do you know who she is? Who helped you kill him?"

"I don't know what you're talking about," she replied in an aloof tone.

"I'd halfway believe you if you weren't in these pictures." He showed her two photos of the crowd at the chess tournament with her and Thad Cameron in them.

"That's not me."

"It sure looks like you. You were there stalking Frank Romine, another friend of Celine's. I bet you and Thad Cameron were planning to kill him. Maybe you already have."

"Enough of that nonsense. Here's something that will be of interest to Nigel." She hit his hand like a hammer with the second folder.

Brock took a minute to read the first document. "So, this is a copy of your mother's last will. Let me guess, it's dated after the one Nigel presented to the court."

"Yes. I was in Grand Cayman when she died and did not learn of her death until after the estate had been settled."

"Why didn't you come forth then or when you got back here two years ago?"

"Because I didn't want to stir up anything—yet. The attorney who prepared this is still at the same firm. He can attest to its authenticity."

Brock carefully read the second sheet in the folder. He said, "And you'll relinquish all claims against Nigel and the estate for a settlement amount of ten million dollars?"

"Yes. Otherwise, I'll go to court and block Nigel from deeding the farm to a corporation as an asset in the distillery deal."

Brock leaned back, threw his arms out, and looked at the ceiling. "Well, you've certainly played your cards right. I'll take this to Nigel, see if he goes for it, and if he does, I'll come back here to get you to sign it. What are you going to do if he pays you off?"

"Disappear again. When you bring back the DNA profile, bring a certified check for ten million."

"If Nigel wants to play ball, I'll join you at your attorney's office in three hours. Have a notary there." Brock found the address of the Louisville lawyer on the will. He said, "Is this where I should meet you?"

"Yes."

When Brock got to Nigel's house, they compared the DNA profile, and he laid out the rest of the deal for him. Nigel bellowed, "I don't have money to pay her!"

"First thing you should do is call that attorney to make sure the will is authentic."

Nigel spent twenty minutes on the phone talking to the law firm, asking them why the will was not presented after his mother's death. The answer he got was that it was the responsibility of the executor of the estate to present the will that Mrs. Barclay had given to the executor, who was none other than Nigel himself. He hung up and said to Brock, "I'll fight her in court. I'm not going to put up with this."

"Then your distillery deal will go up in smoke. Frankly, I see this as a way for you to dispose of a future problem."

"But I don't have ten million!"

"I can help you with that. Sell me *The Birds of America* for that amount."

"Even if I do, it will take too long to move the money around."

"No, it won't," Brock muttered on the heels of Nigel's words. "I've got the ten million in gold coins out in the SUV. Make up a bill of sale for the Audubon, and I'll load it up. Then we can go find a notary that knows you."

Sweat popped out on Nigel's forehead. "I won't have the money to put in the distillery deal if I pay her off." The corners of his mouth went down like those of a painted clown.

"I can help you with that too."

"What, are you made of money?"

"No, but so far, I've bought a book for ten million that I can sell for that amount. I can lend you the ten million you'll need. You'll have to secure the loan with the stock in your distillery deal."

Nigel walked from the hall to the parlor. "That's great. Jaeger gets ten, you get ten or more if you want a return, Clive gets five, and Perry gets five."

"And you'll put the property in worth twenty million and get back sixty if I get twenty million for my trouble. That's forty million left for you. I suggest you quit whining."

Nigel looked crestfallen, but not exactly down and out. "Let's go to my bank for the notary."

"First, make up a bill of sale for *The Birds of America* and a receipt I can get her to sign for the gold. Then we'll go to your bank. I'll meet you next week to give you the signed release and the loan for ten million."

"I want to go with you to see Jaeger."

"No. She refuses to see you. You'll have to trust me."

———

Brock parked the SUV in a secure lot next to the lawyer's office in Louisville. He was directed to the conference room where Jaeger and her legal counsel were waiting for him to arrive. They shook hands in a perfunctory manner and settled in for a frank discussion. Brock announced, "Nigel Barclay has agreed to pay ten million for release of all claims against his estate. Here's the notarized agreement with his signature."

The lawyer sat lifeless, seemingly worried that things were moving too fast. He carefully read the document, and said, "Everything looks to be in order. Miss Barclay, you can sign here, and I'll notarize it. We'll hand this release over to you, Mr. Skinner, when you produce the certified check made out to her for ten million."

"I've got a better idea. I'm ready to hand over five thousand twenty-dollar gold coins instead of a check. I have them in my vehicle outside. They're in six metal cases. I suggest you help me bring the cases up here so you can count them and sign this receipt. I also recommend that you arrange for an armored truck to haul the gold wherever she wants it to go."

The lawyer looked over at Jaeger, and her response was, "Marvelous."

It took twenty-five minutes to count the coins. The lawyer said, "Here is your agreement and receipt for the payment."

Jaeger said, "I also want my DNA profile back."

Brock produced it and asked, "Would you make a copy of it for me?" Jaeger nodded in the affirmative. The lawyer went out and returned with the copy in less than a minute.

222

CHAPTER 26

The four volumes of *The Birds of America* were laid out on the floor in front of the fireplace at the Skinner log cabin on Saturday morning. Cool, dry air wafted through the kitchen and dining room windows, ushering in a crisp cross breeze. Maude was on her hands and knees, carefully turning the pages to inspect the impressive drawings by James John Audubon. She closed each volume, straightened up, and reported, "These are really nice."

Brock helped her up. "I need to store them somewhere until we figure out what we're going to do with them."

"Put them in a crate in your office for a couple of days."

Brock retrieved his coffee cup and sat on the couch. "Maude, I can't believe Jaeger Barclay is behind all the mayhem that's gone on. I just don't see it in her eyes."

"Do you think the trouble will stop now that she's collected ten million?"

"Probably. I haven't stopped, though. I want to know who killed Roy Aldiss, Hogan Barclay, and Thad Cameron, and possibly Frank Romine, and who may still be trying to kill Celine Oliver and Calvin Willett, and potentially Nigel Barclay, Clive Natoli, and Perry Oliver."

"You forgot about yourself."

"I usually do. One of these days the bear's going to get me."

"If you keep talking like that, I'll put you in a cage." She had an angry look on her face.

———

Brock reached Leslie Blazek on the phone after he'd nailed together crates and stored the bird books in his office. "Have you heard from Frank?"

"Yes. He sent me a letter, and there was a video in it."

"What's on the video?"

"It's him, talking in the camera. He's announcing that he's going to take a year off from playing chess so he can travel around the world. His letter asked me to give it to the chess organization to release."

"Thank goodness. That's wonderful news. Means he's still alive. Did the letter say anything else?"

"Since he let me win the chess tournament, he said he needed a favor. He wants me to go to his apartment, load up his stuff, and put it in storage back here in Virginia."

"Call me when you're going to do that. I want to be there to keep you safe."

"I'm flying to Lexington on Monday night. I've rented a small box truck to drive back here after I've loaded up his things on Tuesday morning."

"Let me know what time to meet you there."

"I will. Thanks."

Brock arrived in Danville at 11:45 a.m. The start of the weekend made the town seem empty and subdued. He parked his car two blocks away and stood in front of the restaurant waiting to see if Frank Romine would appear. Lunch patrons began to walk in intermittently. A vehicle pulled up slowly. Frank was driving. He rolled down the window and said, "Get in."

Remarkably, Frank was no worse for wear. He drove onto a residential side street and stopped at a parking spot in front of a white, wood-sided, two-story house with oak trees in the yard. Brock said, "You look like you've just returned from a relaxing vacation. What happened?"

"When I left the hotel, a guy asked me for my car keys and cell phone at gunpoint. I gave them to him, and he handed them to a girl. Then the guy told me to get in the trunk of his car. I think they drove my car back to my apartment and left it there with my phone in it."

"How'd you get away from them?"

"When they stopped to buy gas in Frankfort, I pulled the emergency trunk release and got out. They couldn't do anything because of the people standing around. I taxied over to Georgetown and rented a car and hotel room after they pulled away."

"The letter you sent me said you recognized someone in the crowd at the chess tournament who you thought was looking to kill you. Is he in these pictures?" Brock took the folded photos out of his shirt pocket.

Frank pointed at a short, thin, Slavic-looking character. "That's him."

"Is he the guy who confronted you outside the hotel?"

"Oddly enough, no. It was this guy and this girl."

"That's Thad Cameron, and she's Jaeger Barclay. Thad Cameron blew up Willett's boat. Celine and Calvin dove overboard before the bomb went off. Thad Cameron was found dead a few days later."

"That's Jaeger Barclay?"

"Yes. I guess they were planning to kill you because you're a friend of Celine's."

"I saw her up close. She's gorgeous. Thinner than Celine."

"I've seen her too. She produced a will dated after the one Nigel filed in court that showed she should have inherited everything. Nigel gave her ten million to drop a claim against the estate. She moved into the house Celine moved out of two years ago and has been going by the name Rhonda Hogan. She presented a DNA test proving it was her. I'm sure she's left town by now and will never be seen or heard from again."

"Well, that solves one mystery. What about the trouble swirling around Celine?" Frank asked.

"I haven't completely figured that out yet. I take it you're going to disappear and change your identity to keep from getting killed yourself? Leslie told me she was coming over to gather up your things on Tuesday. I'll give her a hand."

"Thanks. I've put in all the protections needed to safeguard the database at your company. You should be good for a couple of years. I'll send you a letter recommending someone else to pick up where I left off."

"Do you want me to do something with your car?" Brock asked.

"Yes. Take the plate off and park it in the Lexington airport garage. I'll send someone for it in a couple of weeks."

"Do you know who you will become when you disappear?"

"Yes. I've found the identity of a man who I can step in the shoes of. If Celine could do it, I can as well."

Frank drove to where Brock's car was parked. The finality of their meeting took on a sad tone. "When you get settled, write and let me know what address I can reach you at by mail."

"I'll do that." They shook hands, and Frank looked despondent.

Brock knew something wasn't right. On the way back to Hazard, he called Marcel. "I know this is a long shot. You were able to find Jaeger's birth certificate. You said she was born in August thirty-two years ago. Go back and see if you can find anything about her first year of life."

"How am I going to do that?"

"Like you always do. Work a miracle."

———

Sin exists in myriad forms. Legalists keep lists of ones they don't like such as drinking, smoking, dancing, gambling, adultery, lying, and coarse talk. Most lists don't include gluttony since it's a more gentile sin, which is easily excused away.

Pride goes before a fall, the Bible says, and envy and covetousness are across the street waiting for someone to trip and fall on their head. A sin that doesn't get much respect is control, which is pride's brother. Satan was the first to assume control of his own destiny, and from him, no light can escape. He wants to be like God, and he wants you to be your own god, like him. But he is insane, and so are people who think they're in control and don't need God.

Humans on this earth are from the flawed seed of Adam, which means some form of darkness and death are in them. The ultimate in self-examination is to know where Satan has shot the lights out of an otherwise respectable life. For a lot of people, it is control—an unwillingness to submit to God. Like gluttony, it's an excusable sin. People just can't seem to help themselves, in the name of free will. When you think you're in control, things go better—for a while.

Calvin Willett's dock is a small piece of heaven. He sits there among sinners and tax collectors, and the control freaks who don't join in, scoff at him and his epicurean and hedonistic friends. CeCe, Cal's Mary Magdalene, is there too. She's the bridge between him and the masses. When a control freak is unwittingly lured to the dock, one of two things happens: they let go and love their neighbor as themselves or run toward Satan like a scalded dog. In a matter of hours, a person can learn what their parents didn't teach them from birth to adulthood.

A pool party can be a piece of heaven too. It has four important parts: water, refreshments, sunshine, and music. What it doesn't have are boats and waterskiing. If Calvin Willett hadn't been drinking the night he slammed into the dock and almost died, he'd be an accomplished skier by now. He does have a new boat, and his relationship with CeCe has become the joy of his life. All things work together for good, for those who love the Lord.

On Sunday morning, CeCe took control of the kitchen. Cal knew that meant a healthy breakfast and a long bicycle ride to get some exercise. She chirped, "Will you check out this weather? Do you have the crossword puzzle ready?"

"I do. I'm sure we'll get overrun with people today. I'll be spending most of my time in the boat, pulling people on skis. I'm not sure we'll have time to finish the puzzle."

"Sure, we will. I can drive the boat too."

Cal thought the time was right to bring up CeCe's other client and the work she did for him on Friday. "How was your cocktail party the other night?"

"Fine. The politicians look at me, and it's all they can do not to slobber on themselves. It can be rather embarrassing at times."

"You see them quite a bit. Do any of them seem honest?"

CeCe got out the Greek yogurt and put black grapes cut in half on two servings. She beat four eggs and warmed a pan. "They are no different than the general population. A few are sleazy. Some are drunk on power and money. Several are good people—sincere and hardworking. A few are as dumb as a box of rocks. All of them are the kings and queens of networking. And as you might expect, nearly all of them leer at me."

"So, if you were to move in with me more permanently, that would get around." Cal peered at her sideways.

"Why, Cal, that's an awfully bold statement for a gentleman such as yourself. You had better let me know what the terms and conditions of such a move would be. I wouldn't want there to be any misunderstanding." She came over and grabbed his face with both of her hands and stared into his eyes.

"You set the terms. As I've said before, I'm game for whatever pleases you." Cal pursed his lips.

"Do you want to be a pushover?" she asked sternly.

"Want to be? I already am when it comes to you," he replied diffidently.

"Cal, you understand that I can get any man I want." She poured the eggs into the pan and stirred them.

"I do. And you understand I've never been in love with a woman as wonderful as you."

"I can't fault you for trying." She sped up the stirring of the eggs until they were done.

"How's this for trying? I'm asking you to marry me. If you say yes, you won't regret it. I'm a man of strong moral character, and I know that you are a God-fearing woman with a good heart."

"Damn it, Calvin, this conversation makes me extremely uncomfortable." CeCe slid the eggs onto the two plates and brought the plates over to the table.

"Why?" He turned his palms up. "If you say no, then I'll know it's the best thing for you. If you say yes, it'll be the best day of my life. Either way, we can go forward in a good way."

"I'm not so sure about that. It's hard to mix business and pleasure."

"Just think about it. You can give me an answer whenever it suits you. That's today or twenty years from now. I really mean that," he said, blinking his eyes and nodding.

"Okay, I will. Let's have a boisterous party. All your friends will be here to see your new boat." She hugged his neck and sat down to eat breakfast.

Chapter 27

Skinner put a fuzzy yellow blanket in the passenger seat of the Lamborghini for Truman to curl up on while they drove from Hazard to the north end of Herrington Lake. The dog was more interested in watching the road than sleeping. Brock talked to him as though he understood what was being said. As Brock yammered on, Truman broke into a shallow pant and had no interest in keeping eye contact, until he quit talking.

When they got around to the side of Calvin's house and saw the size of the crowd on the dock, they quickly worked their way down the hill. CeCe saw them first. She shuffled over to the gangplank and asked, "Where's Maude?" She had on a dark green one-piece with straps tied in a knot behind her neck. Her stunning beauty never disappointed. Several guests were standing around the orange-and-white speed boat, peering and pointing.

"Slaving away at her winery. She told me to ask you why you haven't taken her up on her offer to run the place."

"Calvin forbade me from considering anything like that. I must get his permission to leave the compound. He said no."

"I'm not surprised." Truman went to Celine as though she were his companion.

She scratched his head between his ears. "What an incredible dog. Where'd you get him?"

"From a breeder. His stud fee is eighty thousand a pop."

Cal came up behind CeCe and said, "Ah, now I see what you meant when you thought this dog could be an advertising star." Truman walked around CeCe to show Cal proper respect. "Come on and join the party." Dean Martin's insouciant voice piped through the speakers, smoothly delivering his version of "Sway" recorded seventy years ago. Makings for tacos were spread out on top of the bar next to the blenders. The guests turned to stare and fawn over the dog. "Folks, this is Brock and his emotional support dog, Truman." Everyone laughed and began talking at once.

When the hubbub died down, Truman went to one of the front corners of the dock and fixed his eyes on a boat across the lake, in the direction of the dam. Brock saw him and asked, "What is it, boy?"

Calvin came over. "What's he staring at?"

"That runabout over there." He jabbed a finger at it. "Do you have any binoculars down here?"

"I'll get them."

Brock adjusted the lenses and kept them focused for twenty seconds. He handed the binocs back to Cal and said, "Bring your inboard around to the front of the dock. I'm going to run up to my car for something. I'll be right back down."

"What's wrong?"

"One of the people in that boat has a rifle with a scope on it."

Brock didn't wait for Calvin's response. Truman stood where he was. Calvin scurried over to the boat, untied it, and threw the binocs in the passenger seat. He commanded, "Get in, Truman." The dog followed orders and lay on the floor. Calvin started the engine and pulled around to the front side of the dock.

Brock retrieved a loaded pistol from under the driver's seat of the Lamborghini and wrapped his windbreaker around it. When he got back down the hill, he stepped into the Nautique and said, "Let's try to find them." What Truman had seen was gone.

Cal came out of the branch of the lake his house was on and sped toward the dam. The craft they were searching for still wasn't in sight. Cal offered, "We better check in the cove on the right. They may be hiding in the stickups." It took five minutes to conduct a search that was unsuccessful.

"Step on it. They're heading south on the main part of the lake." Cal's Correct Craft heaved and leapt forward. Brock caught sight of the quarry ten minutes later, about three hundred yards from the no-wake zone before the bridge. He held up the binocs in time to see the man in a floppy canvas hat throwing the rifle overboard. The man bent over after that and dropped from sight. "There it is." Brock pointed, hoping Cal would see it.

"We'll not be able to gain on them in the idle zone," Cal replied.

"Speed through there and get as close as you can." When they got within two hundred yards, Brock saw the girl driving the boat turn around. *She looks like, or could be, Jaeger Barclay*, he thought.

Suddenly, a siren blared from the gendarme's boat, startling them. The conservation officer picked up his megaphone. "Stop where you are and turn off your engine." Brock surreptitiously took everything out of the glove compartment and stuffed the windbreaker and pistol in it. The officer recognized Willett and said, "Is this your new boat?"

"Yes."

"What are you doing blowing through the idle zone at full speed? You know better than that."

"People in the boat in front of us have a rifle. We're afraid they're going to hurt someone."

"Never mind that. I'm writing you a ticket for speeding." He threw two scuffed white buoys out, so the two vessels wouldn't bang. "I've got a better idea. Why don't I do an inspection of your new machine to make sure you're legal and properly equipped."

"Fine." Cal stared ahead and saw that the boat they were pursuing was running at full speed again on the other side of the no-wake zone.

"Who are your friends?"

"My name's Brock Skinner. This is my dog, Truman."

The water police officer peered at Truman critically, and said, "Nice looking animal." It took fifteen minutes for him to finish checking out Calvin's new rig. When he got back in the police boat, he said, "I'm not going to give you a ticket, but don't go blasting through here like that again. Now, what were you saying about someone having a rifle?"

"We were standing on my dock when Mr. Skinner saw a man in the boat that we were chasing brandish a rifle with a scope."

The gendarme replied, "Leave it to me. I'll check it out."

"Did you recognize the boat?" Cal asked the officer.

"I didn't get a good look at it. Do you remember the letters on the front of it?"

Brock told him what they were. "Can you check the title?" he asked.

The conservation officer tapped the keys of his laptop, and said, "It's not registered here in Kentucky."

Brock flopped down in the padded seat and rubbed his face. "Figures." Truman knew his owner was spoiling for a fight.

On the way home, Calvin wondered out loud, "What was the guy with the rifle going to do?"

"Finish the job that Thad Cameron started: kill you or Celine, or both of you. He couldn't get to either one of you by land because your house is being guarded, so he decided to try by water. What I don't understand is why he ducked down out of sight," said Brock.

Cal had a surprised expression on his face. "That's easy. You must know who he is, and he didn't want to be named."

CeCe was standing on the front of the dock looking troubled when they got back. Cal stood and announced, "It's time for ski runs, everybody. I can take four at a time." Several people huddled around, hoping to be chosen for the first trip.

Brock told the party hosts he was going to take off to check on some things. Truman jumped out of the boat and led the way up the hill. When they were on the road again, Brock called his brother-in-law. "Are you home?"

"Yes. Where are you?"

"Just leaving Willett's place."

"You might want to come by."

"What's up?"

"I've been checking on the life of Jaeger Barclay. Something's fishy."

"I'll be there in fifteen minutes."

Valerie gave Brock a firm hug when he walked into the Sutherland house. She said, "Why didn't you bring Maude? You need to get her more help at that winery."

Truman stared up at Valerie as if he wanted to say, "Don't do that."

"I've tried. It's her baby," Brock said with resignation. He turned to Marcel. "What've you got?"

"I found Hogan Barclay's checking account before and after Jaeger was born. He employed a woman who helped with the baby and around the house."

"Yeah? So what?"

"He paid the woman weekly, but the payments stopped a month after Jaeger was born."

"He must have fired her." Brock spun around, considering what Marcel had said.

"I thought so too, so I found her. She's eighty years old now. I called."

"What did she have to say?"

"She told me when she showed up for work a month after Jaeger was born, Hogan relieved her of her duties. She tried to see the baby to say bye. It was gone, and she didn't know what had happened to it. She went back out to visit Mrs. Barclay for a few weeks, and the baby was never there."

"You find anything that explained the disappearance?"

"No, but the woman told me she saw Mrs. Barclay at the grocery store a year later, and Jaeger was in a stroller."

Brock shared with Marcel what had gone on at the lake. He left the Sutherlands and drove to where Jaeger Barclay had been living, fully expecting to find that she had cleared out for good. He was right, unless he had just seen her on the lake.

They returned to the dock at Willett's house, and this time, Truman ran down the hill ahead of Brock. CeCe was sitting on her favorite seat on the pontoon with her feet up, and the dog had parked himself next to her. Brock said, "Celine, I need you to do something."

"What's that?"

"First thing in the morning, I want you to go to a lab so they can work up a DNA profile on you."

She straightened her back and put her feet on the floor of the pontoon. "What for?"

"Because Perry Oliver is not your father. I plan to prove who is."

"How do you know that?"

"It's too complicated to explain. If you go in first thing, they should have your profile ready by Wednesday morning when they open."

"I'll trust you on this, Brock. What lab should I go to?" He handed her the address.

Brock and Truman got back home at six fifteen just as Maude was getting in from the winery. She asked, "How did you boys do today?"

"Everybody loves Truman, me, not so much."

"And you're surprised at that?"

"No." He went on to tell her about the man with the rifle and the girl driving the boat who looked like Jaeger Barclay. Then he told her the whole story that he had pieced together.

She said, "Are you going to try to stop her?"

"I am."

"When?"

"Wednesday morning. In the meantime, I'm going to pay the Olivers one more visit. I should be back in an hour."

Brock took Maude's SUV to Elm Shoal Branch and parked it facing away from the house in the woods. A gentle breeze was soughing through the trees. The scraggly grass had grown since his last visit. Perry Oliver came to the door. He said, "I'm guessing you've got something you want to say."

"Yes, I would also like to speak to your wife."

"Why?"

"To hear her side of the story. But first, I'm going to tell you what I'm afraid is going to happen. Willard Lentz and Nigel Barclay are meeting in Madison to kick off the distillery on Wednesday morning. I'm afraid he's going to renege on the deal."

"Why would he do that?"

"Because Jaeger Barclay will tell Lentz something that will cause him to back away."

"What would that be?"

"The story of the real Jaeger Barclay."

"I'm not following you," Perry said.

"Yes, you are. No sense trying to play dumb anymore. Remember I told you that I would find out what was going on through DNA testing? Well, it'll all come out on Wednesday."

"So, you're telling me I'm not going to get a payoff?"

"Oh, I'm sure an investor will come along to do the deal. Can I speak to your wife now?"

Perry walked back into the house and said, "Rhonda, this fellow wants to talk to you."

"What does he want?" She looked pitiful. Her blonde hair was unkempt, eyes sullen, and she was wearing tattered clothes.

"How did you decide?"

She gazed at him and said nothing for several seconds. "The eyes. It was her eyes." Her shoulders slumped. "No light could escape from them."

Brock said nothing more. He walked outside. Perry Oliver followed him. He remarked, "All of this should have come out thirty years ago. But I wanted the money and agreed to keep quiet. Look what I've done to her." He rubbed his brow and pounded his thigh with a fist.

Brock returned home to enjoy a relaxing supper with his devoted wife. She told him about her day at the winery, and the interesting customers that came through. He asked, "If you were going to take a boat to Grand Cayman, where would you leave from?"

"Florida."

"Where in Florida?"

"Key West?"

"I suppose so. I'm going to call Nigel Barclay after our tea and give him the bad news."

Brock got him on the line. "Nigel, I told you I'd lend you ten million dollars. I want to warn you, I think Jaeger is going to reveal something that will stop the deal."

"Such as?"

"I'm guessing your mother told her something about the real Jaeger Barclay that will spook investors."

"What do you mean, *real* Jaeger? The DNA testing proves she's my father's daughter."

"There's more that you're not aware of."

"Like what?" Nigel sounded perturbed.

"I'm not sure enough to tell you yet. I'll be in Madison on Wednesday morning, and if Willard Lentz says everything is a go, I'll hand you the certified check made out in your name. You can endorse it over if the papers get signed."

"That's okay with me."

Brock ended the call and began searching the Internet for private boats that leave for Grand Cayman from Key West. He found one and punched in the number to see if anyone would answer. The man who took the call sounded like a sneak and a thief. "I'm trying to find out what it costs to take a boat to Grand Cayman. I heard you make those trips."

"Yes, sir. I leave at seven in the morning and arrive at ten at night. The price is five thousand for the first person and two thousand for everyone else."

"Why is it so expensive?"

"Sir, if I have to tell you that, you should probably take a plane."

"I think I understand. Are you booked this week?"

"I have a trip out on Thursday and will be back on Friday."

"When would I bring my luggage aboard?"

"We do that at eleven o'clock the night before. To be discreet, if you know what I mean."

"I do."

"I'll see you Friday night when you get back. Where is your boat docked?"

"Sunlight Marina, slip F-9. Show yourself by saying you want to go fishing on the edge of the Cayman Trench."

"Will do. See you soon."

Chapter 28

Gray skies that drifted in on Monday morning brought steady rain. The grapevines at the winery would soak up every ounce of moisture that came their way. Maude, like a riverboat gambling farmer, knew the cloud cover and precipitation would be a royal flush for the wine business.

Brock had other things on his mind. Staring out the front window of his home office, he made a call to a private jet company at seven o'clock in the morning. "I can meet you at the London–Corbin airport at ten. I'll be bringing luggage with me."

At 7:45 a.m., Celine was sitting in Calvin's car outside the lab where she would consent to having a DNA profile done. Cal said, "Brock told you Perry Oliver isn't your father. How does he know that?"

"He doesn't act that smart, but he is. And determined. I don't know how he figures things out. According to him, he's about to connect all the dots. I'm a little afraid of finding out who my real father is."

"Your mother didn't tell you? That's peculiar."

"My mother is an emotional basket case. Something traumatic happened to her. She's never recovered from it."

Cal turned in his seat to face Celine. "Let me hazard a guess: she was raped."

"That's what I think."

"And whoever did it is your father."

"That's a logical conclusion." She got out of the car and entered the lab.

At eight fifteen, Clive Natoli placed a call to Nigel Barclay. "T-minus two days. By Wednesday afternoon, the eagle will have landed."

"I'm not so sure. Skinner called me last night and said my sister may tell Lentz something that will scare off the investor."

"About what?"

"He said it may have to do with the real Jaeger Barclay. Do you know what he's talking about?"

Clive knew. He took a quarter of a million dollars in part to keep quiet about it. "I can't say that I do," he lied.

"What does he know?"

Natoli debated whether to tell Nigel the dirty little secret or play dumb and weather the storm. "Whatever it is, you'll just have to address it and keep the deal moving forward."

"Clive, you're holding out on me. If I find out you've not been truthful, I'll cut you out."

"Hey, I'm the one who kept the barrel tax in place. Without it, you'd have no deal."

"And I paid you to do that and could have easily paid someone else."

"Nigel, I recommend you try to keep the friends you've got. You're going to need them."

"Is that a threat?"

"Sort of sounded like one, didn't it." Clive hung up on him.

At nine o'clock in the morning, Leslie Blazek stood in the office of the temperature-controlled bank of glorified garages where she'd be parking Frank Romine's belongings. With her pedigree, the clerk had a hard time believing she'd been tasked with renting such a lowly storage facility. She filled out the forms, handed him a check, and took the key that opened the unit. She worked the lock and determined the best path for a truck to get back to the overhead door.

Leslie's cell phone rang as she was driving back to her apartment. "Hi, Brock."

"Hello, Leslie. How's my favorite Virginian?"

"Lonesome."

"Sorry, I was trying to be funny. Do you need to be cheered up?"

"Go ahead, say it."

"You're high class, beautiful, and smart."

"I'm starting to believe all men are evil creatures."

"You'd be mostly right. Trick is to find one who isn't."

"And you called me for a reason?" she asked.

"I need some information. You said Frank had a wandering eye. How many times did he stray from you?"

"In eight years, I'd say maybe five times." She took the personal question in stride.

"Did you see any of the girls he fell for?"

"Yeah, all of them, I think."

Brock was trying to finesse the point. "Would it be fair to say all were very good looking?"

"Yes. That was the common theme, carrying right over to Celine Oliver."

"Thought so. I had lunch with Frank on Saturday. He was kidnapped after the chess tournament by a very good-looking woman and her henchman. He told me he escaped. I'm not so sure."

"Why do you say that?"

"Because he said she was gorgeous."

"You're implying he might have thrown in with her. Is she bad news?"

"A regular Lizzie Borden. I'm afraid she'll suck him in and kill him."

"Oh, Brock, why'd you tell me that?"

"Hopefully, to save his life. He's going to change his identity. So is his new lady friend."

"And you're thinking they've got some kind of plan?"

"Yes. This time he's run into the black widow. I'll meet you at Frank's tomorrow at nine."

—————————

Brock boarded the private jet after loading the luggage at ten till ten. The flight would be three hours each way. If things went smoothly, he'd get back to Kentucky by six. Before he took off, he asked Marcel to run a complete background check on Willard Lentz. Marcel had quite a bit of information about him by 4:00 p.m. He sent it in an email for Brock to read on the return flight.

Lentz was thirty-five years old. He grew up in Vermont, went to Brown University in Providence, Rhode Island, and took a job on Wall Street. He married Emma Hyde right after he graduated. They stayed in New York City for two years, and when he agreed to go to Kentucky to look for investment opportunities, his wife's family disowned her. They thought Kentucky was flyover country, suited for rednecks and rubes. The couple rented the house they lived in near Three Chimneys Farm, and there was nothing conspicuous in their finances.

On Tuesday morning at eight fifteen, the rain had finally begun to play out. Brock was sitting in Marcel's office at Sutherland Tailoring, drinking a cup of lukewarm coffee. He said, "On the way to the meeting tomorrow in Madison, I'm going to stop at the Lentz residence. After I leave, I want you to follow anybody who comes out and goes anywhere. Text me with updates."

"Where are you going now?" Marcel asked.

"Frank Romine's apartment, to help Leslie Blazek load up his stuff to take back to Virginia."

"If he's going to disappear, what's she going to do with it?"

"Beats me."

Leslie was in Frank's bedroom boxing up clothing and some other small items when Brock came through the door. He jumped right in to help her pack things. She asked, "Did you see the little truck parked outside?"

"I did. Try not to get picked up by some wolf on the way home."

"You're implying I'll attract attention?"

"Like a carbuncle on the nose," Brock answered absurdly.

"Well, if I'm going to get on the road, we need to get the furniture out of here."

"Yes, ma'am."

After everything had been loaded up, Brock sat next to Leslie in the truck's cab. He said, "If Frank turns up dead, the first person the police will chase down is you. Set yourself up to have an ironclad alibi for the next three days. Hopefully, you won't need it, but no sense taking any chances."

"Who would want to kill him?"

"Jaeger Barclay's boyfriend. That is, unless she's planning to hitch her wagon to Frank and kill him."

"Why would she do that?"

"Because he knows the bad things she's done, and probably took part in them. He could hold that over her."

"Is she the one who had Celine's apartment bugged?"

"I think so. She used what information she got to try to hurt people who could unearth her evil deeds."

Leslie put her hands on her face. "That includes you too, I suppose."

"Yes. She's already killed Thad Cameron, the man who'd been doing her bidding."

Leslie glanced in the side mirror, froze for a moment, started the truck, and said, "I've got to get moving if I'm going to make it home before dark." Brock got out and watched her slowly pull away. Frank Romine had laid waste to his own life along with hers. A man with tremendous intelligence and talent who knew better, yet he was on the run, leaving behind the best woman he'd ever have a chance with.

Brock started toward Herrington Lake. He pulled into Willett's driveway shortly after lunch. Calvin came to the door and said, "Why don't you buy a place up the street? You're here more than you're at your house."

"Nice to see you too, Calvin. Are you going to invite me in?"

"Of course. I only wanted to needle you a bit."

Brock crossed his arms and smirked. "In the world of needling, that doesn't even register on the meter."

Celine popped up from the couch. She had workout clothes on. Her hair had been severely pulled back into a ponytail. "Hi, Brock."

"Greetings. I just dropped by to let you know what's happening tomorrow. I need your help."

"What do you have in mind?" Cal asked.

"I'm going to meet you at the lab at eight in the morning. I want to take your DNA profile with me over to a meeting with Nigel Barclay and Willard Lentz that starts at ten o'clock in Madison. Meet me there beforehand outside."

"What for?"

"I want you to follow Lentz when he leaves. There's going to be a revelation at the meeting that'll stop the distillery deal. I think Lentz is taking part in a con, and I want to know where he's off to after things blow up."

"What's this all about?"

Brock ignored the question and went to stand close to Celine. "I might as well break it to you. Hogan Barclay is your father. He raped your mother at the Natoli house in Frankfort right after Christmas nearly thirty-three years ago. Perry Oliver married your mother, which in hindsight, was probably a good thing. It kept her alive."

Celine went over to the window to look out. She showed little emotion. "That means Jaeger is my half sister." Brock said nothing, waiting for her to speak again. "I guess that's why we look somewhat alike."

"Well, I can confirm two things: the real Jaeger Barclay is, in fact, your half sister, and Nigel Barclay your half brother."

"Has Clive known this from the beginning?"

"Yes. Hogan paid him and your stepfather to keep quiet. And they did. I'm the one breaking the silence. More shocking things will come out tomorrow. By Saturday afternoon, I'm expecting this thing to be over."

"What about Frank Romine?"

"I think he survives, never to be seen or heard from again." Brock gave Calvin the address of the Ohio Valley Distillers' Guild.

————————

The day had brightened considerably by midafternoon. The rain on the roads had evaporated so quickly, it almost seemed magical. Brock called ahead to his bank in Hazard, giving them a heads up that he needed a check for ten million made out to Nigel Barclay and would pick it up shortly. He also touched base with his attorney, asking him to hurriedly draft an agreement in the event he had to make good on his promise to front Barclay on his deal, which Brock thought unlikely based on what he felt was going to happen at the meeting. He walked into the log cabin a few minutes after five. His wife was already home from the winery.

Maude asked, "Is the final act in this tragedy going to happen tomorrow?"

"For the most part. I doubt we'll know who will be on Jaeger's arm, when she disappears again, until this weekend."

Later that evening, Nigel Barclay called Brock to make sure everything was set. "You'll be at my meeting with Willard Lentz tomorrow morning at ten o'clock in Madison, right? You know the address?"

"I will, and I do."

"And you'll have a check in your pocket for ten million dollars made out to me?"

"I'm holding the check in my hand this very moment."

"Good. I've never had a friend like you—one who's reliable."

"Sorry to hear that."

————————

At dark, CeCe and Cal were sitting on the back porch of his house. The damp air had turned cool and heavy. She was staring straight into the darkness when she said, "I accept your proposal of marriage."

"Come again?"

"And I'd like to have a small and informal ceremony on the dock this Sunday."

He got up, went over to the love seat she sat in, and sidled up to her. "That's the best thing I've heard in my life. I'll see to it that you never regret the decision. And yes, I love you very much." He leaned in and put his face up against hers. "Do you have a bridesmaid in mind?"

"Leslie Blazek. She understands me. I like her. Who will be your best man?"

"I would prefer it to be Frank Romine, but I guess since he's on the lam, that won't be possible. My second choice is Brock Skinner. I'll ask If he'll do the honors."

"Good. We should invite Maude and the Sutherlands, and a preacher, of course."

"Anybody else?"

"That's up to you. There's no one else on my list."

"What about your mother and 'father'?"

"I suppose it's proper to invite them. I'm sure they won't accept though…" Her voice trailed off, jittery and uncertain. "What about your parents?"

"It would be a happy event for them. We have all of three days to work out the details."

Calvin called Brock to alert him of his duties as best man. Celine did the same with Leslie. She had just gotten home with Frank's stuff in the truck.

Maude asked her husband who had called him. He said, "You're not going to believe this: Calvin is marrying Celine on the dock this Sunday. I'm the best man."

"How about that?" Her face turned farcical to go with her seraphic smile.

Chapter 29

Celine walked out of the lab on Wednesday morning with the DNA workup in her hand. Calvin was leaning on the Lamborghini, talking about his wedding plan. She shoved the folder through Brock's open window. He took the paperwork out and put it alongside the copy of the other DNA profile he had. Celine asked, "What's that you've got there?"

"Proof that aliens have visited this earth."

"I should have known better than to ask." She rolled her eyes.

Cal said, "We'll meet you in Madison a little before ten."

"Thanks. See you then. And thanks, Celine, for doing this. You'll see the wisdom in it shortly." Brock fired up the car and whizzed away.

Brock drove past the Lentz residence ten minutes later and pulled in behind Marcel's car that was sitting on an asphalt outcropping across the street. He got out and said, "As soon as Willard leaves, I'll park in front and walk up to the house."

Lentz was gone before 9:00 a.m. His purported wife, going by the name Emma Lentz, swung open the door and said nothing. Her eyes were evil and brooding, so much so that even light could not escape from them. Brock said obsequiously, "Ma'am, my car has broken down on the road. Can I borrow your phone to call a wrecker?" She went into another room to retrieve her mobile, came back, and gave it to him. He entered the house and closed the front door while she was gone. "Thank you." He slipped the phone into his jacket pocket.

"Aren't you going to call a wrecker?"

"Let's not carry on with this charade, Jaeger." Brock moved like a cat, reached for her long black hair, and yanked the wig off her head.

She bellowed, "Stop it! Don't touch me." Her real hair was the same style and color as Celine's and Jaeger Barclay number four who recently lived where Celine used to live.

Brock walked into the first room he came to. It was completely empty. He threw down the wig and said, "Looks like you're going somewhere, and won't be coming back."

"Get out, or I'll call the police." She had morphed into a satanic siren.

"With what? I've got your phone. And besides, if you call, I'll let them know about the people you've killed, and there are many."

"Looks like I should have killed you."

"You had your chance when you and Willard were on Lake Herrington. I saw him throw the rifle overboard."

"You can never rely on men."

"The ones you hang with, I suppose not. That was a cute trick getting a woman who looked like you to be your shill. You went to the lab to get the DNA profile and gave it to her to extort Nigel. Where's the ten million in gold?"

"I don't know. Why don't you ask her. Now, get out of here!"

Brock moved in closer. "You should thank me. I'm going to let you make a run for it. The only thing left for me to learn is whether Frank Romine has landed on red or black. If you harm him, I'll come after you."

"You're getting a little too big for your britches," she replied confidently, as her mind stopped spinning.

"And you better disappear to a place where no one can ever find you. I can prove instantly that you're not Emma Lentz. It won't take much for your boyfriend to flip and claim you killed her."

"You talk big. I wonder how good you are at dodging bullets."

"Apparently, pretty good. Here's the bottom line: if I ever see you again, I'll haul you in." He left with her phone in his pocket and ran to his car just in case she had the ability to get a gun quickly and shoot him in the back.

Brock broke the speed limit to get to Madison by 9:55 a.m. He saw Calvin's 1967 Ford parked in a meter space a block past the Ohio Valley Distillers' Guild. He wheeled into a spot further down the road, got out, and knelt on the passenger side of Cal's car where Celine was sitting. The folder he was carrying was tucked under his arm. She rolled down the window and asked, "Any final instructions?"

"Yes. Give Calvin your phone. I want you to come with me."

Calvin sat up and commented pointedly, "You keep her safe."

"I will. When Willard Lentz tears out of here, follow him. Call to let me know where he's going. You do know how to use a cell phone, correct?"

"I showed him," Celine confirmed. She got out of the car and fluffed her hair. "Let's go."

Pearl saw Celine first and then recognized Brock as he stepped in behind her. She said, "Well, hello. This must be your wife."

"No, actually. My wife's way better looking than her." He gave Celine a silly grin. She rolled her eyes again.

"That's a lie, and you know it. But I'm not going to get in the middle of it." Pearl didn't take guff from anybody. "Go on back. I presume you're meeting with Nigel and Willard."

"As a matter of fact, we are. What kind of mood are they in?"

"Bad."

"Don't forget, I promised to send you a birthday present," Brock reminded her.

"Oh, I haven't forgotten. Maybe you can give me some fairy dust that'll make me look like her." She threw a finger at Celine and turned into an angry schoolmarm.

As they walked back to the bland conference room, Celine said, "The way you talk to women is embarrassing, bordering on demeaning."

"I'll remember that."

Nigel Barclay recognized Celine Oliver and chortled, "What's *she* doing here?"

"I brought her along because you told me you were mean to her when she lived in your house, and you wanted to apologize to her."

Nigel threw his hands out to the side and pronounced, "This is hardly the time or the place."

"I'm kidding. Lighten up." He turned to Lentz. "Willard, this is the third Jaeger Barclay. Her real name is Celine Oliver."

"What do you mean third?"

"Well, there have been four of them."

Nigel rubbed his head and said to Lentz, "I don't know what he's talking about."

Everyone sat down. Nigel probed, "Are we ready to sign the paperwork?"

"There's a bit of a problem, Nigel. I got this in the mail yesterday." He took a yellow envelope with a note in it out of his sports coat pocket. "Let me read it to you. Dear Mr. Lentz, I think you should know that the real Jaeger Barclay died when she was only four weeks old. The Barclay parents buried the child on the property without letting the state know she was dead. I suggest you find where the child is buried and dig her up to confirm her identity before you consider building a distillery on the site. It's signed Jaeger Barclay."

Nigel stood and growled, "What the hell is this?"

"I can straighten things out," Brock responded smoothly. "The girl you knew as Jaeger Barclay when you were young is the person your parents used to hide the death of your real sister."

"Where is she now? I want to talk to her."

"She's been living with Willard here for the last twelve years."

"How can that be?"

Lentz put his hands on his thighs and elbows out to the side. "That's a lie."

Brock started in again: "Things went bad when Mrs. Barclay told the second Jaeger that she wasn't her mother, and that her husband had had an affair with another woman, and that woman was her mother."

"And you claim there are four Jaegers?"

"Yes. The one who died at a month old, the one Nigel knew when he was young who disappeared, this beautiful lady here who impersonated the one who vanished, and the last one who shook you down for ten million."

"How did Jaeger number two get tangled up with Willard here?"

"After you let her strip in front of him, she looked him up and offered herself to him. His real wife's parents had disowned their daughter, and she wasn't cut out for life in Kentucky. So, the two of them killed her, and she took her place, now living under the name Emma Lentz."

"That's unbelievable," Nigel belted out as he threw his head to the side.

"You haven't heard half of it. When Mrs. Barclay told Jaeger number two that her father was a philanderer, she killed him. Suffocation, I presume. Everything blew apart when she found out that Jaeger number three, a.k.a. Celine Oliver, was her twin sister."

Celine leaned forward and barked, "What do you mean, she's my twin sister?"

Brock emphatically opened the folder he had brought and pushed the two DNA profiles to the center of the table. "Your DNA is identical to that of Jaeger number two who disappeared."

"How did the Barclays get her?"

"Rhonda Cunningham got pregnant with twins. Perry Oliver and Clive Natoli asked Hogan if he wanted to buy one of them. He said yes. I asked Rhonda how she decided which child to sell. She told me that the look in the eyes of Jaeger number two was pure evil. Rhonda has been torn up emotionally ever since she agreed to sell one of her children."

Celine leaned back and started crying audibly. She got up and went to sit at the end of the row of plastic tables.

"Jaeger had already killed her father and Willard's wife, and killing was getting easier for her. She became angry and jealous of her twin sister, so the first thing she did was go to Richmond to kill Celine's friend, Roy Aldiss. Willard helped her."

Celine yelled at Lentz, "You animal!"

"Hey, I didn't kill anyone, and this story he's telling is nothing but a pack of lies. I don't have to sit here and listen to this garbage."

"Oh, yes you do," Brock said. "Jaeger number two flew off to Grand Cayman after killing Roy, and I'm sure she came back under a false name to live as Emma Lentz. When Mrs. Barclay died, Celine went back to living under her own name, after she collected a million dollars from Nigel. Jaeger number two hired Jaeger number four and told her to go by the name Rhonda Hogan. She was to keep an eye on Celine. When she found out Celine planned to move from the house she was renting to an apartment, Jaeger number two hired Thad Cameron to put microphones in her new place. Rhonda Hogan moved into the house Celine had vacated."

Nigel asked, "Why all the machinations?"

"Mrs. Barclay gave Jaeger number two a will that she could use to extort money from you. The plan needed a fourth Jaeger who could come out in the open. I'm sure she's been paid off and is long gone."

Nigel asked brusquely, "Do you want me to call the police?"

"No. We're going to let him make a run for it. Jaeger number two, posing as his wife, Emma Lentz, is a bigger fish than he is. Given the chance, he'll flip on her. Jaeger number two has been trying to kill the people around Celine who could expose her. She hired Thad Cameron to put a bomb in Calvin Willett's boat and to help her kidnap Frank Romine, and then she killed Cameron to cover her tracks. I'm letting Willard go in exchange for him not killing Frank Romine." Brock turned to Lentz. "I'm going to tell you the same thing I told your girlfriend: if Frank Romine doesn't turn up, I'll come for you personally." He stuck his arm straight out and pointed at Willard's head.

Lentz dropped his pretense of innocence and said, "Hell, man, I'm afraid Romine has wooed my girlfriend, and the two of them are going to kill me."

"Ah. You may be on to something. Since you've been part of her killing spree, it's you who could testify against her, and she knows it. I'm guessing you'll try to kill him before she has a chance to bump you off. Sort of puts you in a bind, doesn't it?"

"Yes. Can I leave now?"

"Be my guest."

In a split second, Willard Lentz bolted out into the street and ran toward his car.

A text message appeared on Brock's phone from Marcel: *She dropped off a rental car and flew to Florida from the Lexington airport.* "Let's go, Celine. Nigel, I'll talk to you later. Sorry about the distillery deal." He waved at Pearl on the way out. They got in his car and headed for Celine's apartment. He said to her, "I'm going to drive Frank's car to the airport in Lexington. I need for you to drive my car and keep it at Cal's until I get back from a quick trip I'm taking."

"Okay. I'm emotionally drained. I hope Cal gets home quickly."

"He will."

Frank had asked Brock to take the license plate off and leave his car at the airport in Lexington. He threw the plate in the trunk and put the keys under a floor mat in the back seat. The private jet he had arranged for was waiting at the FBO terminal to the south. It took him ten minutes to walk over. As he boarded the plane, a call came in from Willett. Lentz turned in the rental car he was driving and cleared security at the Louisville airport. Calvin didn't know what flight he was taking.

Brock arrived in Key West three hours later. He went to the vehicle he'd rented on his earlier visit, which was parked in an outdoor lot. He got a couple of sandwiches and drinks, and then parked where he could see the empty slip F-9 at Sunlight Marina.

The first person he saw was Jaeger number two. She pulled up to the dock in an SUV, got out, looked around, got back in the vehicle, and drove away. Near dark, Frank Romine, wearing a hat as a disguise, slinked by. At ten o'clock, Willard Lentz appeared. Jaeger drove up and parked the SUV. He got the luggage out and rolled the six cases to the empty boat slip. The boat motored in a few minutes later. The luggage was taken onboard after the five passengers disembarked.

It was midnight before the lights of the boat were turned off, and the crew went ashore. Brock looked at his watch. He put the seat back to catch a quick nap.

CHAPTER 30

Brock arrived back in Lexington dead tired at seven o'clock Thursday morning. He unloaded the luggage from the plane and hired a ride to Sutherland Tailoring in Harrodsburg. Marcel entered his office at eight fifteen to find Brock sitting in the chair across from his desk. Marcel said, "Tell me what you know."

It took Brock nearly half an hour to recite the thirty-three-year history of Hogan Barclay's twin daughters. He ended the dissertation by saying, "I'm sure Jaeger Barclay, a.k.a. Emma Lentz, caught a boat to Grand Cayman. What I'm not sure about is who went with her—Willard Lentz or Frank Romine."

"How do we find that out?"

"If Frank went, or he's dead, we'll never hear from him. If Willard went, I'll get a note in the mail from Frank, letting us know he's alive. We'll just have to wait and see."

"What will Jaeger do when she finds out what happened?"

"She might try to come after me."

"Damn it, Brock, you had better keep that to yourself. My sister will come unglued if she thinks that's a possibility."

"Yeah. Can we take these and put them in the company safe?" Brock looked at the six metal cases by the door that he'd brought from the airport. They rolled them down the hall and took the elevator to the basement where the IT backups were kept in the walk-in, fireproof room.

Marcel took Brock to Willett's house to pick up his Lamborghini. The sky was a radiant blue, and the heat of the sun felt good on their faces. The deciduous trees were turning colors quickly. Calvin and Celine moseyed out of the house to greet them. Celine had on a chartreuse terrycloth onesie that accentuated her full figure. Calvin offered, "So, they've run off to Grand Cayman. That island's a haven for drug runners, a regular Sodom and Gomorrah. Do you know the story, Brock?"

"Sodom and Gomorrah? Abraham's nephew, Lot, and his family lived in Sodom. God warned he was going to destroy the cities because of the sinfulness of the people. Abraham negotiated with God to spare them if ten righteous people could be found. Unfortunately, only Lot's family was righteous. They were instructed to flee the city and not look back. Lot's wife didn't heed the warning, and when she looked back, she turned into a pillar of salt."

"Right. CeCe, tell Marcel and Brock where Satan lives," said Cal.

"According to you, him and his fallen angels live in a black hole graveyard three times the size of our galaxy."

"But I bet you don't know where he stays when he's here on earth."

She replied, "I'm sure you're going to tell us."

"The Cayman Trench is nearly five miles deep off the coast of Grand Cayman. Over three miles down, there are black-smoker volcano vents spewing black water hot enough to melt lead. Hell is under those vents. You can find Satan there when he's resting, which I'm not sure he does much of."

"Cal, you'll need to behave better in front of people if we're to get along with folks. These crackpot theories of yours will scare them off, and we don't want 'em to think you're one brick short of a load."

Calvin made eye contact with Marcel and Brock. "Do I sound like a kook?"

Marcel said, "I can tell you that Valerie doesn't think anyone's a kook. And since we got married, I've come over to her way of thinking, except for one person, my brother-in-law here. Now, he's a kook." Cal and CeCe laughed. Brock snickered himself.

Celine asked, "Do you guys want to come in?"

"No, I'm tired. I'm heading home to take a nap," Brock said. "Tell me again about the wedding plans before I take off."

"I've arranged for a minister who isn't preaching this Sunday to perform the service on the dock at eleven in the morning. Marcel and Valerie, you and Maude, my parents, and Leslie Blazek are attending. The dress code is casual for everyone except us. CeCe is the most beautiful lady this side of Eden, and she'll be wearing a stunning dress for the ceremony and pictures. Afterward, a lunch will be served in the house."

"Congratulations to both of you! We'll see you on Sunday," Marcel said in a heartfelt voice.

About a third of the way home, after dodging a deer in the road, Brock called Nigel Barclay. "Things have been a little rough for you the last couple of weeks. Are you holding up okay?"

"Pretty good. I'm still smarting over being fleeced for ten million dollars."

"It ain't over till it's over," Brock added to cheer him up.

"If my parents buried my dead sister somewhere on the property, I think I know where."

"Yes?"

"The family has had a pet cemetery out back for two hundred years. She's likely there."

"Are you going to try to dig her up?"

"No. On this one, I'm going to contact the police, tell them the story, and ask what to do."

"Smart move. When you get that business cleared up, you can search for another investor for the distillery."

"That's my thought."

"I've got another suggestion for you."

"What's that?"

"Why don't you strike up a relationship with Pearl over at the guild?"

"Pearl?"

"Yeah. What's wrong with her?" Brock asked.

"Nothing. I've treated her poorly over the years, and I'm sure she thinks I'm a bad person," said Nigel.

"Go see her and beg for forgiveness. You'll have to be a nicer person from here on out if you want to entertain lady friends."

Nigel's snort came through the phone. "What, are you a matchmaker now?"

"I've gotten to know Pearl a little bit. She could add spark to your life."

"I'm hanging up now," Nigel replied arrogantly.

Brock went straight to the winery when he drove into town. Maude was in an exuberant mood, thinking everything had been closed out. She could be right, and he answered her questions succinctly, but didn't volunteer any additional information. "Best I can tell, Willard Lentz and Jaeger Barclay took a boat to Grand Cayman, and Frank Romine has dropped out of sight. We may hear from him in the future."

"What are we going to do with the bird books?"

"Sell them back to Nigel or the highest bidder. I'm going to go home and take a nap."

"Are you getting old?"

"I feel old after all this."

"I'll see you tonight," Maude said as she went about her business.

———

Brock showed up at Nigel's place unannounced late on Saturday morning. A brisk, cool wind was swirling the row of pampas grass between the trees along the black fence that lined the driveway up to the two-hundred-year-old brick house. "What are you doing here?" Nigel asked when he saw him.

"I'm curious to know what the police said about your sister."

"A crew of people came by yesterday to dig around in the pet cemetery. They found a container with an infant's body in it. They're checking the DNA to make a positive identification. If it's her, a death certificate will be issued, and a proper burial will be arranged."

"Sad. I guess it'll be good to resolve the matter."

"Yes." Nigel seemed to be in a daze. He walked back inside. Brock followed him.

"I also wanted to let you know that I'll still give you the ten million dollars if you find someone else to back your distillery deal. You can pay me back when you cash in. Also, if you'd like to buy *The Birds of America* back, I'll sell it to you for what I paid."

"That's generous of you. I might want it sometime in the future. There have been a couple of calls from potential investors in the distillery. I've got meetings with them next week."

"That's fantastic news."

"One more thing: I made my pitch to Pearl. She's playing hard to get. I think she'll forgive me, eventually."

"You're on a roll. When she finally weakens, you should bring her over to my wife's winery in Hazard. Would make a good first date."

"Count on it. I take it Willard Lentz and my half sister are on the run? What do you know about them?"

"They're in Grand Cayman. I'm not sure Willard is going to pass the accelerated life test for very long."

"You think she'd kill him too?"

"Hard to tell. If so, we'll never hear about it."

Nigel stuck his hand out unexpectedly to shake, and said, "Thanks for being a friend."

———————

Everyone arrived at Willett's house by ten o'clock on Sunday morning, and there was excitement in the air. The food caterers were busy in the kitchen preparing to put out the spread at noon. Maude said to Leslie Blazek, "It's nice to see you again so soon." The chatter of small talk increased in volume among the entourage as they waited for the bride and groom to appear. When they did, no one had words to describe how beautiful they were as a couple.

After the preacher came in and introduced himself, the throng of people made their way down the hill. The green lake water had a little chop to it, and the subdued sloshing noises echoing under the wood floor of the dock reduced the formality of the occasion. When the short-but-sweet service was over, Cal opened a bottle of champagne. A toast was offered by several of the attendees, making the whole affair joyous. Brock asked Cal, "Do you know what happened on this day in 1967?"

"No, what?"

"Che Guevara was killed."

"I told you it was a very good year," he replied gleefully.

The photographer got pictures of the couple sitting in the new Ski Nautique, and then some up in the house in front of the fireplace. CeCe changed clothes and Cal ditched his tuxedo before the food was served. He went to the radio and tuned to a jazz station that played music from the fifties and sixties. A prayer was offered by the preacher before the meal, and the chatter got lively as everyone dug in.

Over the din, Calvin faintly heard the announcer of the jazz station mention a news alert that had just come in, so he turned up the volume to hear what was being said. Conversation in the room ceased.

"It appears that the Cayman Islands have shifted and sunk into the sea. Reports indicate that a large land mass has separated from the wall of the Cayman Trench, likely falling several miles below the surface. The fate of the seventy thousand inhabitants and tourists on the islands is currently unknown. This event is being called one of the greatest natural disasters in history. Scientists believe that the backwash over the descending mass will cause massive drowning, foundering of boats, and a tsunami. Ships throughout the Caribbean are on alert and preparing for rough seas."

The group was stunned. Celine said, "Turn on the television."

Clicking through the channels, each was covering the horrific event, speculating as to what might have happened. The euphoria of the wonderful wedding had dissipated, replaced by sadness for the lives lost. It put the good times experienced every weekend by the crowd at Herrington Lake in perspective. Life was indeed uncertain, and making sure people were ready for what came next was foremost in Calvin's mind. He spoke up, "What a tragedy."

Brock thought for sure that Jaeger Barclay and either Willard Lentz or Frank Romine had died in the earthquake. He tried to blame himself for causing them to run off to Grand Cayman, but knew they'd planned to go there regardless of what he had done. He peered at Leslie Blazek and felt pity for her. He hadn't done much to make her life better.

An hour later, as the coverage of the disaster continued, the front door of Calvin's house eased open. Frank Romine was standing there, vacant and listless. Leslie sprang up and ran in his direction. "Frank! You're alive." She hugged him and urged him to come in. Everyone stood and gathered around.

Brock asked, "Are you okay?"

He had on khaki pants, a checkered button-down shirt, and light Polo jacket—all wrinkled. "Yes. I identified the man who I thought was here from a foreign country to kill me. Turns out, he is just an avid chess fan who attends tournaments when he can."

"That means you're in the clear and can come out of hiding," Marcel suggested.

"It does."

"Have you heard about the Grand Cayman catastrophe?"

"Yes, it was on the car radio."

"Do you know if Willard Lentz and Jaeger Barclay were there when the island fell?"

"I suppose so. By the grace of God, I'm not there too. She almost had me convinced to go with her and leave Lentz behind. But it was the look in her eyes that scared me."

Calvin commented wanly, "So evil, even light cannot escape from them."

Brock drifted off by himself and walked over to a tall, narrow window on the front of the house. Frank's disregard for the feelings of Leslie Blazek angered him to the point where he wasn't sure if he could control himself. He didn't believe Romine, and halfway expected to see Jaeger Barclay sitting in the passenger seat of Frank's car. He found Maude and said, "Let's go home."

She had a troubled look on her face. "What's wrong?"

"I need to get out of here before I kill him with my bare hands."

Maude whispered to Cal and CeCe to explain what was going on. She waved to everyone else on the way out. The Lamborghini was running, and when Maude got strapped in, she said, "This is the first time I've seen you like this."

"And I hope it's the last." When he got up on the main road, he burned rubber getting away.